ALSO BY SHANNON WORK

Now I See You
Everything To Lose
The Killing Storm

MURDER IN THE SAN JUANS

A NOVEL

SHANNON WORK

MURDER IN THE SAN JUANS
by Shannon Work
COPYRIGHT © 2022 Shannon Work

ISBN: 978-1-7354353-9-8 (paperback)
ISBN: 979-8-9869376-1-8 (large print paperback)
ISBN: 979-8-9869376-0-1 (eBook)

www.shannonwork.com

"The madman thinks he is sane."

Salvador Dali

CHAPTER 1

Wednesday, May 11

CONGRESSMAN CLIFF ROBERTS stood on the tarmac holding his laptop in one hand and a large envelope in the other. He studied the sawtooth ridge to the north. It was mid-May, but the mountain peaks were still blanketed with snow. It was a gorgeous morning, the sky a vivid shade of turquoise. Cliff drew in a deep breath. The air was cold and still, but he knew the winds were coming.

"We've got just enough time," Alan Krueger, Cliff's pilot, assured him. He held a clipboard, rechecking the flight plan with the weather report. "We'll take off to the west, then circle around and head back over the canyon, slip under the winds before we turn north. Might take us a few more minutes, but we should make DC in time for a late lunch."

Alan was wearing dark slacks and a pressed white shirt with gold and black epaulets buttoned onto the shoulders. A black cap with a gold braid across the crown was tucked under his arm. He looked every inch the commercial pilot, a fact that both amused and annoyed Cliff.

Cliff had spent years insisting he didn't expect the rigid formality his late father had, to no avail. The two men were the same age, fifty-eight, and Cliff had long ago considered their relationship as friends rather than employer-employee.

Alan had been his father's pilot for as long as Cliff could remember, ferrying Colorado's elder senator back and forth between Denver and Washington, DC, until the statesman's sudden death the year before his son was elected to the House. Alan had continued on as the Robertses' private pilot.

"Still with the monkey suit?" Cliff teased, shaking his head.

Alan clapped him on a shoulder and smiled. "Let's get you to DC, Congressman."

Cliff climbed the steps into the King Air, and Alan followed, closing and latching the door behind them. Although Cliff wasn't a pilot, he took the seat in the front, to Alan's right, preferring the view and the company in the cockpit to sitting alone in the rear of the plane like his father always had.

Cliff tucked the envelope and his laptop between the seat and the fuselage. He didn't want to think about the envelope's contents. It reminded him of Susan. He should have woken her before he left and kissed her goodbye, but he hadn't. He regretted that now. He would call her as soon as they landed.

Alan had on a headset and fiddled with the controls. He started the turbo-prop engines, and the plane shook to life.

As they taxied, Cliff looked south to Wilson Peak, its summit soaring over fourteen thousand feet. The highest point in San Miguel County, the mountain loomed over the landscape like a protective overlord. Still covered in snow but with grass greening at its base, it looked spectacular in the morning light.

The engines revved and the King Air sped down the runway. It lifted and shivered as it took flight, the runway suddenly dropping away as if the earth had fallen out from underneath them.

Dozens of people had told Cliff they'd never fly in or out of Telluride. Perched over nine thousand feet above sea level, it was the highest commercial airport in North America and was surrounded by the Rocky Mountains on three sides. Taking off and landing at Telluride was not for the faint of heart. But it was an adrenaline rush, one Cliff thought was exhilarating.

He watched the valley slip past for several minutes before Alan banked the plane sharply to the north and started the turn back. Soon, the entire valley floor was in view, with Telluride nestled near the end of the box canyon, the Rockies towering over the town on three sides.

The plane rose steadily, the props whining on either side of the fuselage, straining against the climb.

Cliff looked north to the sharp peak of Mount Sneffels and the mountains surrounding it. It reminded him of what he had to do when he got to the Capitol. The vote would be the following week. His decision would make some people angry, but it was unavoidable. Such was the life of a politician. He thought again about the contents of the envelope but pushed the thought quickly out of his mind.

The plane continued its climb as they flew over town and headed toward Savage Basin. Cliff turned and looked south, following the faint outline of Bear Creek Trail through the trees to the base of the falls in the distance. He would miss Telluride—he always did when he was gone. But he loved DC even more, and the thought of being back in the city invigorated him.

"Imogene Pass dead ahead," Alan announced.

Cliff knew the pass was just over thirteen thousand feet and estimated the plane was already a good three or four thousand feet above it.

He looked ahead to the mountains in the distance around Crested Butte, and the plane suddenly jolted to one side as if struck by a fist. Cliff stiffened in his seat. He had never considered himself a nervous flier, but turbulence always got his attention.

"Wind shear," Alan said. "Nothing to worry about."

A few seconds later, they hit a second, smaller pocket of air, but Alan didn't seem to notice.

Cliff gripped the arms of his seat and took in a deep breath, steadying his nerves.

Then it happened.

An explosion.

His thoughts came in short clips.

The back of the plane.

Peeling metal and wind.

The plane shuddered violently.

Alan struggled with the controls and grabbed the radio. He cried out, "Telluride!—"

His voice sounded strange. . . distant.

Cliff felt the plane fall.

Upside down. Spiraling. Snowy mountains.

The seat belt cutting into his lap.

His head.

Dizzy.

Didn't kiss her goodbye.

CHAPTER 2

FOR JACK MARTIN, home was a 1982 Airstream trailer, parked on campsite twenty of the Town Park Campground in Telluride, Colorado. At least for the time being, it was.

He sat in a metal folding chair leaned against the trailer, it's silvery skin cold on his back. He'd been lost in a chapter of *The Crossing*, a novel by Cormac McCarthy that his neighbor, Otto, had suggested on their latest trip to the library, when he heard the faint sound of an explosion in the distance.

The air was crisp and still, and Jack knew the sound had come from miles away. But he dropped his chair back onto four legs and stood up, then strained to listen but didn't hear anything over the gurgle of the river that bordered the eastern edge of the campground. He took several steps away from the trailer and turned toward the end of the canyon where Ingram Falls dropped nearly two thousand feet in a series of steps from a high-mountain basin above. The view was spectacular, but this morning Jack didn't notice. Something about the sound had been unsettling.

Crockett became aware of Jack's movement and abandoned his early-morning hunt for mice. He stood panting at his master's feet, wagging his tail.

Jack reached down and scratched the brown dog behind an ear. "What was it, boy?" he asked, still looking east.

After a few seconds, Jack gave up, tossed the book onto the chair, and started through the trees for campsite twenty-one, Crockett following close on his heels. The wind began to kick up slightly, swaying the branches of the pines. As he got closer, he heard the muffled chorus of George Strait's "Amarillo by Morning" coming from inside the tattered army surplus tent.

The campground had started filling up again. Jack had been there since January. By late March, the winter tourists had moved on and the town became the province of the locals. It was now mid-May, and the tourists were trickling back. For two months, Jack and Otto had had the campground practically to themselves. But things were changing.

Jack noticed Otto's cane propped against the tent and realized he hadn't seen the old guy use it since the weather had warmed.

"Otto," Jack hollered through the tent wall.

The music inside was turned down, and Jack watched as the door flap was slowly unzipped from the inside.

"Mornin'," Otto said, his wild gray hair and beard sticking out in every direction. He stepped out of the tent and bent carefully to pet the dog. "Mornin', Crockett."

Otto Finn was dressed in a plaid flannel shirt and tattered canvas pants, the same pair he'd worn every day of the four months Jack had known him, the bottoms of which were tucked into old work boots that didn't match. His shriveled face was permanently tanned from decades spent in the mountains, but his eyes were crystal blue and still danced with life.

Jack met Otto when he and Crockett had moved the trailer to Telluride from a campground outside Durango. The old guy was eccentric and prone to pulling the occasional prank, but

Jack had grown fond of him. The two had spent countless hours sitting along the banks of Bear Creek discussing the world's problems. Otto had some pretty unconventional suggestions on how to solve them, and Jack was surprised to find that he often agreed with the crazy old coot.

Jack had also learned about living and working in the mountains. Otto had grown up in the San Juans around Telluride, taught to live off the land and mine for silver and gold by his father, who'd emigrated from Scandinavia a hundred years earlier. Even nearing the age of eighty, Otto still mined somewhere in the surrounding mountains when the weather was warm. The location of his mine was a secret Otto had yet to reveal. With the snow in the higher elevations melting faster each day, Jack knew the old guy would soon set off and spend the rest of the summer in the high country.

It was Otto who had told Jack about the howitzer that was fired in the early mornings during ski season to lessen the risk of avalanches. But what Jack heard that morning hadn't sounded like a howitzer.

"There was an explosion a while ago," Jack said. "I guess you didn't hear it."

"Didn't hear nothin'." Otto's gray beard fluttered with the increasing breeze. He rubbed at it, thinking. "Was it gunfire?"

"It didn't sound like it." Having spent close to fifteen years with the FBI and a year with the Aspen Police Department, Jack was no stranger to the sound of guns, both on the range and on the job.

"Where'd it come from?"

"Somewhere up there." Jack pointed east toward the end of the canyon.

Otto turned and looked. "Still plenty of snow, but no avalanche worries this late. Could've been dynamite, but the big mines still operatin' are all over the ridge. You couldn't have heard anything that far away."

Jack stood quiet, letting Otto think.

"Could've been poachers," Otto said, still pulling on his beard. "But you said it didn't sound like gunfire." He thought about it a moment longer, then shook his head. "Beats me, Jack. Wish I'd heard it. But I'll listen in on the scanner and let you know if somethin' turns up."

It amused Jack that Otto kept a police scanner handy. Judith Hadley, the owner of Pandora Café in town, had alluded to Otto using it when he was in the mountains mining. She hadn't admitted as much, but Jack guessed from the conversation that Otto's mine could be on government land.

"Need a cup of coffee?" Otto asked. "I was just about to come out and make me some."

"Thank you, I think I will."

Otto's coffee looked like road tar. He brewed it in a speckled enameled pot over a tabletop charcoal grill. The first time Otto had offered it to him, Jack had hesitated and then was surprised to find out how good it was.

The two men sat listening to the river while they drank, Jack straddling one side of the picnic table secured to the ground of the campsite and Otto in a folding chair at the far end.

The frigid morning temperature was warming quickly with the rising sun. As Otto reminisced, Jack let his thoughts wander.

He'd spent the last couple of years in Colorado. First in Aspen as a detective with the Aspen Police Department, then at two different campgrounds with Crockett until they'd finally settled in Telluride.

In the few months he'd been there, Jack had grown to love Telluride. Even before the ski resort closed for the season in

April, he and Crockett had hit the hiking trails around town. They had trudged through sloshy mixes of snow and mud until the ground at the lower elevations had finally dried a few weeks earlier. But Jack was looking forward to hiking higher as soon as enough snow melted and the trails were opened.

As much as he had grown to love Colorado, Texas was always in the back of his mind. He hadn't had a paying job since he resigned from the Aspen Police Department over a year earlier. Since then, except for a homicide investigation he'd been paid for in Vail, he had lived off his savings, which were growing precariously thin.

In January, he had solved the murder of a missing Telluride woman. No one had hired him, but he had been determined to find the woman's killer. It had been Jack's first pro bono investigation, and he hoped it would be his last.

But the case had brought him to Telluride, and for that, he was grateful. He planned to spend the summer there, hiking the San Juan Mountains with Crockett. Before the snow returned in the fall, he would head back to Texas, where there were always jobs in construction or the oil fields. What he really wanted—a job in law enforcement—was probably a pipe dream. Although he had solved the notorious Hermes Strangler case while working as a detective in Aspen, he doubted the short time he'd been employed there would help him secure a meaningful job once back in Texas. Several years earlier, he had been forced to resign from the FBI following a shooting incident in Houston. It would no doubt hurt his chances of finding another job in law enforcement, but he would try. Until then, he would enjoy the time he had left in Colorado.

Otto was saying something about the explosion, which brought Jack around.

"Could've been a sonic boom," Otto said. "We get them on occasion."

Jack drained the last of his coffee and set the tin cup down on the table. "It sounded more like dynamite. Maybe someone's mining closer to town than they're supposed to," he said, trying to goad his old friend. "Somewhere on government property."

It worked.

Otto was lifting his cup to his mouth but stopped. There was a glint in his eyes. "Now you got me thinkin'." He set the cup on the table and struggled to push himself up out of the chair. "I'm gonna get that scanner. Let's find out what's going on."

Otto turned and disappeared into the tent, and Jack smiled.

CHAPTER 3

THE TELLURIDE AIRPORT was perched high on a plateau six miles west of town. There was no control tower, but William Palmer sat behind a radio that monitored air traffic coming and going. He tried making contact with the King Air on a different frequency. He had already tried a dozen.

There was no reply.

"Danny, I think you need to get in here," he called out to his boss.

A few seconds later, Danny Hodges strolled out of his office with a doughnut in one hand and a paper cup from The Coffee Cowboy in the other. "What is it?"

William took off the headset and tossed it onto the table in front of him. "I can't reach the King Air that flew out of here earlier."

Danny wiped doughnut glaze from his mouth, and some of it fell to the floor. "Why're you trying?"

"We received an incomplete transmission several minutes ago. It had to have come from the pilot of the King Air. The only other traffic we've had this morning was the Gulfstream that flew in just after the King Air left."

"You're talking about the King Air that Congressman Roberts was on?"

William nodded.

"Well, what did they say?"

"That's just it. They didn't say anything. Just 'Telluride,' then nothing. Like he was cut off before he was finished talking."

"Maybe he changed his mind. Decided he didn't need to talk to us and shut off his radio."

"I thought about that, but it was the tone of his voice—like he was yelling. And there was other static."

"What kind of static?"

"I'm not sure." William frowned, looking up at his boss. "But it sounded like wind."

CHAPTER 4

SHERIFF TONY BURNS had been at his desk since before dawn, going over the activity report for the week. There had been multiple traffic incidents; two abandoned vehicles; four DUIs; three cases of illegal dumping; a disturbance at Town Park in which a male had thrown a rock through the window of a parked car; a parole violation; a medical assist; two domestic disturbances; and the capture and return of one loose dog.

He tossed the activity report aside, screwed his eyes shut, and massaged the bridge of his nose. It was the same week after week. Although it had been only sixteen years since he'd been elected sheriff of San Miguel County, Tony had spent his life in law enforcement. And although he was only forty-three, he was already starting to think about retirement.

He could join his older brother, a fly-fishing guide in Montana, who often bragged about the tips he made. Maybe he'd head farther north, to Alaska, where his sister and brother-in-law ran a salmon hatchery outside of Ketchikan. They were always looking for help. He could work a few days a week and hunt and fish the rest.

Tony had been the only one to follow in their father's footsteps—and *his* father's before him—both of whom had worked their entire careers in law enforcement. His siblings had willfully resisted going into the family profession and set out on their own soon after high school. But Tony had been the dutiful middle child and done what was expected of him.

Except for a double-homicide case in Norwood several years earlier that CBI, Colorado Bureau of Investigations, eventually stepped in and took over, there had been only one case in his career that had held any real excitement for him. And even *that* one had been solved by someone else. Not by CBI again but by a private investigator—an outsider.

But that was months ago. And since then, there had been a nearly endless stream of traffic violations, disabled vehicles, domestic calls, and the occasional stolen bicycle.

Tony wanted a change. No, he *needed* a change. But he'd think about that later. He drew in and released a deep breath, then opened his eyes and pulled the inmate log from the corner of his desk.

There were currently two incarcerations: one of the DUIs, who had resisted arrest, and the Town Park rock thrower.

Deputy O'Connor knocked on his open door. "Can I interrupt?"

Tony tossed the inmate log aside. "Please."

Kim stepped into the office. "We just got a call from some guys in Ingram Basin—"

"Skinning?" Tony asked, referring to the practice of clipping synthetic skins onto the bottom of skis, climbing a mountain, and then skiing down. It was a popular activity in the mountains after the ski resort closed for the season.

"No. They're hiking."

"Hiking? It's too early to be up there."

"Agree."

They'd had record snows that winter and spring. And although the grass was green in town, the snow was still deep at higher altitudes. It infuriated Tony when, every spring, he'd have to send search and rescue to hunt for lost or stranded hikers.

"They need help?"

Kim shook her head. "Not them but possibly someone else." Tony frowned. "They said they saw a plane fly in the vicinity of Savage Basin headed east. Heard a pop of some kind, and a few seconds later heard what they thought was a crash. Happened about thirty minutes ago."

"They think the plane crashed?"

"That's what they're saying. But they couldn't see it because they're on the other side of Ajax," she said, referring to the mountain at the eastern edge of the canyon.

"Why did they wait to report it?"

"No cell service—they were out of range."

Just then Deputy Travis Barry stuck his head in the office. "Sheriff, sorry to bother you. Dispatch just got a call from someone in Pandora. Said they think a plane went down this side of Imogene Pass about a half hour ago."

"Why am I just now hearing about it?" Travis started to speak, but Tony got to it first. "Let me guess. No cell service?"

The deputy nodded. "It was Lon Remine who called it in. He was walking his dog out by the old mill."

Tony sighed. With all the advances in technology, cellular service in the mountains was still spotty and grossly unreliable. He thought about the call a moment. Pandora was the area just east of town at the end of the box canyon.

"Lon would've had a better visual than the hikers," Tony said, then turned to Kim. "Call the airport. See if they know about any of this." He looked at Travis next. "Call search and rescue. Just in case, let's get everyone assembled at the base of Tomboy Road. If we need to, we'll head up."

Tony had a feeling his morning was about to get crazy.

CHAPTER 5

JACK WAS STILL sitting at the picnic table when Otto emerged from the tent, radio scanner in hand.

Otto shuffled to his chair and dropped into it. "Might take me a while to find the right frequency," he said, turning the dials with clumsy, weathered fingers.

There was a commotion several campsites over, and Jack saw a group of four or five twentysomethings who had emerged from a cluster of tents pitched in a circle. A couple of them were arguing about something. He knew from trips to the public showers, passing their campsite, that the kids had a makeshift propane-powered cooktop in the center with a handful of chairs and benches scattered around it.

Otto was still searching for the right frequency. "I'll be glad when they're gone."

The group had shown up a few weeks earlier. They were boisterous and rowdy, often killing the serenity of what had been a peaceful campsite. Jack agreed with Otto; he was ready for them to move on.

"Have you ever seen them here before?" he asked.

Otto stopped fiddling with the scanner and glanced over at the group. "Don't think so. We've had some cause disturbances before but not as often as this lot." He shook his head and turned his attention back to the scanner.

Jack heard a crash and realized a fight had broken out. He saw one of the guys land a punch, sending another staggering. He fell back onto one of the girls in the group, who ended up on the ground, spewing expletives.

An aging hippie opened the door of a nearby trailer. "Knock it off!" he yelled. "Some of us are still trying to sleep!"

"Shut up, old man!" one of the kids hollered back. One of the others laughed.

The man disappeared into his trailer in a huff, slamming the door behind him.

It had been weeks of the same. The kids would get drunk or high, then fight among themselves. The town marshals had been called out several times, threatening to throw them out of town, but things had only gotten worse.

Through talk at Pandora Café, Jack had found out the kids were recruits paid to travel the country and protest for whichever cause was paying them for their services. This time, they'd been hired by someone funding Wilderness Keepers. Jack had done some digging and found out the environmental group was legitimate but these particular protesters weren't.

"They're a bad lot," Otto said, shaking his head. "Best keep your distance. From what I hear, they stirred up quite the hornets' nest at the town hall meetin' a couple of nights ago."

One of them noticed Jack and Otto watching. "What d'*you* want?" he hollered across the campground, jerking his chin and posturing.

Jack had had enough. He swung a leg over the bench at the table and stood up. "Crockett, stay." The dog was standing next to Otto's chair and sat. "Excuse me for a minute, Otto."

"You're gonna open a bag of nails," Otto said. "I wouldn't do that if I were you."

"I'm just going to talk to them."

"You're outnumbered."

"Yeah, but they're hungover," Jack said, starting in the direction of the campsite. There would be more of them in the tents sleeping. Jack counted on all of them being hungover or high.

"Don't make me have to come help ya," Otto called out to him and laughed.

The one who'd jerked his chin noticed Jack headed in his direction and elbowed the guy standing next to him. Both took a few steps toward Jack, their chests puffed out and arms bowed and swinging with too much swagger. One wore a Black Sabbath hoodie; the other was shirtless, bare chested despite the morning chill.

Jack had come into contact with plenty of guys just like these two. Bullies in high school trying to make their mark, drunk frat guys in college wanting to one-up a football player. Jack sized them up quickly. If he could keep it to just the two, they wouldn't be much of a problem.

As he approached, Jack held up his hands. "Listen, guys, this is a peaceful campground."

"We bothering you, old man?" The shirtless one staggered closer, squinting his eyes. "Why don't you mind your own business?"

Jack stopped a few feet from him. "Listen, I don't want any trouble."

The muscles in Shirtless Guy's neck tensed. He looked ready to pounce when a third man stepped from behind a tent. He was larger than the other two, with a buzz cut and a bearing that marked him as the leader.

"What's going on?" Buzz Cut asked, holding up a hand to call off his minions.

Shirtless backed down.

Jack stood his ground. "Some of us are tired of the racket."

Buzz Cut took a step closer, swaying slightly. "As far as I know, this is still a free country, old man."

"You're disturbing the peace."

Shirtless spat on the ground at Jack's feet, just missing the tips of his cowboy boots. "Wyatt Earp, here, wants us to settle down, Dewane."

"Shut up, Thomas." Buzz Cut turned his attention back to Jack and spread his arms wide. "It's our campsite, old man. And we have a policy against trespassers." When Jack didn't reply, he added, "And a policy against people buttin' in when it ain't their business."

"That's a lot of policies."

Buzz Cut's eyes narrowed. "You need to leave," he said. "You have no legal standing here."

The fight in the tent circle had broken out again. The same two guys were rolling on the ground, throwing punches. A couple of the girls in the group were screaming at them.

Jack stared at Buzz Cut, but in his peripheral vision he saw Shirtless and Hoodie each take a couple of steps to either side. They were trying to flank him. *So, this is the way it's going to be,* Jack thought, silently cursing himself for not listening to Otto.

He had three—maybe four—seconds to assess the situation. Out of the corner of his eye, he saw Shirtless crouch in a ridiculous attempt at some sort of ninja pose. Buzz Cut didn't move, but Hoodie had taken a slight step backward. Because of the hangover? Or was he having second thoughts? Either way, Hoodie was going to be the weakest threat.

Buzz Cut was the first to make a move. From experience, Jack knew those wanting to reinforce their leadership position typically did.

But Jack was ready. It took a split second, no more.

When Buzz Cut lunged, Jack spun out of the way, throwing his right elbow up and catching him in the throat, sending him staggering.

Shirtless Ninja's reaction was delayed—not surprising given his intoxication. He made a half-hearted jump toward Jack and was met with a sweep to his standing knee—one meant to render him helpless but not permanently maimed. Yelping in pain, he dropped like a stone.

Hoodie was breathing hard, his eyes bulging. Holding shaking hands aloft, he took another step back.

Buzz clutched his throat, coughing.

Jack was catching his breath and preparing for round two when a white truck with Marshal emblazoned on the side emerged from the trees and approached the campsite.

The officer parked the truck and got out. He glanced at Shirtless still on the ground, groaning and holding his knee, then at Buzz. "What's going on this time, Dewane?"

Buzz coughed. "Simple misunderstanding, Marshal," he said in a strained voice. "We're all good now."

The insignia on the officer's uniform identified him as Deputy Marshal Croix. He was built squat but solid. Jack had seen him at the campground before.

Croix glanced at Hoodie, still on the ground, then made eye contact with Jack, and a look of confusion crossed his face. It took a second for it to register. "Jack Martin?"

Jack nodded. "Marshal."

Croix was silent a moment, then turned back to Dewane. "We got a call you guys were disturbing the peace."

"Not us, Marshal." Dewane coughed again. "But if we hear anything, we'll let you know."

The deputy stared at Buzz a moment, then glanced down to where Hoodie was helping Shirtless up from the ground.

"Next time I'm called out here, I'm going to give you guys a ticket," Croix said. "Don't make me come out again. Understand?"

"Yes, sir," Dewane answered.

Croix turned to Jack. "Can I speak with you a moment?"

Dewane hustled his two companions back toward the tent circle where a couple of the others had been watching the events unfold. Before he disappeared, he shot a look of warning over his shoulder at Jack, indicating their business wasn't finished.

Jack followed Croix to his truck.

"Listen, I know these guys are trouble," the deputy said. "If it were up to me, I'd haul all of them in right now. But the marshal is hoping they'll be gone soon. He doesn't want a stink over arresting any of them. It'd be bad publicity. But in the meantime, if you see or hear anything you think we need to know about, I'd appreciate a call." He handed Jack his card.

In the few months Jack had been in Telluride, he'd learned that, although Sheriff Tony Burns had jurisdiction over San Miguel County, the marshals were responsible for law enforcement within the city limits.

He watched the truck pull away and cast a glance over his shoulder, noticing Otto waiving at him. Satisfied Dewane and his crew were no longer a threat—at least for now—Jack turned toward his own campsite. Otto held Crockett by the collar with one hand and was smoking a cigarette with the other. He was grinning ear to ear and shaking his head. The scanner was on his lap.

"Son, I had to have me a Camel you were so entertaining," he said, waving the cigarette and belting out the gritty laugh of a lifelong smoker. "Watchin' that was more fun than I've had in a long time."

"You didn't come help."

"No, but I almost released the hound."

Otto let go of Crockett, and the dog immediately rushed to Jack's side, wagging his tail. Jack switched the marshal's card from his right hand to his left and bent to pet him.

Otto set the scanner on the table, shaking his head. "I tried warnin' you—every one of those kids is a bubble off plumb, raising hell like they do."

Jack gestured toward the scanner. "Did you find out what happened?"

"Plane went down in Savage Basin." He pointed to an area near the top of the canyon. "That's what you must've heard."

Jack looked to where Otto was pointing. The basin was a large scooped area tucked just below the highest peaks northeast of town. Everything up there was still blanketed in snow.

"Search and rescue will head up soon, I figure," Otto said, turning around. "But that's gonna be a *recovery*, not a rescue."

The two men were quiet a moment.

"The marshal give you a ticket?" Otto asked.

Jack was confused, then remembered the card he was holding and tucked it into a back pocket. "He gave me his number." He glanced in the direction of the tent circle. "In case we have any more problems."

CHAPTER 6

TED HAWTHORNE WAS a little man with a giant chip on his shoulder. He was small and thin, with a wisp of hair that he greased and swept sideways over a tall forehead. He sat drumming his fingers on the oversize pine desk in his office at the back of Telluride Bank & Trust.

Dressed in wool pants and a chunky cardigan vest, to the casual observer, Ted would seem more the quirky academic than the president of Telluride's oldest bank. With his penny loafers and fastidious manner, he was easily mistaken as an outsider, but his roots in the old mining town ran deep.

Ted had grown up in Telluride. His father had been the president of Telluride Bank & Trust, as had his grandfather and great-grandfather before him.

The Hawthornes had settled in the canyon soon after gold was discovered in the mountains above town. The gold rush that ensued had swelled the settlement's population, attracting fortune seekers from across the globe. Along with the miners came outlaws, women of ill repute, and businessmen looking to cash in on the new riches. Among the businessmen was Abraham Theodore Hawthorne, who had emigrated as a young man from New York and established the town's first chartered bank.

Over a century later, the Telluride Bank & Trust was still privately owned and run by Abraham's great-grandson.

That morning, Ted had come in early—well before the bank opened—just as he had every working day for the last three decades. He rarely took time off. His last vacation had been to a banking conference in Scottsdale, Arizona, nearly a decade earlier.

Ted didn't hike or fish or ski. He worked. And the harder he worked, the more things seemed to stay the same. But not for much longer, he thought with nervous satisfaction.

Congressman Cliff Roberts would finally get what was coming to him. He was up for reelection, and the brewing land controversy couldn't have come at a better time. Ted smiled remembering the outbursts shouted at Cliff during the town hall meeting held several nights earlier at the old Opera House. *Dirty politician! You're a sellout!*

But it wasn't just the rowdy crowd inside. Outside, a band of protesters chanted, carrying homemade signs that read Keep it Wild, Not Defiled. Stop the Steal. Out with Cliff!

Ted had feigned indignation, telling anyone who'd listen that the hoodlums should have been "run out of town before the meeting" and that "someone's head should roll in the Marshal's Department for letting things get out of hand."

Eric Dale and his group, Wilderness Keepers, had been in town for several weeks protesting a land trade being negotiated between the federal government and a local millionaire rancher, Hank Wade.

Wade wanted three hundred acres of high-alpine land adjacent to the venerable Mount Sneffels, one of the area's fourteen-thousand-foot peaks. In exchange, Wade pledged to give the government a parcel nearly seven times that size closer to the nearby town of Ridgway. The land Wade offered the government was considered a crucial migratory corridor for deer and elk. But many people, including Eric Dale, considered the proposed swap an unequal exchange at best and, at worst, a greedy land grab of one of the most pristine wilderness areas left in the San Juan Mountains.

Caught in the center of the controversy was Cliff Roberts, representing Colorado's Third Congressional District. He was considered the state's "golden boy," the son of Colorado's longest-serving senator, the late Edward Roberts.

But Ted knew the truth, knew that the golden boy had been exiled as an adolescent, sent to live in the family's vacation home in Telluride with a caretaker following multiple run-ins with law enforcement in DC.

"He could have at least let me live at the house in Denver," Cliff had complained to Ted years ago when the two were in junior high. "Instead, the old man shipped me out here to the middle of nowhere."

At first, Cliff had continued his wild ways, running afoul of the town marshals on more than one occasion. But over the years, he'd slowly turned himself around, working nights at the local radio station and eventually graduating salutatorian of their high school class. Of course, Ted had been valedictorian.

The two men had remained friends over the years, Ted regularly donating to Cliff's political campaigns and Cliff dazzling everyone he came into contact with. Ted's resentment of Cliff had grown over the years, and it was a struggle to keep his feelings in check.

But there was no time for reminiscing. Ted pulled his reading glasses down from the top of his head and turned his attention back to the stack of reports on his desk. Two hours later, he barely noticed when Gretchen, the bank's cashier and only full-time teller, showed up for work.

"Good morning, Mr. Hawthorne," she called out in a singsong voice, pushing her bulk through the low, saloon-like swinging doors that separated the bank's lobby from the work areas. "Wind's starting to kick up a gale out there."

Ted grunted a reply and adjusted the glasses on his nose.

An hour later, he'd finished going through the stack of reports. Deposits were up and delinquencies on loan payments were down. Business was good in Telluride, but Ted wasn't happy. He'd turned fifty-eight the year before but felt middle age slipping through his fingers. Before it was too late, he wanted something more. He tapped a Bic pen on the top of the desk, thinking.

The bank's front door swung open, and Chuck Daniels, the part-time teller, stumbled inside. The kid was dressed in jeans and a button-down shirt that wasn't fully tucked in. He was out of breath, like he'd been running.

He spoke to Gretchen. "A plane went down in Savage Basin. They say it was that congressman."

"Cliff Roberts?" Gretchen gasped.

"Yeah, him."

Ted Hawthorne felt the color drain from his face.

CHAPTER 7

IT WAS THE TYPE of call Tony Burns had spent his career hoping to avoid. He parked the white Tahoe at the curb along Columbia Avenue and killed the ignition.

"Ever done one of these?" Deputy Kim O'Connor asked, sitting in the passenger seat next to him.

"Yeah. It's the worst part of the job."

"It's my first." She sounded apprehensive. "We can't wait to tell her until after it's confirmed?"

Tony sighed. "With all the snow up there, it could take search and rescue hours to confirm it." He shook his head. "I don't want Susan spending the day trying to reach him and not knowing. Word is going to get out about a crash. I don't want her to find out about it from conversation in town."

Sheriff and deputy sat a moment, both dreading what they had to do.

Tony studied the home, one of the oldest in Telluride. It sat facing south and was bathed in the rising sun on two sides. It was a two-story Victorian that sat on a corner and was painted a deep shade of blue, the trim and porch railings a stark white. It was the biggest of the old houses in town, set on what Tony thought had to be the largest residential lot—and one of the prettiest. Mature trees dotted the front and side yards. An enormous spruce stood guard near the street and swayed in the wind.

There was some historical significance to the home, but Tony couldn't remember what it was. Probably built by an early town leader, maybe the owner of one of the mines somewhere in the mountains. But currently it was the residence of Congressman Cliff Roberts—probably the *late* Congressman Cliff Roberts—and his wife, Susan. They didn't know for sure, but Tony didn't think there was any way Cliff or his pilot could have survived the crash. But he wouldn't tell that to Susan; he would only tell her that Cliff was missing.

"Let's get this over with," Tony said. He was grateful Kim had volunteered to come with him.

Kim had a small, birdlike build and wore her red hair in a ponytail that blew furiously in the wind as they took the sidewalk to the front door. Although she was the least intimidating deputy on Tony's staff, she had the biggest heart. Kim had grown up in Telluride, and the locals loved her. She knew everyone in town, including Susan.

At the door, Kim stood to the side. Tony knocked, then cleared his throat. A few seconds later, the door opened.

Susan Roberts was in her midforties with hair the same shade as the morning sun. She wore designer jeans and a cashmere sweater. Tony thought she was beautiful.

She seemed surprised to see them.

"Sheriff," Susan said, then nodded at his deputy. "Kim." Her smile slowly morphed into a look of concern. "Is there something wrong?"

"Susan, may we come in?"

She stared at him a moment, then pulled the door open further. "Of course. Please come in."

Tony stepped inside and glanced around. The old woodwork had been meticulously restored. The floors—probably pine—were stained a caramel color and coated with a heavy polyurethane. The furniture and art were antique and looked expensive. Despite being updated, the house retained the old-wood smell typical of a late Victorian.

Susan ushered them into the nearby living room. "Would you like to have a seat?"

Tony shook his head. "No, but thank you." He drew in a deep breath, steadying his nerves. "Susan, Kim and I have come to tell you that a plane went down in Savage Basin this morning."

It took a moment; then she brought her hand to her throat. "Cliff's?"

Tony felt his heart sink. "We believe so."

Her voice shook. "What do you mean *believe*? Was it his plane or not?"

"We believe so, but—"

"But it might not be." Her eyes were pleading with him. She wanted him to give her hope, leave a door open that it wasn't her husband.

Tony wished he could tell her what she wanted to hear, but he knew it would be a lie. "There were eyewitnesses that saw it go down— "

"But there's a chance it wasn't Cliff's. You just said you weren't sure." Her eyes were welling with tears, and her voice was growing angry. "It could have been someone else's."

Tony shook his head. "The control tower in Denver that was tracking the flight said it disappeared from radar. The guys at the airport here said they lost radio contact and haven't been able to reestablish it. They've been trying for almost an hour."

"But there's a chance? You don't know for sure."

"Search and rescue is assembling now. Once they get up there, they'll be able to confirm it."

"Can't you send a helicopter?"

"The wind has picked up. We can't risk flying."

Susan started to cry.

Kim stepped toward her. "I'm sorry," she said, laying a hand on her arm, but Susan pushed it away.

"No." She staggered back into a side table, nearly toppling a lamp. "You don't know for sure. The radio could be turned off."

The conversation was going worse than Tony had expected. "No other plane has flown out this morning." He shook his head again. "I'm sorry, Susan."

Kim guided her to a couch, where she sat down and dropped her face into her hands. They let her cry.

Tony wasn't sure how much time had passed, but it seemed like an eternity—an awkward, excruciating eternity. When she finished crying, she stood up, her face swollen and flushed but stoic.

She wiped mascara from under her eyes. "Where did the witnesses say it went down?"

"Savage Basin."

Susan walked to a window and stared up at the mountains. After a long minute, she turned around. "Thank you for coming." Her voice had changed. It was distant, almost mechanical. "But I need you to leave now. There are people I need to call."

Tony was struck by the dramatic change in her demeanor. From the sensitivity training he'd had years earlier, he recognized the different stages of grief. She had already gone through denial and anger, and now reality was setting in. Or was it shock? He would send someone to check on her in a few hours.

Outside, Kim was the first one to speak. "I hope I never have to do that again."

Tony agreed.

In the Tahoe, she turned to him. "Let me go with search and rescue," she said.

Tony started the ignition. "Kim, it's not your job."

"But I want to go."

"It'll be too dangerous. The road will be closed before they get anywhere near the basin."

"I don't care. I've done it before."

Tony knew that she had volunteered for search and rescue missions in the past. But she was older now, probably nearing forty, and had two small children.

"I can't let you—"

"Please, Tony."

"Your last search and rescue was what? Ten years ago? Before you had Samantha and Jake?"

She slumped back in the seat as he pulled away from the curb.

"Besides," he said. "I know Daryl wouldn't like it either."

Kim and Daryl had split up the year before. Tony knew that he had moved to Grand Junction and taken a job with one of the wineries, leaving Kim and the kids in Telluride. Although they'd never been married, they'd had a long-term relationship—one of those newfangled "marriages in spirit" that Tony never understood. And despite the split, their relationship was still an amicable one.

"I'll call him and ask," Kim said. "If he's all right with it, will you let me go?"

Tony turned the corner onto Main Street. He didn't like it, but if Daryl said okay, he didn't know how he could keep her from going.

Kim's father had died when she was a teenager. Callum O'Connor had been a stocky redhead who'd emigrated from Ireland before she was born. From the stories Tony had heard, he knew Callum had hit town like a copper-colored whirlwind. He was fun-loving and boisterous and a regular at the Last Dollar Saloon, often buying rounds of drinks for locals at the bar. But his time in Telluride had been cut tragically short when he and two co-workers from the Camp Bird Mine were caught in a deadly avalanche.

After the accident, Kim's mother moved east to Chicago, but Kim had stayed. She started volunteering with search and rescue before she was out of high school, and Tony suspected her father's accident had been the reason why.

But Telluride wasn't an easy place to raise children alone. So after Kim's split with Daryl, Tony had asked her why she didn't move as well. "The mountains are in my blood," she had said. He understood.

They sat in the truck for a while longer, the wind kicking up and starting to roar.

"All right," Tony finally said. "If Daryl's okay with it, you can go."

"Thank y—"

"But for the record, *I'm* not okay with it." He saw several trees along Main Street sway with the wind. "It's going to be a dangerous climb."

"I'll be fine," Kim said, trying to reassure him.

Tony thought of Samantha and Jake and what Kim meant to the office—hell, what she meant to just about everyone in Telluride.

He squeezed the steering wheel and pushed down on the accelerator. "You better be."

CHAPTER 8

JACK REMAINED AT the picnic table drinking coffee with Otto until the rowdy activists had dispersed—some disappearing back into their tents, the others leaving on foot in the direction of town.

Satisfied there wouldn't be any more problems, Jack stood up. "I'm going to Judith's for breakfast," he told Otto, referring to the café where he'd eaten at least one meal a day since arriving in Telluride. "Care to join me?"

Otto shook his head and laid a weathered hand on Crockett. "You go on. Leave him here with me."

"You sure?"

"We'll be fine, boy, won't we?" he said, patting the dog's head.

Jack was leaving Crockett with him more and more, and suspected the dog was enjoying it as much as Otto was.

Jack started for town, making his way through the campground on foot. Campsite twenty was located at the far end, the farthest from Main Street. In January, when he had decided to stay in Telluride through the summer, he had briefly considered asking for a space closer to the entrance. He walked almost everywhere he went—the market, the library, the café—and being closer to the entrance would shave several minutes off each trip. But he had quickly realized how much he enjoyed Otto's company and camping next to the river and so dismissed the idea of moving. And now, four months later, he wasn't sure he wanted to leave Telluride at the end of the summer. He would let his bank account balance dictate how long he and Crockett could stay.

On Main Street, Jack headed west toward downtown. He felt his cell phone buzz and pulled it from his pocket, then glanced at the caller ID. Buckley Bailey.

Bailey, the former governor of Texas, and his wife, Celeste, lived in Austin but had a second home in Telluride. Jack hadn't talked to him in months. The last time having been the day Jack solved the murder of Alice Fremont. Alice had been a longtime friend of Buckley's, and he'd called to congratulate Jack on the arrest.

Jack was curious why he was calling now.

"Hello, Buckley."

"Jack! Thank God you answered." Buckley's voice thundered through the phone. He sounded frantic. "Where are you? Still in Telluride, I hope."

Jack pictured Buckley leaning back, his cowboy boots resting atop the oversize desk in the study of the Baileys' giant log home in Mountain Village. "I'm still here," he said.

"Great!" Buckley boomed. "I need you to do something for me."

Jack wondered what was going on. Was it Celeste? Before he could ask, Buckley continued.

"I need you to get to the base of Tomboy Road. Do you know where it is?"

"No."

"From Main Street, head north on North Oak. It's at the top of the hill. Search and rescue is gearing up. I want you to go with them." He was talking loud and fast.

Jack stopped walking. Surely he had misunderstood what Buckley said. "Search and rescue?"

"A plane went down above town a little while ago. I need you to go with them to find it."

Jack turned and looked east, to the area high in the mountains where Otto had pointed to earlier. It was still covered in snow.

"Buckley, I can't—"

"But you're a hiker," he said. "I've heard."

The conversation was ridiculous. "I *hike*," Jack replied, "but—"

"Jack, I need you to go with them."

"Why?"

"Where are you now?" Buckley asked. "How soon can you get there?"

Jack was growing frustrated. "Even if I agreed to go, they wouldn't let me."

"It's already been arranged."

"What?" Jack blew out air. "What do you mean it's been arranged?"

"It's been arranged. They're expecting you."

This was crazy. Jack had hiked countless miles with Crockett in the last year, but hiking into the snow with a search and rescue team was different. He looked back up at the frozen basin perched high above the canyon.

"I'll pay you." Buckley's tone had lost its frantic edge. "Jack, I need you to go. Please get to the base of Tomboy Road as soon as you can. A friend of mine was on that plane. His wife just called me." When Jack hesitated, he added: "He's a congress-man. You know how these things go. It won't be long before the media finds out about the crash, and then all hell will break loose. Law enforcement won't tell us a damn thing until some committee of bureaucrats decides it's time to make a public statement. I don't want to wait that long. He's my friend."

Jack thought about it a moment, then crossed the street to-ward the campground, his cowboy boots clomping on the pave-ment. "All right, I'll go. But I've got to change clothes."

"Hurry."

Jack started to jog, still holding his phone to his ear while Buckley filled him in on Congressman Cliff Roberts and what he knew about the plane crash—which wasn't much.

Buckley was insistent Jack be with search and rescue when they found the plane, but he wasn't making it clear why. It was true, the government was typically slow to release information. The details behind the crash wouldn't be reported immediately, but if the congressman was dead, they would at least report *that*. What else did Buckley want to know?

When Jack reached the campground, he ran through the trees toward the trailer. "Buckley, from what you're telling me, it sounds like it'll be a recovery, not a rescue."

"Just go," Buckley said. "The basin is high up—it could take all day. You won't have cell service for most of it, but call me when you can." The usually cheerful Texan sounded worried.

Jack ended the call and ran faster despite being out of breath. Buckley would have had to pull some serious strings to secure Jack a spot on search and rescue to hunt for a downed plane carrying a US congressman. The FBI and Secret Service were probably already on their way to Telluride.

Something didn't add up.

CHAPTER 9

LESS THAN FIVE minutes after he ended the call from Buckley, Jack was in the truck on the way to meet up with search and rescue. It was the off season in Telluride, and not hard to find a parking spot. Driving would save several minutes.

Jack drove several blocks up Main Street, turned right on North Oak, and parked next to the curb. He was only a couple of blocks away, but it would be a steep climb to the end of the street, where a couple of Tahoes and several trucks with trailers and snowmobiles were parked near the top. A dozen or so people milled about in some sort of organized chaos.

Jack got out of the truck and jogged toward them, a feat made more difficult wearing his winter boots. At the trailer, he had changed out of his jeans and cowboy boots into canvas pants and the insulated winter boots he'd purchased a few months before and still didn't like. But they served a purpose. And if he was going to be hiking in snow, his leather ropers weren't an option.

On the way out the door, he'd grabbed his Carhartt jacket, then asked Otto if he'd mind watching Crockett for the rest of the day, explaining what was going on. As he'd expected, the old man readily agreed.

As he jogged the hill, Jack noticed the sheriff among the group at the top of the street. He was talking with a tall, athletic-looking man in his early thirties with white-blond hair. They were studying a map that had been lain on the open tailgate of one of the trucks.

Tony looked up when Jack approached. He didn't look happy. "I understand you're going up with search and rescue."

"Seems like it."

"You an EMT?"

"No."

"A mountain medic?"

"A what?"

"Never mind."

The blond man folded the map and shut the tailgate.

"Anders this is Jack Martin," Tony said to the blond man. "He's coming with you."

Anders nodded, then turned to the sheriff. "I think we're ready." Tony handed him a radio, and Anders shut the tailgate, then started for the driver's-side door. "Load up!" he hollered to the group.

A dozen or so men, two women, and a dog started piling into the vehicles.

Tony turned to Jack. "If it were up to me, you wouldn't be going," he said. "But Buckley Bailey pulls enough political weight around here to insist that you do." When Jack didn't reply, he added, "He says you're an experienced hiker."

"I hike."

The sheriff scrutinized Jack's coat and pants and didn't seem impressed. His gaze slid down to his boots. Jack thought they were ridiculous looking but noticed that almost everyone was wearing something similar.

"At least you've got on decent boots," Tony said, nodding his approval. "You're going to need them." He gestured toward the bed of the truck. "Climb in."

Jack stepped onto the rear bumper and swung a leg over the tailgate. A deputy was already seated in the back of the truck. She introduced herself as Kim O'Connor and didn't seem to mind that Jack was there. He noticed that she wore a down coat and insulated pants. Her red hair was pulled back in a ponytail that blew sideways in the wind under a knit cap.

"What's the latest on the hikers?" Tony asked her. "They okay?"

Kim nodded. "Local kids. Already headed back down."

Tony slapped the top of the tailgate. "Good." He looked over the small caravan and back to Kim. "You guys be careful."

The group headed up the canyon. Anders's truck took the lead, and a Tahoe brought up the rear. In the back of the truck with Jack and Kim were three men, all with long faces. Everyone was aware of the gravity of what they were about to do.

They drove a single-lane gravel road cut from the side of the mountains that soared high to their left. To their right was a steep drop to the valley floor below. The wind roared around them, and the cold soon penetrated Jack's canvas pants and jacket. He saw Kim pull up the hood of her down coat and bury her face inside.

They bounced over the gravel road without speaking, and Jack studied the valley below, green with the beginnings of summer. After a few minutes, he noticed a waterfall in the distance, tucked in a corner of the canyon, south of Ingram Falls. He had never seen it before, the mountains behind the campground having blocked it from view. The falls spilled over a cliff face and plummeted a few hundred feet to the ground below. Beside the falls a white building sat precariously on the cliff's edge. The view of it from across the canyon was spectacular.

Jack shifted his gaze over, squinting against the wind, and scrutinized the ridge line that loomed above them. The uppermost rocky crags were still covered in snow, the peaks seeming to reach up and touch the turquoise sky. The basin where they were headed looked much the same. It looked beautiful but menacing.

"Seems like heaven up here, doesn't it?" Kim had emerged from the dark confines of her coat and was looking up at the peaks. Just then a gust of wind flung grit off the mountain, and they turned their faces away. "But maybe it's hell."

The temperature dropped, and Jack zipped his coat to his neck. The farther they drove, the more rugged the road and the mountains became. Soon, except for the pines, nothing was green. And above the approaching tree line, everything was covered in snow. Jack noticed the road had turned to a mix of rock and mud.

Sometime later, they came to a stop. The guy seated in the passenger seat of Anders's truck jumped out and unchained a single-arm gate that blocked the road. It was painted yellow, and there was a sign mounted on it warning that the road ahead was closed. The guy held the gate aloft while the small convoy rolled through, then pulled it down and locked it behind them.

They continued on.

Kim had her face huddled inside her coat again, the hood pulled down as far as it would go, shielding her from the biting wind and growing cold.

"How close will we get?" Jack hollered out to her, wondering when the road would end and they'd be forced to continue on the snowmobiles.

Kim peered out from the hood. "To the point where we can still turn the trucks around and head back," she said. "Or the snow gets too deep."

After a while, they entered an area where the road hung precariously to a cliff face that blocked the north wind. They were approaching a hairpin turn. Jack glanced over the side of the truck and immediately wished he hadn't. The edge of the road dropped away probably a thousand feet to the ground below.

"We're in Royer's Gulch," Kim said when she noticed him looking. "We'll be fine." She must have seen the worry on his face. "I've been through here a thousand times," she added, trying to reassure him. She didn't.

Jack held his breath as they drove across a makeshift bridge of poured concrete that somehow clung to the mountainside, the truck bouncing left and right. He took another quick glance over the side, and what he saw made his heart skip a beat. There now couldn't have had more than eight inches to spare between the wheel and the road. He imagined a sudden strong gust of wind hurling them off into the ravine below.

There were a few more turns in what was easily the worst section of road Jack had ever experienced. Next they drove through a small tunnel blasted through solid rock, then around a few more bends. Jack sighed in relief when they cleared the last turn and the road widened a bit.

Kim emerged from her coat's hood and laughed. She had been watching him. "See? Piece of cake."

The convoy trudged on.

After what seemed like hours, Anders finally stopped the truck. He got out and gestured to the driver of the vehicle behind them.

"This is as far as we go," he hollered over the wind. "We're on snowmobiles or foot from here."

Jack climbed over the tailgate and stared up at where they were headed. Each breath he exhaled fogged in front of him.

"Next stop Savage Basin," Kim said. She had come up behind him and was pulling on a backpack.

Jack didn't know what to say. It was worse than he had expected. Except for the cliffs and rocky peaks, everything was buried in snow. The basin lay due east of where they'd stopped and looked like God had taken a giant scoop out of the mountains and replaced it with an enormous bowl of snow. Directly behind the basin was the steep incline that Jack had heard the locals refer to as Imogene Pass. The ridge line continued west and south, encircling the basin on three sides—much of it with sawtooth peaks that looked like the teeth of a giant wild animal.

Jack took it all in while icy winds swirled around him. It was the last place someone would want to be stranded, he thought. And a falling aircraft wouldn't stand a chance.

For the first time since he'd gotten the call from Buckley Bailey, Jack worried about what they might find.

CHAPTER 10

THE MOUNTAINSIDE WAS soon a flurry of activity. Jack watched as a couple of guys divided an assortment of ropes. Two others were packing something onto the backs of the snowmobiles that looked like folded tents. Jack wasn't sure what to think. He wasn't prepared to spend the night outdoors.

He saw others dig through the contents of their backpacks. They had flashlights, knives, and food. He watched as they pulled on gloves and helmets—most of them with headlamps.

Anders hoisted a large canvas bag from the bed of the truck and noticed Jack watching. "Where's your gear?"

Jack felt woefully unprepared. His fingers were numb, and he silently cursed himself for forgetting to grab his gloves. His body burned with cold beneath his jacket and pants. He'd been a fool to think canvas would be enough. But he hadn't been given any time. Buckley had insisted Jack go with search and rescue immediately, which he had. How could he have known he needed "gear"? Hell, he didn't even *own* gear.

With the tall Nordic glaring at him, waiting for a response, Jack felt like an idiot. "I don't have any."

The look of disdain on Anders's face could have sliced metal. Without comment, he jerked open the door to the truck and leaned in. Jack heard him open and rifle through the console, then slam it shut. Next, he reached farther in and pulled something from the passenger-side floorboard.

"Put this on," he said, handing Jack a yellow helmet. "And these."

To Jack's relief, it was a pair of black insulated gloves. "Thank you."

"Don't lose them." He looked down at Jack's boots, then reached back into the truck and came out with a set of snow-shoes. "Don't lose these, either." He turned to the group and began giving instructions.

Jack watched as they unloaded and mounted the snowmo-biles. Kim called to him and offered him a spot behind her. And although he was grateful for the ride, he felt emasculated riding shotgun behind the hundred-pound redhead.

Several minutes later they were on their way. The pecking order was made clear. Anders took the lead, along with another capable-looking thirtysomething. Jack had heard Anders refer to him as Smith. Smith had a full beard and the bearing of a man at home in the mountains. Jack wasn't sure if Smith was his first name or last, but it probably wouldn't matter. Except for Kim, the rest of the group seemed to resent him being there. He didn't blame them for it. If he were in their shoes, he'd probably feel the same way about an unprepared interloper stuck in their group at the behest of an obnoxious politician pulling strings behind the scenes.

They drove through the snow for less than an hour when Anders stopped the group again and announced they would have to go the rest of the way on foot. The snow was too deep and the ledges hugging the mountainside, too narrow to cross safely. Jack couldn't believe they were still following a road.

"It's under there," Kim said when he asked. "And Imogene Pass—near where we're headed—is a great excursion in the summer. You should try it."

Jack leaned over and looked down the cliff face to the ground below and doubted he ever would.

Kim gave him a pair of waterproof pants to pull over his canvas ones, then helped him strap on the snowshoes. She must have seen the worry in his eyes. "Your first search and rescue?"

Jack nodded.

"You'll be all right," she said and smiled reassuringly.

The group set off again. Jack took the pecking-order clues and dropped to the back. He would bring up the rear. He didn't mind pulling drag. The views were stunning, and he was still figuring out how to hike in snowshoes.

He looked back down the valley, where they had come from. The sun was shining, but Telluride was small and hazy in the distance below.

"We'll be about four thousand feet above town when we get up to Savage Basin." Kim had dropped back beside him. She talked loudly, making sure he could hear her over the wind.

Jack looked at where they were headed. "There's a lot of snow up there," he said. "I'm not prepared. I wasn't told—"

"Ah, that's no problem," she said, punching the sleeve of his Carhartt jacket. "Between the rest of us, we got you covered."

They walked in silence for a while, following the others.

"What do you know about the crash?" Jack asked.

Kim shook her head. "Not much. Just that they think it's a King Air carrying Cliff Roberts. He's our local congressman."

"Would they send you guys up here if it wasn't a congressman?"

"You mean, if it wasn't someone as important?"

Jack nodded.

"Absolutely they would," Kim replied. "Under normal circumstances, if there's no inclement weather, they'd send a chopper up. But not in this wind. And until it dies down, we're on our own."

Jack knew from the forecast that the high winds were supposed to last throughout the day, not slowing until nightfall. It was unlikely a helicopter would be able to get to the crash site until the next morning.

Jack surveyed the rugged mountainside. To his left, the slope rose sharply, probably a thousand feet. To the right, it dropped dramatically away probably another thousand. He again imagined a strong gust of wind sending them all hurdling over the edge. He angled closer to the mountainside, hugging the uphill slope.

After a while, the road curved, temporarily blocking them from the wind, making conversation easier.

"Have any planes crashed up here before?"

"Unfortunately, yes," Kim answered. "It doesn't happen often, but we've had a few. Mainly due to wind sheers and pilots underestimating how hard it is to gain enough altitude to clear the peaks. The air's thin up here."

Jack wondered about the King Air. "Maybe that's what happened this time."

"Doesn't sound like it. From what the hikers said, it sounds like the plane was already above the mountains. And they reported hearing an explosion."

Jack had heard the explosion, too. But it would have been much louder for anyone up this high when it occurred.

"It'll be interesting to find out what happened," Kim said. "But usually these investigations last months. We won't know for a while."

"What about a flight recorder?"

Kim shook her head. "Private planes aren't required to have them."

"Cockpit voice recorder?"

She shook her head again. "They've been trying to get a signal from an ELT."

"What's that?"

"Emergency locator transmitter. In the event of a crash, an ELT is designed to send a signal that, when triangulated by satellites, will pinpoint a plane's location."

"They haven't located the signal?"

"No. And that's not good." When Jack didn't reply, she explained. "It's likely the ELT was destroyed in the explosion. Which all but kills any hope of finding survivors."

Three hours later, snow covered everything, and there was no longer any evidence of anything resembling a road. They had made it to a clearing near the bottom of the basin, and Anders held up a hand, stopping the group.

"Take a break," he called out.

Jack watched him pull binoculars out of a bag and scan their surroundings.

Kim offered Jack a granola bar. "Eat this," she said. "It might be a while before we get another chance."

Jack took it and thanked her. "We're in Savage Basin?"

"This is it," she said, sweeping an arm toward the snowy slopes. She unwrapped her bar and took a bite.

It was an immense open area, enclosed by steep mountain buttresses on three sides. The winds swirled around them, seeming to come from every direction. Jack squinted, looking over it all. Except for their small band of searchers, there were no signs of life—flora or fauna.

"I can see why it's named Savage Basin," he said.

Kim finished a bite and wiped her mouth. "Believe it or not, this was a hub of mining activity back in the day. Nearly a thousand people lived up here."

Jack couldn't imagine such a thing. And if this was what it was like in May, he wondered what frozen hell on earth it must be in the dead of winter. He turned and looked back toward Telluride, now barely visible in the distance.

"Four and a half miles from town by road," Kim said when she saw him looking. "And four thousand feet above it."

Jack finished the granola bar and stuffed the wrapper in the pocket of his jacket. He looked up into the basin. "How much farther? Do they have any idea where the plane is?"

"According to the report from the hikers, it probably came down somewhere on the flats." She pointed to a spot high in the basin. "See how it rises and levels off a couple different times? Sort of plateaus at the top? That's the flats. It's where the mining bosses and their families had houses. Above the noise and grime where the miners lived and worked. See the old columns?" She was pointing lower, to a spot closer to them.

"I do," Jack said. It was an odd-looking array of concrete columns, four wide and twelve deep, sticking up about fifteen feet out of the snow.

"That was the site of the old boarding house."

Jack looked past the columns to the flats above. It would be a formidable climb. "Are we hiking all the way to the top?"

Kim patted the sleeve of his jacket. "Don't worry," she said. "We're about halfway there."

The rest of the way, the group struggled, breathing hard and puffing out clouds of vapor as they clambered through the snow in the thin air. Jack's lungs and thighs were burning. His hands had gone numb hours earlier. Nothing about the grueling football practices in the blazing Texas sun compared to the pain and exhaustion he felt at that moment. He glanced over at the others trudging ahead of him with a new sense of admiration and respect. They had volunteered for this.

When the group finally reached the flats, Anders stopped them and pulled the binoculars from his bag again. Jack watched as he swept the area.

"There it is," Anders said, pointing toward the southeast corner of the basin.

Jack could just make it out—a dark tangle of metal in the expanse of white. It was sunk deep in the drifts and partially hidden by the shadow of the southern ridge line. The wreckage was still fifty or more yards away, and it was already midafternoon. The sun was beginning its descent toward the horizon. Daylight would start dwindling soon, and Jack hoped they wouldn't need the tents he had seen being packed on the snowmobiles earlier.

"Smith," Anders called out. "Come with me. The rest of you stay here. We're going to see if there are any survivors." He shook his head when he said it. They all knew there wouldn't be any. "Kim, call Tony with our coordinates."

Kim rifled through her backpack.

"Why doesn't he want us to go with them?" Jack asked her.

She had pulled out a handheld radio. "He's trying not to disturb the scene. Except for reporting the location, there's probably nothing else we can do." There was a calm resignation in her voice that Jack suspected came from experience.

He watched the men as they approached the wreckage. The mass of twisted metal was beyond recognition. Even up close, Jack didn't think the charred debris would resemble an airplane. From where he was, he couldn't make out wings or a tail, nothing that looked like a fuselage. Most of it had probably been buried in the snow upon impact. Someone could have told him it was the ruins of a semitruck or a locomotive. And, if he didn't know where they were, he would have been inclined to believe them.

From the distance, Jack watched Anders take photographs of the wreckage from different angles. Smith disappeared from view for several minutes. Jack guessed he was searching the wreckage for survivors.

After several minutes, Anders and Smith returned. Anders asked if Kim had relayed their coordinates, then told her to radio the sheriff again, tell him that whoever had been on the flight was dead. They had found human remains.

Next, Anders instructed the group to turn around. There was no more they could do.

By the time the group reached town, it was after ten o'clock. The climb down from the basin had been nearly as punishing as the climb up. Jack couldn't remember being more exhausted. Every muscle in his body ached, and he vowed to never strap on snowshoes again.

On the drive back to the trailer, he called Buckley. The phone was answered immediately.

"Jack, where've you been?" He must have been sitting on it, waiting. "Did y'all find the plane?"

Jack let out a tired sigh. "We did."

Buckley peppered him with more questions, some of which Jack could answer, others he couldn't. He was too tired to think. He told Buckley he'd be by in the morning to give him a full report. Buckley reluctantly agreed and ended the call.

At the campground, Jack found Crockett in Otto's tent. He thanked the old man and told him he'd fill him in on what had happened the next day.

When Jack finally lay down on the bunk in his trailer, he was sure he would immediately fall dead asleep, but he didn't. He lay in the dark going over everything that had happened that day. He thought of Buckley's questions and wondered about the former governor's relationship with the deceased congressman. Why had he been so intent on Jack going with search and rescue? What had he expected them to find?

Before he fell asleep, Jack decided that when he met with Buckley the next morning, he would have a few questions of his own.

CHAPTER 11

Thursday, May 12

THE NEXT MORNING came early—too early. It was still an hour before daylight, but Jack couldn't sleep. He'd spent the night struggling to find a comfortable position. But no matter what he tried, some part of his body ached.

He'd finally given up sometime around three o'clock, rolled off the bunk, and dug through a drawer for painkillers. They had helped, but not for long.

He tossed the blanket off and gingerly dropped his feet to the floor. It was dark, but he could hear Crockett dancing at his feet.

"Give me a second," Jack said, rubbing the back of his neck, trying to work out a kink. He finally stood up and felt like someone had taken a sledgehammer to his legs.

He let Crockett outside for a few minutes. When the dog was back inside, Jack headed to the public bathroom. He stood under the hot water and couldn't remember a shower that had ever felt so good.

Back at the trailer, he stood on the outside stoop, staring up into the canyon. The sun was still below the horizon, but it cast the mountains in a soft pink silhouette.

Jack glanced at the time on his cell phone. It was still too early to call Buckley. But as he stepped into the trailer, his phone buzzed.

"Jack, you coming?" Buckley sounded like he'd been awake for hours. The man was relentless.

Buckley Bailey was a loudmouthed Texas politician prone to hyperbole and exaggeration. His constituents either loved or hated him; there didn't seem to be much middle ground. He was obnoxious and loud. But for some reason Jack couldn't explain, he liked him.

Jack took in and released a long breath, causing the muscles in his chest to ache. "Give me half an hour," he said, massaging the back of his neck. "I've got to feed my dog."

Exactly twenty-five minutes later, Jack pulled off the highway and through the entrance to Mountain Village, marveling at how much it had changed since January, when he'd last seen it. What had been open fields of snow were now golf greens and fairways. Farther up the road, spring grass blanketed what had been ski slopes.

Unlike Telluride, which had been founded during the region's burgeoning mining days in the nineteenth century, Mountain Village was a relatively young community. Designed to accommodate the growing number of tourists and second homeowners, it had sprung up around Telluride's ski resort in the 1990s.

Sitting a thousand feet above the valley floor, Mountain Village was connected to Telluride by a gondola system that whisked visitors and residents between the two communities in a matter of minutes.

Jack drove the tree-lined boulevard toward the village center. A group of kids was already out fishing from the banks of a small pond that had been frozen over when he last saw it. He weaved past a cluster of condominiums at the town's center and continued on.

A quarter mile farther, he neared the end of the boulevard and turned onto the winding driveway that led to the Baileys' home. It was a massive structure built of stacked logs with an impressive array of steep gables and covered balconies. Large plate-glass windows reflected the surrounding forest. The house was flanked on both sides by tall aspens, their bare branches showing the signs of early buds. Jack had been there before, and looking at it all, he thought it was still the most beautiful house he'd ever seen.

He parked the truck in the circular driveway, took a set of flagstone stairs to the front doors, and was just about to knock when one of them swung open.

Buckley had been waiting for him.

"Jack," Buckley roared. "Come in." A black Lab stood wagging its tail at his feet.

"Hello, Bo," Jack said, bending to pet the dog as he stepped inside.

"He remembers you." Buckley shut the door behind them and shook Jack's hand. "Come in. I want to hear all about what happened yesterday."

Dressed in a pearl-button shirt and jeans and alligator boots that Jack knew would have cost a fortune, Buckley was the living caricature of a larger-than-life Texan. The only thing missing was a cowboy hat. Then Jack saw it across the room, hung on a mounted set of deer antlers.

Buckley led him to a pair of couches set facing each other against a glass wall. The mountain views were stunning.

Jack sank down into one of the sofas. "How's the exploratory committee going?"

Buckley Bailey had been a three-term governor of the Lone Star State before an unfavorable exposé in the *Dallas Morning News* had set off a political firestorm and cost him a run for the Senate. But four months earlier, the last time Jack had talked to him, he had set his political sights even higher and was planning to run for president.

Buckley sat on the sofa facing him. "I think I'm going to sit this one out," he said, referring to the upcoming presidential election. "I've got too many irons in the fire at the moment. But enough about that. Tell me what happened yesterday."

Jack told him about the trek up to the basin with search and rescue and about finding the plane buried in the snow. When he was finished talking, Buckley ran a hand through his mane of salt-and-pepper hair and leaned back on the couch, resting a foot on his knee. He was silent a moment, thinking.

"It's a crying shame," he finally said, picking at a spot on his boot. "Cliff was a good man."

It was the opening Jack was hoping for. "How'd you know him?"

"Cliff?" Buckley shook his head. "I've known him for years. He's the main reason Celeste and I are here in Telluride." He became more animated as he talked. "Cliff's father was Edward Roberts."

"The senator?" Jack had heard of him.

"The very one. Practically a legend in this state." Buckley swung his foot to the floor and crossed the other over the opposite knee. "Edward was a close friend of Celeste's family. That's how I met him. He and Margaret—his wife—came to our wedding. For years, the families vacationed together—hunting, fishing. We'd be at the same high-falutin' charity galas. It's a strange thing how the *big* rich"—he said the word "big" while making air quotes—"all seem to know each other."

Buckley said it in a way that excluded himself. Jack knew he had grown up poor in the Texas Panhandle and had managed to claw his way to the top echelon of the state's political class. But when it came to the ultra-wealthy circles his wife's family ran in, it was obvious Buckley still considered himself an outsider.

"Anyway," he continued. "Edward helped with political connections when I first ran for governor. He was a good man. So was his son."

Jack had heard the media stories and knew Senator Edward Roberts had been a political figure as polarizing as Buckley. His constituents had either loved or hated him. But despite his mixed popularity, Edward Roberts had been one of the longest-serving US Senators in Congress before he died suddenly of a stroke almost a decade earlier.

"So that's how you met Cliff," Jack said. "Through his father."

Buckley nodded somberly. "Cliff was a good friend. He and Susan—his wife—had us out to Telluride years ago. We came every summer for a bit, and they started bugging us about getting our own place up here. Didn't take much to convince Celeste." He spread his arms wide. "Here we are."

Buckley turned his face to the window. The view across the valley to the ridge that hung above town was spectacular, but Buckley didn't seem to notice. He was lost in thought, and Jack gave him a moment. When he turned back, it was as if a switch inside him had been flipped. His face had grown hard, and Jack saw his jaw muscles tense.

"What did they find at the crash?"

Jack was taken aback by the question. "Just the wreckage of the plane."

"Besides that. I don't want gruesome details about the bodies or anything—Alan Krueger, the pilot, was a friend of mine, too—but what did they *find*? A black box? A voice recorder?"

"They weren't looking for any of that," Jack said. "From what I understand, search and rescue's mission was to check for survivors and determine the plane's location for whoever goes up next. Since there's no wind this morning, my guess is they'll send a helicopter up and do a more thorough search."

Buckley frowned. He didn't seem happy with Jack's answer. "What about suitcases or personal effects?" he asked. "Did you get close enough to see anything like that?"

The question didn't make sense. Why would Buckley ask about luggage? Jack described what little of the scene he saw.

"That's it? That's not enough."

"Enough of what?" Jack was confused.

"Not enough information." Buckley swung his foot to the floor and leaned toward him. "This was no accident," he said, pointing a finger at Jack. "Someone wanted Cliff dead, and I have a good idea who. But that plane didn't go down on its own, and I want you to look into it."

The directive took Jack by surprise, but he let Buckley continue.

"I want you to look into a group called the Wilderness Keepers. It's one of those wacko environmentalist groups that goes around bombing and setting things on fire in the name of conservation—that sort of thing. Eric Dale's the ringleader. The guy's a rattlesnake. Raised all sorts of hell at Cliff's town hall a couple of nights ago. Had his henchmen hollering threats and badgering people to sign their petition against Cliff. It would have been bad enough in an odd year, but Cliff was up for reelection." Buckley shook his head.

"You think someone took the plane down on purpose?"

"I know so. They wanted Cliff out of the way."

"Who?"

"Wilderness Keepers." Buckley was growing frustrated, but Jack still didn't understand. He thought the accusation was a bit dramatic but wanted more information.

"Why would they want to kill him?"

"It's a long story," Buckley replied. "It's over a land deal Cliff was going to recommend to Congress."

"And now that he's dead, he won't be around to recommend it." Jack was thinking out loud.

"Exactly."

It hardly seemed like a motive for murder—an environmentalist group angry with a politician. But Jack had known killers who'd murdered for less. "So what happens now?"

"With the election?" Buckley shrugged. "The governor will probably appoint a temporary replacement to fill Cliff's seat. Who knows what happens between now and November," he said, referring to Election Day. "You just look into Dale. My money's on them being behind this."

"Behind the crash?" The idea still seemed ludicrous.

"They're going to find out this wasn't an accident." Buckley pointed his finger again. "This was murder. Someone brought that plane down on purpose, and I want you to find out who. And the first place I want you to look is at Eric Dale and Wilderness Keepers."

Jack thought of the rowdy activists at the campground. He knew about Wilderness Keepers and knew the group had a violent reputation, but he thought it was a stretch to accuse them of murdering a sitting US congressman.

"But why would they do it?" Jack asked.

"They're up in arms about a proposed land swap. And Cliff was chair of the house committee responsible for making the decision on whether to approve it or not. Cliff's recommendation—one way or the other—would likely have swayed the rest of the committee. The vote was supposed to be next week."

"That's what the town hall was about?"

Buckley nodded. "Cliff was going to recommend that the committee approve the trade. It would have been a done deal."

"And Wilderness Keepers is against it."

Buckley shifted on the couch, growing visibly agitated. "Dale's group is a bunch of rabid, tree-hugging socialists hell-bent on doing whatever it takes to get their way."

"Even murder?" Jack didn't bother hiding his skepticism. In all his years in law enforcement, he'd come into contact with plenty of political activist groups but could count on one hand those he'd dealt with that had actually committed outright murder. He wasn't buying it.

"What about his reelection?" Jack asked.

"What about it?"

"How was it going?"

"Fine." Buckley waved a hand dismissively. "Cliff was going to be easily reelected. He was leading in the polls."

Jack wondered about Cliff's opponent. It wouldn't be the first time one political rival offed the other. It was an intriguing scenario, but Jack wasn't sure he wanted to get involved. Looking into the death of a sitting congressman wasn't how he had planned to spend the summer. There was an almost endless list of things he'd rather do instead.

"Listen, Jack." Buckley had dropped his voice. "Cliff was a great guy and an honest politician. There are rumors out there that he wasn't, but they're not true. In politics, the nature of the job draws crazies like flies to honey. The crash wasn't an accident."

"The authorities are going to investigate—"

"I don't want to leave this to the authorities. I've been in government long enough to know how slow their wheels turn. We're going to have the FAA, the FBI, NTSB, the local sheriff, and God knows who else looking into this. It could take months—years!" He shook his head. "In the meantime, I want *you* looking into it."

Jack still wasn't convinced. "There's a good chance they'll find out it was mechanical failure—or pilot error."

"I'm telling you it wasn't," Buckley argued. "But even if they do, it's going to take them months to figure it out. I want you on this *now*. Start with Dale."

The idea was crazy. There were probably half a dozen government agencies already investigating the crash. Yet for some reason, Buckley wanted Jack to conduct his own investigation. Why?

"Listen," Buckley began. His tone had eased further. "Just poke around and see what you can find out. I'll pay you by the week. Check out Dale and his band of nutjobs. Keep in contact with the sheriff's office. I hear Tony Burns likes you. Keep your ear to the ground and keep me posted on whatever you find out about their investigations. Maybe you can call one of your old FBI contacts. Get them to fill you in."

Jack thought about it. His head was telling him to get up and walk out, tell Buckley he wouldn't do it, then spend the summer as he'd planned—hiking the mountains with Crockett. That's what he knew he *should* do. But Buckley had planted a seed, and Jack felt the familiar gnawing at his gut that he got at the possibility of an intriguing case.

He thought of the explosion he'd heard the morning before and wondered if Buckley was right.

Had the death of a sitting congressman been an assassination?

CHAPTER 12

LEA SCOTSMAN HAD been up since before dawn. It didn't matter what day of the week it was; her routine had been the same every morning as far back as she could remember.

Lose an hour in the morning, and you'll spend all day hunting for it. She'd heard her father say it countless times. As a child, she'd resented having to rise early, but as the years passed, she had grown to understand its significance. Especially after her father died and Lea was left to run the ranch by herself.

Home was a sprawling lodge on a 16,800-acre spread in Ouray County, not far from the small town of Ridgway. The area's claim to fame was being the movie location for Hollywood's 1969 version of *True Grit*. Locals who'd been around at the time still told stories about running into John Wayne while the movie was being filmed. Lea had been just a toddler when the movie premiered, but she appreciated the local restaurant that had been named after it, its walls covered with John Wayne memorabilia. The older she got, the more seldom Lea left the ranch, but when she did, she would often stop at the True Grit Café for a bite to eat and a dose of local gossip, making the trip into town more tolerable.

Lea hadn't always been a recluse. She had attended school in Ridgway, then spent two years at Colorado State in Fort Collins. At the time, she'd dreamed of becoming a veterinarian. But the dream had been cut short when, in the spring of her junior year, her father died suddenly from a heart attack while working cattle.

Lea was an only child, and her mother had been a city girl from Denver and completely incapable of taking care of the ranch. After Lea's father died, her mother had lasted another year before announcing she couldn't take the seclusion any longer, packed up her belongings, and moved back to Denver.

Lea had been left virtually alone. Aside from a couple of old schoolmates, the kids in town she'd grown up with had moved on years ago. She thanked God every night for Percy Ferguson, her father's top hand, who'd stayed on and still worked the ranch with her.

For the first few years that she was back home, Lea would head into town most weekends and had even gone on a few dates. She was five seven with a slim build, ebony hair, and vivid hazel eyes. She had always been told she was attractive. *Our very own Liz Taylor,* her paternal grandmother had once remarked. Lea knew it was a stretch but had never forgotten the compliment. But a lot of time had passed since then. She'd had her heart broken years earlier and had given up on love long ago.

But she loved the ranch, loved the wide-open pastures and rolling foothills—especially in springtime, when the new grass was in but the Sneffels Range, which soared in the distance, was still blanketed with snow. She loved the cold, crisp mornings and the gentle coos of the doves that returned every spring.

If she had once harbored any regrets over choosing life on the ranch alone, they had been set free long ago.

Lea poured coffee into a heavy mug and carried it to the table, cradling it with both hands, letting it warm them. She settled down into a chair.

The kitchen was large, the walls made of enormous logs that had been meticulously stacked a century earlier. Pinewood cabinets lined two of the walls, and a row of windows lined another. In the center of the room was an old banquet table that could accommodate twelve but rarely sat more than two. Lea rubbed the table's surface with her free hand as she sipped the coffee.

The older she got, the more rooted to the ranch she became. Except for trips to Ridgway for supplies or mail, or the occasional trip to the bank in Telluride, she rarely left it anymore.

Although the lodge was remote, it was one of the few that had cell service and decent Wi-Fi. And every morning without fail, Lea made a pot of black coffee and read the news on her laptop while she waited for Percy.

She had just started reading a story about the latest uptick in inflation when she heard footsteps in the large front hall that led back to the kitchen.

"Morning," Percy hollered from down the hall.

Lea heard Percy's heavy footfalls on the pine floor grow louder as he neared the kitchen. He was a squat in stature but solid muscle. And although he was pushing seventy, he could still do anything on the ranch he asked the younger hands to do.

"Morning, Percy," Lea said, lifting her mug and gesturing at the coffeepot. "Help yourself."

Percy pulled a cup from the cabinet. "I thought I'd ride the west pasture this morning, make sure there aren't any signs of that lion before we release the calves into it."

"Can't Cody do that for you?"

"On vacation, remember?" Percy rolled his brown eyes.

"I forgot he was gone. Two weeks, right?"

"Y-ep." Percy drew the word out into two syllables.

Lea caught the judgment in his voice and smiled. "Unlike us, Percy, most people do have lives." She took another sip of coffee.

Percy dropped his bulk into a chair across the table from her. They sat in silence for a few minutes, each mentally preparing for the day ahead in their own way. Lea taking a few minutes to catch up on the news outside the ranch and Percy enjoying the calm before their work began. It was the same every morning.

Percy blew over the hot coffee, staring out the window.

Outside, the world was mostly dark, but the sun was on the verge of cresting the mountains on the horizon. Inside, except for the soft murmur of the refrigerator, the house was quiet.

Lea took another sip and held the mug aloft, staring at the computer monitor.

Percy was the first to break the silence. "Anything interesting in the news today?"

"Nothing," she replied. "Unless you consider the Federal Reserve raising interest rates interesting."

"Nope."

She laughed, then clicked on a website for local news, expecting to see another headline about the proposed condominium development in Telluride that had residents up in arms. But that wasn't what she saw.

She felt the color drain from her face and realized her hand was shaking. She set the mug down. "Percy..." She struggled to talk. Her mouth had gone dry.

Percy turned from the window. He was lifting the coffee to his lips, but when he saw the look on her face, he stopped. "What is it?"

"Cliff..." Lea felt her eyes begin to well.

Percy hesitated a moment. "Cliff Roberts?"

Her history with Cliff was no secret.

"Yes," she replied, her voice quivering.

"What about him?"

"He's dead."

CHAPTER 13

ON THE WAY back to Telluride, Jack's stomach growled. He knew there was one place in town he could get a great breakfast *and* local gossip—Pandora Café.

He wanted to research Cliff Roberts, see what he could dig up about the late congressman. And talking with Judith Hadley, the owner of Pandora Café, was as good a place as any to start.

He parked the truck along the curb and got out. It was still early, and the streets were quiet. A few locals shuffled along the sidewalks on their way to work.

Jack pushed open the door to the café and stepped inside, where he was immediately met with the aroma of bacon. He was glad to see his favorite table, the one set adjacent to the large stone fireplace, was empty. He pulled out a chair and took a seat facing the front door.

"What'll you have, stranger?" Judith set a plate of biscuits on the table and wiped her hands on her burlap apron.

Jack was anything but a stranger. In the four months he'd been in town, Judith had become as near a friend as he'd had since his days in school.

"What's the special?" he asked.

Judith pulled an order pad from a pocket and a pen from behind her ear. "Today we've got a mile-high stack of buttermilk pancakes and a side of sausage. It's not really a mile-high, but you get the point."

"I'll take it."

She studied him for a moment. "Let me get this started, and then I'll be back. You look like a man needing to talk."

She turned and disappeared behind a swinging door that led to the kitchen. Jack wasn't sure how she did it, but he was sure Judith could read his mind. It was a talent he swore his late grandmother had when he was growing up and suspected it was one of the many reasons he liked Judith as much as he did.

But there were plenty of other reasons to like her. Judith Hadley was the type of person who befriended everyone. She was medium-built and late middle-aged, with cropped gray hair and a penchant for gossip. But it was never vindictive. Judith was interested in the welfare of her local clientele as if they were family. Jack couldn't remember his mother but liked to think she had been something like Judith.

She reappeared through the swinging door with a tall glass of orange juice in one hand and a cup of coffee in the other and set both down on the table in front of him.

She pulled out an empty chair and sat. She offered a concerned smile. "Now tell me what's going on."

Jack wasn't sure where to start. "You heard about the congressman?"

An expression of sorrow instantly clouded her face. "I have." She took a moment to regroup. "I heard about the crash yesterday but didn't find out it was Cliff until this morning."

"You knew him?"

Judith nodded slowly. "Practically his whole life. He was in here a few nights ago. We had us a good visit." There was a deep sadness in her eyes.

Jack gave her a second, then asked, "Can you tell me about him?"

Judith laid her forearms gently on the table. "What do you want to know?"

Jack wasn't sure. Like anyone paying even the least bit of attention to the news, he'd heard of Cliff's father. The late Senator Edward Roberts was a legend in Washington and had been constantly embroiled in political turmoil of some sort or another that was reported in the national media.

But Jack knew almost nothing about the senator's son and wondered if he was as controversial. Jack still believed the plane crash was likely the result of mechanical failure or pilot error, but Buckley Bailey had gotten under his skin. And a part of Jack was curious to know if something the congressman had been involved in could have gotten him killed.

"If you've got time," Jack said, glancing over the café—there were only a handful of diners. "Start at the beginning."

Judith spread her fingers on the table and studied them as she talked. She told Jack how Cliff had gotten into trouble in DC as an adolescent and was sent to live at the family's vacation home in Telluride—away from the scrutiny of the media and out of his father's hair. Judith shook her head as she talked. Jack could tell she didn't approve of how he had been treated.

"Why didn't they send him to live in Denver?" Jack asked. "Why Telluride?"

"Too many temptations in the city, I guess. So they banished the poor kid to their vacation home, out of reach of the media. . . and his family." Her tone dripped with scorn. "Oh, Edward or Margaret would come visit every few months or so.

And Cliff would go to Denver or DC on holidays. But he didn't see them much."

"He lived here alone?"

She shook her head. "There was always a caretaker or a housekeeper with him."

"You knew him back then?"

A faint smile crossed her lips as she remembered. "He came in here all the time. Sometimes he'd stay and help me close up when he wasn't with friends. We had some good talks. He liked my apple pie."

Jack saw Judith's eyes grow glassy and suspected the young Cliff Roberts had come for more than apple pie. Like Jack, the kid probably needed a friend.

"Did he get in trouble after he moved here?" he asked.

"He did at first. He had a rough couple of years but then settled down and ended up a really good kid. He went off to college somewhere back East, then into politics like his father." She paused a moment, and her face hardened a bit. "But he was nothing like his father."

Jack came forward in his chair. "How so?"

"Edward Roberts was a typical politician—arrogant, self-centered. But everyone loved Cliff." She hesitated. "Well, almost everyone."

"Did he have any enemies?"

"He was a politician," she replied. "They always have enemies. You can have honest differences of opinion with people, and some of them are going to hate you for it." She shook her head and drew in a deep breath. "It can be an ugly world sometimes."

Jack had to agree with her. He'd seen his share of intolerance and hate.

"What do you know about Wilderness Keepers?" he asked.

"The protest group?"

He nodded.

"Not much," she replied. "Just that they caused a stink the other night when Cliff spoke at the Opera House."

Jack remembered the town hall Buckley had mentioned. "What happened?"

"They were interrupting and yelling at him. Accusing him of being a crooked politician and taking bribes."

"But you don't think he *was* crooked."

"Not at all."

"I heard they were upset about some land trade Cliff was involved in."

Jack wanted as much information out of her as he could get. Judith spent the next several minutes explaining the proposed land deal, how a multimillionaire landowner, Hank Wade, had offered the federal government nearly two thousand acres near the town of Ridgway, not far from Telluride, in exchange for a three-hundred-acre tract near some mountaintop.

Judith still stared at her hands. "They say the land Hank Wade is offering the government is part of some migratory corridor for deer and elk. And that there's not even road access to the land he wants. Doesn't make sense."

"Sounds like a good deal for the government."

Judith nodded in agreement. "That's what Cliff thought, too."

"And that's what the town hall was about?"

"That and a few other housekeeping items."

"Do you remember what those were?"

Judith thought a minute. "One was the federal grant the airport is trying to get for more hangars." She drummed her fingers on the table. "Another was a highway project Cliff was helping us lobby the state for. Stuff like that."

"Nothing controversial like the land trade?"

"Not even close."

Jack thought about it for a moment. "How will Cliff's death affect the deal now?" he asked himself as much as Judith, thinking aloud.

"My guess is that it can't be good for Hank," Judith replied. "Cliff was the committee chair. His vote was going to influence the rest of the committee members. He'll have to be replaced now, so it'll probably hold up the government's decision."

Even after years as an FBI agent, Jack didn't pretend to understand the workings of the federal government. But if the congressman was going to recommend the trade, his death could be a huge blow to Hank Wade. And now the committee's decision will likely be delayed until a replacement chair was appointed. And who's to say his successor would vote *for* the deal?

But Wade's loss would be someone else's gain—Eric Dale's. And Wilderness Keepers.

Jack's phone buzzed in the pocket of his jeans, and he dug it out. He glanced at the caller ID, then up at Judith. "Excuse me for a second."

"Take your time." She stood up and pointed at his empty coffee cup. "I'll get you a refill."

A few seconds later, Jack hung up the call, and Judith reappeared with a coffeepot. He rose from the chair and pulled out his wallet.

"Thank you, Judith, but I've got to go."

"That was quick."

Jack laid a five on the table for the coffee and a tip. Breakfast would have to wait.

"Was that about Cliff?" Judith watched him closely. When he didn't answer, she asked, "You're investigating the crash, aren't you?"

Jack hesitated for several more beats, then nodded.

"You getting paid for this one?"

He debated how much to tell her but decided that she'd find out somehow anyway. He pushed his chair back under the table. "Buckley Bailey."

Judith whistled through her teeth. "Well, he's got plenty to pay you with." She chuckled. "At least his wife does."

Jack didn't know how much Buckley would be paying him, but he didn't care. There was a good chance federal investigators were going to discover the crash had been caused by mechanical failure or pilot error. But the more Jack thought about it, the more he thought it was caused by something else.

Judith's expression was serious. "You take Buckley Bailey's money," she said. "But don't trust him any farther than you can throw him."

CHAPTER 14

AS HE DID every morning, Ted Hawthorne had walked the six blocks from his condo along the river to work. He stood on the stoop of Telluride Bank & Trust and fumbled through a leather satchel for his keys.

When he found them, he looked cautiously over one shoulder and then the other. He had heard too many stories over the years of thieves lying in wait as a banker unlocked the door. The Telluride Bank & Trust had been robbed once, years ago, but Ted was determined it would never happen again—not on his watch.

The bank was a small two-story white building with ornamental columns and finials attached to the exterior wall. Above the second floor, a deep overhanging cornice was adorned with decorative brackets. Ted thought the little building was the most impressive in town, a testament to the significance of the bank and its founder.

He slid the key into the deadbolt and opened the door wide enough to slip inside, then turned and relocked it. Gretchen wouldn't be in for at least an hour.

As he turned away, something through the plate-glass window next to the door caught his eye. A man walked briskly up the sidewalk. For a moment, as he passed the bank, Ted thought he was going to try the door, but to his relief, the man kept going. He knew he was being paranoid, but it was part of the job. Bankers had to be cautious. But something about the man seemed familiar.

Ted watched through the window as the man continued past the adjacent building. He was tall, much taller than Ted, had an athletic build, and walked with a confident stride. Probably early forties. The man needed a haircut. He had wavy brown hair that brushed the top of his shirt collar and was wearing jeans and scruffy-looking cowboy boots. As he turned the corner, Ted caught a glimpse of his profile and suddenly realized who he was. That detective.

But why was he still in town?

Ted turned from the window, hurried into his office, and shut the door. What was the man's name? He'd been all over the news. But Ted couldn't remember.

Like everyone in town, Ted had devoured the media coverage of Alice Fremont's murder several months earlier. He knew that the detective had helped the sheriff solve the case and had solved cases in Aspen and Vail the year before.

Ted took a seat behind his pine desk, pulled a stack of papers toward him, and realized his hands were shaking. He went through the pages one by one, but as hard as he tried, he couldn't concentrate on his work. After several minutes, he gave up.

Ted pushed the papers aside and booted up his computer. He googled *Alice Fremont murder detective* and immediately found what he was looking for.

Jack Martin.

That was his name.

Ted swallowed.

Why was Jack Martin still in Telluride?

CHAPTER 15

JACK REPLAYED THE call from Buckley in his head. It had been brief.

As soon as Jack answered the phone, Buckley had blurted, "Meet me at 401 West Columbia. Susan is asking to see you. Get here as soon as you can." That was it. Buckley had ended the call without waiting for a reply. His voice had sounded strained. He hadn't mentioned a last name, but Jack assumed the Susan he referred to was Susan Roberts, the wife of the late congressman.

As he climbed the sidewalk from Main Street toward West Columbia, Jack wondered why he'd been summoned so abruptly. If he weren't so curious about what was going on, Buckley's demand would have offended him.

At West Columbia, Jack checked the address and turned west. He found the house two blocks farther. It was a pretty Victorian on a huge lot.

He took the steps to the porch two at a time and knocked on the front door. From the urgency in his voice, Jack expected Buckley to be watching for him. But he wasn't.

Finally, Buckley answered the door and ushered him inside. "Come in, Jack. Susan wants to talk to you."

In the living room, a woman rose from a velvet sofa and extended a small pale hand. "Mr. Martin. Thank you for coming. I'm Susan Roberts."

Despite her swollen eyes and that she was not wearing a stitch of makeup, Jack thought she was beautiful. She was about his age, with wavy blond hair that fell to just below her shoulders and eyes the same shade of blue as a high-mountain lake. Her hand was cold to the touch, and it brought him around.

"I was just down the street," Jack said, stumbling over his words. "At the café." He was sure he sounded like an idiot.

Susan returned to her spot on the sofa. "Please, Detective. Have a seat."

Buckley took one of two wingback chairs, and Jack sat down in the other.

"Buckley told me you were looking into my husband's accident."

"I am," he said, hoping she was okay with it.

Buckley leaned in his direction. "I told Susan that we couldn't leave this up to the government. We needed someone else looking into the crash."

"At first I resisted the idea of getting you involved," Susan began. "I thought we should let the official investigation run its course. But since Buckley had you go with search and rescue, I guess you're involved already."

There was a hint of reprimand in her voice, and Buckley sank back in his chair.

"I don't have to be," Jack answered.

"But you already are," she replied. She turned to a side table, took a crumpled sheet of paper lying next to a rock, and held it out to him.

Jack got out of his seat and took it from her.

"That was thrown through a back window of my house this morning," she said, tucking her feet under her. "It was attached to a rock with a rubber band."

Jack had returned to his chair and glanced at the paper. Photoshopped jail bars had been superimposed over the black-and-white photo of a man. Below it, a headline blared Kick Out Cliff.

"They've been putting them up all over town." There was a quiver in her voice. She sounded angry. "And now they've thrown one through my widow."

Jack studied the paper further. Under the headline there was a short paragraph protesting the government's proposed land trade with Hank Wade. And below that was a call to vote Cliff Roberts out of office in the upcoming November election.

"Did you report it?"

"I called the marshals this morning. They sent a deputy over to take a statement, but they didn't seem overly concerned."

Probably because Cliff was now dead, Jack thought, but he kept the sentiment to himself. "What time did it happen?"

"Early. Just after six."

Jack wondered why the rock had been thrown through the Robertses' window the morning *after* the plane crash. The person who had done it either didn't know that Cliff was dead, or they didn't care.

"Buckley says you can help find out who did this," she said.

Jack still held the paper. "You want me to find out who's behind the rock?"

"That"—she stole a quick glance at Buckley before continuing—"and who killed Cliff. I believe they're one and the same."

Jack knew that a slew of government agencies would already be investigating the crash. He had argued the same point with Buckley, but now was being asked to look into the congressman's death by his widow. Had Buckley, for some reason, talked her into this? Jack wanted to test her resolve.

"There are already people investigating—"

"No." She swung her feet to the floor. "They'll be studying the plane for months."

Buckley spoke next. "We want you to look into Eric Dale and his group."

"Wilderness Keepers?" Jack asked.

"They wanted my husband dead, Detective. They said as much during the town hall a few nights ago." She pointed to the paper. Her face was hard, and she fought back tears. "The government won't look at Dale right away. They're scared of the activist groups—scared of bad publicity. And when they *do* investigate them, they'll do it in secret, not wanting the media to find out."

"They treat these people with kid gloves," Buckley said. "Look at the half-hearted investigations that were done in Montana."

Jack knew Buckley was referring to the two buildings that had been bombed—one occupied by a forestry company, the other, a real estate development firm. According to the authorities, the investigations had gone cold, despite rumors that Wilderness Keepers had been behind both incidents. Some people accused the government of covering up, but Jack knew from his time with the FBI that small ecoterrorist cells were hard to catch, and most attacks went unsolved.

"But the cause of the crash is still unknown," Jack said.

Susan spoke first. "Cliff's pilot has been with his family for years. He was a decorated military veteran. Alan oversaw the maintenance of the plane personally." She shook her head. "The crash wasn't an accident."

"Can you think of anyone who'd want your husband dead?" Jack asked.

"He was a politician—threats came with the job. But none of them seemed credible enough to worry about...until now." There was a steely resolve in her eyes. "Wilderness Keepers did this, Detective. I'm sure of it."

There was a knock at the door.

Buckley rose from his chair. "I'll get it."

Jack heard him talking with a woman in the foyer. He returned a few seconds later.

"Susan, it's Lea. She'd like to—"

"No," Susan interrupted. Her face was flushed with emotion—anger or frustration, Jack wasn't sure which. "It's too soon," she said. "Please ask her to leave."

Buckley looked like he was about to say something but then turned toward the foyer.

Jack took the opportunity to leave and stood up. "I'm sorry about your husband, Mrs. Roberts."

Susan got up and stepped toward him. "Thank you for coming. Buckley obviously thinks very highly of you." She held out her hand, and Jack shook it. "Will you be looking into the crash?"

Jack saw something in her eyes besides sadness. It was desperation...or fear. He knew he should refuse to take the case. Investigating a politician's death would attract the wrong kind of attention. He should have refused to look into it when Buckley had asked him earlier—but he hadn't. And he wouldn't refuse the dead congressman's beautiful widow now.

Besides, the case was intriguing, and Buckley was going to pay him. And after almost a year without a paycheck, Jack knew that any money he could make from investigating the crash would go a long way in helping his dwindling finances.

"I'll look into it," he told her.

"Thank you."

Susan led him into the foyer but hesitated at the door. "Please let yourself out, Detective." Her voice was shaking slightly. "Thank you again for coming." Without waiting for a reply, she turned and disappeared back into the living room.

Jack was confused by the sudden change in her behavior. Then, through a window adjacent to the door, he saw Buckley talking to a woman on the sidewalk. It looked like he was apologizing.

The woman was probably in her midfifties. Medium height with a slim build, she was dressed in jeans and a patterned wool coat. Jack thought she was pretty.

She had come to the house to see Susan. But for some reason, Susan wanted to avoid her.

Jack wondered why.

CHAPTER 16

WHEN JACK STEPPED onto the porch, Buckley and the woman stopped talking.

"Jack, this is Lea Scotsman," Buckley said. "An old friend of Cliff's. Lea, Jack Martin."

Jack took the steps to the sidewalk, and the woman came toward him and held out a hand. It was small, but her handshake was firm.

"It's nice to meet you," she said, smiling softly.

Buckley clapped Jack on the shoulder. "Stay here. I'm going to tell Susan goodbye, but I want to talk to you before you leave. See you later, Lea." He took the steps to the porch and disappeared inside.

"Did you know Cliff?" Lea asked.

Jack thought he detected a hint of sadness in her voice. "I didn't."

"That's too bad. He was a good man." She was quiet a moment.

Jack wasn't sure what to say. He wanted to know how she knew Cliff and Susan Roberts and why Susan had refused to see her. But he decided to ask Buckley later instead.

"I need to be going, too," she said. "It was nice to meet you."

Jack watched Lea climb into a tan Tahoe and pull away from the curb. She gave him a slight wave as she left.

A few minutes later, Buckley emerged from the house. He took the steps to the sidewalk two at a time and seemed agitated briefly but recovered quickly.

"Thank you for coming," he said, slapping Jack's shoulder again. "Get on this as soon as you can. Talk to Dale or one of his henchmen at Wilderness Keepers. Let me know what you find out. But don't stop there. Buddy up to Tony Burns. He'll insist on the feds keeping the sheriff's office informed on their investigation. You find out what's going on, and then you let me know."

Buckley dug into a pocket and pulled out his wallet. "Here," he said, counting out five one-hundred-dollar bills and handing them to Jack. "This should be enough to get you started."

Jack took the money and stuck it into a front pocket of his jeans. "This could all be a waste of time and money if the crash is ruled an accident."

"It won't be," Buckley said. "You just let me know what you find out."

Jack nodded. He wasn't sure what he was getting himself into, but the cash in his pocket felt good. Plus, he didn't have anything better to do. He'd give it a week. See what he could dig up. It wasn't as if he were signing an employment contract. Knowing he could give the money back to Buckley at any time made the decision easier.

"I'll start today."

Buckley flashed a toothy politician's grin, reminding Jack of Judith's warning not to trust him farther than he could throw him.

They took the sidewalk to the street where Buckley had parked his black Navigator. But Jack wasn't going to let him get away just yet.

"Who was the woman?"

"Lea?"

Jack nodded.

"I don't know her well," Buckley said. "But she's an old friend of Cliff's. Grew up in the area."

"What does she do now?"

"She's a rancher. Inherited some family land near Ridgway. *A lot* of land, from what I hear."

"But you don't know her?"

Buckley shook his head. "Not well." He must have seen the skepticism on Jack's face. "I know a lot of people in town, Jack, but I don't know all of them. And from what Cliff's told me, Lea stays out of politics and doesn't donate to campaigns, so why bother?" He said it with a smile.

"Why wouldn't Susan see her?"

Buckley seemed thrown by the question. "Uh. . . I think it's too early for Susan. She's very private and hasn't wanted to receive visitors." He yanked open the door to the Navigator and got in. "Let me give you a ride back to. . ." His voice trailed off. "Well, danged if I don't know where you're staying—you've never said."

"Town Park Campground."

"The campground?" Buckley spat it back at him as if Jack had said he was staying on the moon.

"I'll walk," Jack told him. "But thank you."

Buckley thought about it a moment, then shrugged. "Suit yourself. But call me as soon as you uncover something. Start with Dale. The rumor is they've got a temporary place in town somewhere they're using as an office. Good luck." He shut the door and drove away.

Jack headed in the opposite direction. At the corner, he heard something inside the Robertses' home and stopped. A single window was pushed open an inch or two, enough for the muffled sound of someone crying to escape. It had to be Susan. While he was there, he hadn't seen anyone else inside except Buckley.

Jack paused at the curb, recognizing the sound of pain that was still raw, the early stages of grief. He had felt it himself decades earlier when his grandparents had been murdered.

For a moment, his heart clenched as he remembered.

CHAPTER 17

JACK HAD PLANNED on returning to the trailer to research Wilderness Keepers before paying Eric Dale a visit. But plans change.

He noticed one of the guys he'd tussled with the morning before step out of an alley onto Main Street and turn in the direction of the campground. The offices of Wilderness Keepers would probably be nearby.

Jack headed for the alley, pulling his phone from his pocket as he passed outdoor diners seated along the sidewalk. The tables were covered in white cloths and set with china and silver. Too rich for his blood, but the smell of their breakfasts reminded him he hadn't eaten.

A middle-aged woman wrapped in a fur-trimmed throw and sitting with a friend watched him appreciably as he passed. Jack tipped his head and kept walking.

He stopped at the entrance to the alley and tapped at his phone. It was unlikely the temporary address for Wilderness Keepers was published online, but it was worth a shot. A quick search proved him right. But he had a backup plan.

Jack scrolled through his contacts until he found the one he was looking for. It took several rings before the call was answered. There was talking and laughing in the background.

"Pandora Café."

"Judith, it's Jack."

"Jack." She sounded surprised but happy to hear from him. "Did you change your mind about breakfast?"

Jack glanced back at the diners sitting outside Chop House. The offer was tempting. "I'll come by later," he said. "But I have a question for you first."

As he'd hoped, he hit a home run by calling Judith Hadley, beloved town gossip with a heart of gold. Jack thanked her for the information and ended the call.

He took the alley to another that ran parallel behind the buildings lining Main Street. The asphalt surface was uneven, pocked by endless seasons of freeze and thaw. He dodged a garbage truck emptying waste from a dumpster and found the small, nondescript entrance exactly where Judith said it would be.

He could have easily walked past it without noticing. The frame of the screen door was painted a deep rust, the same color as the peeling paint on the building. Two windows, one on each side, were coated with dirt and grime, making seeing into the building impossible.

Jack pulled open the screen door, then the door behind it, and stepped inside. He squinted, letting his eyes adjust to the dimly lit room, then glanced around.

Unlike other activist groups he'd dealt with, this one didn't appear to be well funded. The office was one room. Homemade signs were propped against the far wall. The top one read KICK OUT CLIFF.

"Can I help you?"

Jack turned to his left and saw a man sitting at a cheap metal desk. He looked to be in his early thirties. He was dressed well but had unkempt shaggy hair that hung below his shoulders and an overgrown beard to match.

"I'm looking for Eric Dale."

The stranger stood up and eyed Jack suspiciously. "You found him."

Jack stuck out his hand and stepped forward, his boots clomping on the chipped linoleum floor. "My name's Jack Martin. I'd like to ask you a few questions."

Dale examined the outstretched hand and hesitated. Just when Jack thought he was going to refuse to shake it, he reached out and shook.

"You law enforcement?"

"Not exactly."

Dale studied his face, still sizing him up. And probably wondering if Jack was lying. He gestured to a chair next to the desk, and Jack sat.

There were mounds of paper on the desk. Jack noticed one was a stack of the same flyers that had been thrown through Susan Roberts's window.

Dale pulled a clipboard from a desk drawer and pushed it in Jack's direction. "Have you signed this yet?"

It was an odd start to the conversation.

Jack glanced at the paper on the clipboard and saw the word "petition" printed at the top. There were already dozens of signatures scrawled on the page.

"What is it?" Jack asked.

"It's an appeal to stop a millionaire from screwing taxpayers."

The land swap.

Jack should have known. "Hank Wade."

The look on Dale's face hardened. "You know him?"

Jack shook his head.

Dale dug through the drawer again. "If you don't want to sign that one, here's another." He slapped a second clipboard down on the desk.

Jack picked it up. "What's this one?"

"Logging company wants to turn a small piece of heaven in Minnesota into an arboreal graveyard."

Jack set it back down.

Dale pulled a third clipboard from the drawer. "How about this one?" He laid it on top of the first two. "Oil company wants to defile federal lands in New Mexico."

He left the petitions sitting in front of Jack, then pulled a pen from a small cup and dropped it on the top one. The gesture felt like a dare, and Jack felt his pulse quicken.

Dale waited a moment. "I didn't think so," he said. "You swagger in here with your jeans and cowboy boots. You've got Texas wildcatter written all over you."

Jack didn't reply.

Dale leaned back in his chair and looked down his nose. "So, what do you want from me, Tex?"

"I'm from Louisiana."

The two men stared at each other for several uncomfortable seconds. Then Dale laughed and came forward in his chair.

"All right, Louisiana. You said you had some questions for me. What are they?"

His tone had changed. It was less threatening but not exactly friendly. Jack hoped they had broken the ice. A testosterone standoff wasn't a successful strategy for extracting information. He wouldn't pretend to be Dale's friend, but he didn't want to immediately come across as a foe, either.

Jack would ease the subject of Cliff Roberts into the conversation later. Asking about the dead congressman right out of the gate would probably kill any chance of Dale talking candidly.

Jack pointed to the first clipboard. "Tell me about this one."

Dale looked at the petition and frowned. "The land trade? What do you want to know?"

"Everything."

Dale hesitated. "Who are you again?"

"Jack Ma—"

"Jack Martin. I got that. And you're not law enforcement. So, who are you?"

Jack had to tread lightly. The last thing he wanted to do was scare Dale into clamming up. "Let's just say I'm an interested citizen wanting more information."

Dale frowned. "Did Wade send you?"

"Never met the man."

"And you're not FBI?"

Jack didn't see any sense in letting him know he'd previously worked for the FBI. He shook his head.

"All right, Louisiana. I'll tell you what it's about."

For the next several minutes, Dale filled Jack in on the details of the proposed land trade between the government and the millionaire rancher. Jack knew to take the information with a grain of salt—he was getting one side of the story.

Dale was animated, fidgeting and throwing his arms in the air as he talked. "The land Hank Wade wants is a high-mountain tract that he would have everyone believe is practically worthless. It's extremely remote. No road access. His argument is that the land he's willing to trade for it is larger and closer to town, so more valuable."

"I was told Wade's property near Ridgway is a crucial migratory corridor for elk and deer."

Dale waved a hand dismissively. "Maybe. But what he doesn't say is that there were a couple of kids camping on the land that he wants who reported seeing a moose." He leaned forward in his chair and raised his eyebrows. "And if *that's* true, that moose are repopulating the area after all these years, that's huge." He leaned back and shook his head. "It trumps any migratory corridor."

"What about the value of the properties?" Jack asked. "A larger tract closer to town would be more valuable."

Dale blew out a frustrated breath. "That's what they'd like everyone to think." He got up from the desk and walked to a large map that had been tacked to the grungy Sheetrock wall.

Jack joined him.

"Here," Dale said, pointing to a spot on the map that had been outlined in red marker; it was close to Ridgway and bordered the highway. "This is the tract Wade wants to give the government."

Next, Dale slid his finger to a smaller section outlined in red that appeared to be in the middle of nowhere. "And *this* is the property he wants."

Jack studied the two areas. The tract Hank Wade wanted to give the government was bordered by national forest on three sides and by all accounts looked like the better property. "Why does he want the smaller area?"

Dale took his finger off the map and pointed it at Jack's chest. "*That's* the question we can't get the media to ask. And the question Hank Wade won't answer. But it's the linchpin."

Jack didn't understand. Why would Wade want a much smaller, secluded tract? But of greater significance was, why was it important enough for Dale to threaten a sitting congressman?

He didn't have to ask. Dale continued. "What's not being reported in the media is that Wade already owns the adjacent land—here." He slid his finger just below the high-mountain area. "He's been adding parcels to this ranch for years. And if he's able to get his hands on this last tract, he will control the largest area of remote forest left in the Rocky Mountains."

Jack suspected Dale was holding something back. "It's not just about the trade, though, is it?" he asked. "I take it you don't like Hank Wade."

Dale's face hardened, and he turned back to the desk. "He's a capitalist vulture," he said, gathering up the clipboards and shoving them back in the drawer. "He bribes people to get what he wants. He's done it his entire life. Now he's bribed a congressman—someone who is supposed to represent us, the taxpayers."

"Congressman Roberts?"

Dale nodded.

"That's a pretty strong accusation," Jack replied, wanting to steer the conversation to the dead congressman. "I take it you didn't like Roberts, either."

Dale hesitated, and Jack figured what came out of his mouth next would be a lie.

"My problem wasn't ever with Roberts. It's what he stands for. . ." His voice trailed off. "Stood for," he corrected himself. "There are too many men like him in positions of authority taking money for favors."

"And you think Congressman Roberts took money from Hank Wade?"

"I know he did." Dale walked to the door and opened it. "Now, if you'll excuse me, I've got a speech to give in Bozeman in a few days that I need to prepare for." He pushed open the screen door, signaling their conversation was over.

Jack stepped outside. "I'll probably have more questions."

"It'll be my pleasure," Dale said sarcastically.

Jack started for Main Street but glanced back. Eric Dale had been more forthcoming than he'd expected, talking freely about the land swap and the dead congressman that some people suspected he was responsible for assassinating. He hadn't been friendly, but he hadn't seemed particularly menacing, either— not the type to bomb logging company offices, and certainly not the type to sabotage a congressman's plane.

Then again, some of the most seemingly candid people Jack had questioned while working for the FBI had ended up being stone-cold killers.

And there had been a glint in Dale's eyes that Jack had seen in men before, men skilled at covering up their emotions but ones who would do almost anything to get what they wanted.

CHAPTER 18

ON HIS WAY back to the campground, Jack dug his phone from his pocket and searched for the number of an old colleague he hoped still worked in financial crimes at the Houston FBI office.

He hit the call button and held his breath, relieved when the phone was answered on the other end.

"Archibald Rochambeau." It was said with a thick Cajun accent Jack recognized immediately.

He sounded bored. Jack hoped he was.

"Archie, it's Jack Martin."

"Martin! Long time no hear! Whatcha been up to? Well, that's a stupid question. I know what you've been up to—you've been all over the news. But seriously, old buddy, how you doing?"

They spent the next few minutes catching up. Archie talked about his wife and two sons. After suffering through several minutes of play-by-play of the latest peewee soccer games, Jack got to the point of the call.

"Archie, I need to ask a favor."

"I figured. Something told me you weren't calling just to shoot the bull after all these years." There was no resentment in his tone. "But it just so happens I'm not too busy at the moment—as long as you don't get me arrested." He laughed at his own joke.

Jack knew Archie was kidding but could hear the curiosity in his voice. Jack felt a tinge of guilt. Archie would know that when Jack asked for a "favor," he would end up skirting—if not breaking—the law.

But Archie Rochambeau was a computer whiz and a financial genius and one of only a handful of people in the country who could help find out what Jack needed to know.

Jack pictured his old friend sitting at his desk surrounded by computer monitors in the basement of the FBI building. His office was a dreary, windowless space not much larger than a cubical. It had been plastered with photographs of Archie's large family—brothers, sisters, and cousins. Jack could only imagine how many now were photos of his two boys—probably dressed in their soccer uniforms.

He and Archie had always enjoyed a cordial working relationship. Jack suspected part of the reason they got along so well was that Archie was also from Baton Rouge. But that didn't explain it all. Despite their personality differences, Jack genuinely liked and respected Archie and knew the feeling was mutual.

"I need you to dig up some financials on someone."

"I'm shocked," Archie teased with a quick laugh. "Some things never change, do they? Let me guess. You're on another one of your one-man crusades?"

"Something like that."

"Who's the lucky target this time?"

"Cliff Roberts."

"Pretty common name. Hold on, I need a pen." There was a rattling noise in the background, then a click. "I'm ready. Cliff

Roberts. Sounds familiar, but I don't know why. What else you got for me? How do I find the right Cliff Roberts?"

"He's from Colorado," Jack said. "He's a congressman."

There was silence on the other end of the line, and then Archie whistled through his teeth. "US or state?" He sounded hesitant, and Jack grew nervous it would be the first time Archie refused to help.

"US," Jack replied and held his breath.

"Uh-huh." Archie took a moment, considering the request. "Going for a big dog this time. Well, *go broke or go home*, is what I always say. What'd he do?"

"He might have taken a bribe."

More silence. "And what if he did? You going to pass along the info? Get the crooked SOB busted?"

"He's dead."

"Dead?"

"Still don't watch the news, Arch?"

"Not if I can help it."

Jack told him about the crash.

"So he's no longer around to prosecute," Archie said. "But you still want to know if he took a bribe?"

Jack knew it sounded crazy. But if the crash *wasn't* an accident and the congressman had been murdered, knowing if he had been bribed could help him figure out who would've wanted him dead.

"It's important," Jack said.

He could hear Archie tapping the pen on his desk while he thought about the request.

"All right," he said. "I'll do it. What do you need?"

Jack let out the breath he'd been holding and ran his free hand through his hair. "Start with bank records. Check the large nationals first, but if you don't find anything there, check regional ones in Colorado and DC. If you can't find anything there, either, check local banks in Telluride."

The line was quiet, and Jack knew Archie was taking notes.

There was a click of a pen. "Got it. Give me twenty-four hours."

"Thanks, Archie. I owe you one."

"How about another case of that lager brewed in Lafayette like you sent me last time?"

Jack screwed up his nose. "You still drink that stuff?"

"Every chance I get, Martin. Every chance I get."

Jack smiled. He missed his old friend. "Give that beautiful wife of yours a kiss for me."

"If I do, she'll be disappointed it wasn't authentic. You're famous in these parts now. You don't go quietly, do ya?" He laughed again at his own joke.

Jack realized he was referring to the high-profile cases he'd solved since he'd been in Colorado. He should have known word would have gotten back to the bureau's office in Houston.

"And from what it sounds like," Archie continued, "this latest case of yours is going to attract even more attention." He laughed again. "Just so you keep my name out of it. Deal?"

Jack was afraid Archie was right. He wanted to know what had happened to Cliff Roberts. And if it turned out it was murder, Jack wanted to help find the killer. But the media uproar following his previous cases had him gun-shy. The thought of being suffocated by the media again was his biggest nightmare. He didn't blame Archie for wanting to keep his name out of it. If Jack could figure out a way, he would help solve the case and keep *his* name out of the press, too.

"Deal?" Archie asked again, sounding more insistent.

"Deal."

They ended the call, and Jack crossed the street in the direction of Pandora Café. He would finally have breakfast, then head back to the trailer. He had Archie looking into Roberts's finances. But he wanted to do his own research on the late congressman.

In the last two days, Jack had gotten conflicting opinions about the kind of man Cliff Roberts had been. He wanted to find out for himself.

CHAPTER 19

Friday, May 13

THE NEXT MORNING, Jack loaded Crockett into the truck and drove out of the campground onto Main Street. Despite the cold, he rolled down the passenger window far enough for the dog to hang his head out and lap at the frosty morning air.

It was early. There weren't any tourists out yet, only a handful of locals milling about on the sidewalks, probably on their way to work.

As he entered downtown, Jack slowed to let a guy on a bike cross the road. He was white with dreadlocks and looked as if he hadn't bathed in days, but he lifted his hand in thanks as he passed in front of the truck.

Jack had grown fond of Telluride. As long as he didn't mention that he was from Texas, the locals were typically friendly. When asked, he often said he was from Louisiana despite not having lived in the state for decades.

Jack could understand some of the animosity against Texans. Tourists from the Lone Star state were sometimes loud and pushy. But more often than not, they weren't. From what Jack could tell, they were no different from anyone else visiting the mountain town. And in the few months he'd lived there, Jack had learned that most of the locals weren't really "local" anyway. They'd moved there from all over the country, states like California and Arizona, even Florida and Illinois.

Telluride was a melting pot, just like anywhere else. Rare were the denizens who were truly native, people like Judith Hadley and Otto Finn, who had actually grown up there.

And the longer he stayed, the more Jack felt like part of the community. It was a feeling he'd missed since leaving Houston two years earlier. His plan had been to stay in Telluride through the summer, then leave come fall. But he was having second thoughts.

He rolled the driver's-side window down, letting cold air fill the cab from both sides, and thought about what he had decided the night before. He would see the case through. If it was determined the plane crash was an accident, his work would be done. He had the five hundred dollars from Buckley that would help him get through the summer. He would decide in the fall what to do next.

But if his instincts were correct, if Cliff Roberts had been assassinated, he would assist in the investigation... as much as law enforcement would let him. Jack wasn't concerned about Tony Burns. He was confident he had built enough rapport with the local sheriff to be able to keep a hand in the case. It was the federal agencies that concerned him. If the NTSB and the FBI shut out the local guys, Jack would be out of luck.

He saw someone pull open the door to Pandora Café and wished there were time to stop in for breakfast. The protein bar he had eaten at the trailer wouldn't keep him full for long. But he wanted to catch Hank Wade early and knew that ranchers typically started their days just after dawn. He hoped he wouldn't be too late.

Jack had spent the previous afternoon and well into the evening researching Roberts. He'd read countless media stories of the dead congressman and his famous senator father. Many people had commended both father and son on their tireless service to the state of Colorado and the country. But other articles had been less flattering and accused one or the other—or both—of having spent their careers accepting bribes for political favors. Jack hoped a visit with Hank Wade would help him determine which portrayal of Cliff Roberts was accurate.

Despite the glowing testaments to Roberts's character from Judith and Buckley, Jack wanted to know more. He would make the decision about Cliff's character himself.

Judith seemed genuinely fond of Roberts, and Jack didn't doubt her sincerity. But Buckley was different. Buckley was a seasoned politician skilled at lying. And Jack still wondered why he had insisted he accompany search and rescue to the crash site. Jack remembered his questions about luggage and personal effects. Had there been something Buckley wanted them to find—or something he hoped they wouldn't?

A large black and white bird flew in front of the truck, nearly hitting the windshield, and Crockett barked. A man on the sidewalk unlocking a door a few feet away jumped. He spun in their direction and frowned. But his expression immediately changed. His eyes grew wide, and he quickly turned his attention back to unlocking the door. He looked scared. But why?

The encounter lasted only a few seconds, but something had been unsettling. Jack turned again to look. The man was small and wiry, dressed in a funny tweed getup that reminded Jack of several of his old college professors. The sign on the building read Telluride Bank & Trust.

Jack turned his attention back to the road. He drove the rest of the way through town, then took Highway 145 toward

Placerville, where he would turn north toward Ridgway. They were the directions Otto had given him.

After Placerville, Jack would be on his own. He didn't have an address but knew Wade's ranch would be somewhere before he got to Ridgway. "A large gate made of logs fit for a king," Otto had said. "Or a king in his own mind."

Otto's disdain had been palpable. It seemed everyone knew—or knew *about*—Hank Wade. And very few of them had anything good to say.

Jack was ready to meet the man himself.

CHAPTER 20

IT WAS THAT detective again. Ted was sure that Jack Martin was watching him.

As soon as he drove by, Ted unlocked the door, stepped inside the bank, and immediately relocked it.

He watched the truck through the window until it disappeared down the street, then scurried into his office, shrugged off his jacket, and hung it on the brass coatrack in the corner. His heart was pounding in his chest. He decided to skip his usual cup of coffee but went into the small break room and poured himself a glass of water. Back in his office, he sat down at his desk and took a bottle of pills from the top drawer. He shook two into his palm, then swallowed them, washing them down with the water.

The pills had been prescribed by his doctor years earlier to help settle his nerves. In thirty minutes, everything would be fine, he reassured himself. Or would it?

Ted drew in and released several deep breaths, trying to slow his heart rate, then pulled the local paper from his satchel and laid it on the desk.

He should have expected it—Cliff's obituary. A large photograph dominated the top half of the front page. Surrounding it were large blocks of text. Ted knew it would be the glowing account of Cliff's life—growing up in Telluride, his stellar athletic achievements while in high school. It would extoll his academic accolades in college and law school. There would be mentions of his legislative accomplishments while in Congress. Ted couldn't bring himself to read it.

He stared down at the smiling face of his old friend. There had been so much history between them. Some of it had been good, yet so much had been bad.

Ted quickly flipped through the remaining pages of the newspaper, hoping to find something else of interest. He skimmed an article about a mountain lion sighting on the west side of town, then gave up. He folded the paper and tossed it in the waste bin next to the desk.

But visions of Cliff's crash haunted him. Ted could only imagine how terrified Cliff must have been. Had he been killed instantly? Or had he been alive until the plane slammed into the snow? Ted shuddered. He wouldn't think about that now. There was work to do.

He booted up his computer and printed out the new accounts log from the day before, then spent the next twenty minutes staring blankly at the top page. It was useless.

He shoved the stack of papers to one side, then crossed his forearms on his desk and buried his head in them. All the rage and pain that had been building for years was catching up with him. His nerves were shredded.

When he saw people he knew in the bank or on the street, they looked at him differently. Even the way his employees acted around him had changed. Everyone looked at him as if they knew what he'd done. The day before, he had caught Gretchen watching him from her desk. He was sure she knew.

Ted's heart raced as he waited for the pills to kick in.

Cliff's funeral would be in a few days. The date would be included in the obituary.

Ted knew he should pull it from the waste bin and read it. But he left it in the trash.

CHAPTER 21

ONCE THEY CLEARED town, Jack wound up the windows, and Crockett laid down on the passenger seat next to him and fell asleep.

For miles, the highway was two lanes perched on the side of a red rock mountain. The road was steep and curved. Jack stuck the transmission in manual and downshifted to save his brakes—a lesson he'd learned the hard way while living outside of Aspen.

Neither side of the road had a shoulder, and just beyond the opposite lane, the mountain fell away in a sheer drop to the San Miguel River below. It was an unforgiving stretch of highway that Jack suspected had seen its share of tragic accidents. He drove the speed limit, taking care to keep the truck centered in his lane.

As they approached the town of Sawpit, the land flattened, and Jack felt his body relax. He noticed someone fly-fishing in the river, which was now only a few feet below the highway. The sun reflected off the moving water like thousands of shimmering diamonds. It looked peaceful, like a scene from a movie. Outside of baiting hooks with pieces of hot dog as a kid, Jack had never fished before but decided one day he'd like to try.

He dug his cell phone from under Crockett and found the number Buckley had given him for Hank Wade. He pressed it, but immediately got a message that the call had failed. He tried a second time and got the same result, then gave up and tossed the phone aside.

Twenty minutes later, not far outside of Ridgway, Jack noticed an elaborate stacked-log entrance and slowed the truck. As he drew closer, he saw two massive *W*'s sculpted from wrought iron and set into the logs on either side.

"Fit for a king," he said aloud. Crockett lifted his head and looked at him.

Jack turned through the entrance onto a gravel road. The foothills were green and rolling. Large, open fields were covered in lush spring grass. Behind them, the mountains were blanketed in pines and soared to rocky peaks that were still covered with snow.

Jack drove slowly, winding his way through pastures and over cattle guards. Less-traveled roads branched off in different directions. He stayed the course, following the one he hoped would eventually lead him to a house or barn.

In the distance, several men on horseback were driving a herd of cattle toward an unknown destination. A cloud of dust trailed behind them. Jack wondered if Wade was among the group.

The gravel road rose up and crested a hill, then turned and plunged into a forest. A few minutes later, the truck cleared the trees, and a cluster of buildings and livestock pens came into view. It was a compound.

The house was simple but large—two stories clad in lap siding and painted a pale green. The trim around the second-floor windows was painted bright white and matched the porch railings, which extended the length of the house. It was an old home, but it appeared well maintained.

Roughly fifty yards to the south was a barn. Three horses stood idle in a wood-railed pen to one side.

Jack pulled to the front of the house and got out.

"Stay here, Crockett," he said, shutting the door.

A red hound lying on the porch bawled once, then got up to greet Jack, wagging his tail.

Jack bent over. "What's your name, old fella?" he asked, scratching the dog behind his ears.

"I could ask you the same thing." A man had swung open the screen door and stood on the threshold watching. He was tall, maybe an inch shorter than Jack, and fit. Probably mid-forties, with close-cut dark hair sprinkled with gray and a matching beard. Wearing a black Stetson, faded jeans, and a plaid flannel shirt, the guy could have been straight out of casting for *Yellowstone*.

Jack stood up and approached him. "Name's Jack Martin. I'm looking for Hank Wade."

The man glanced toward the barn as if searching for someone, but immediately turned back. "You found him." He stepped onto the porch, letting the screen door shut behind him, then took the steps to the yard.

Wade's handshake was firm, and he didn't break eye contact until the shake was released. A strong personality, Jack decided. Confident and decisive. Hopefully honest.

"I'd like to ask you a few questions about Cliff Roberts."

Wade's gaze gave nothing away. There was a moment of silence before he replied. "Come on in," he said, turning toward the house, then stopped. "You're dog friendly?"

Jack glanced at Crockett still sitting in the truck. "The friendliest."

The harsh look on Wade's face relaxed, and he smiled. "Then let it out of there. Red would love the company."

Jack opened the door, and Crockett immediately bounded out and headed for the hound. The two sniffed each other cautiously with tense wagging tails. Crockett dropped onto his front legs, throwing his haunches in the air, and the two began running circles in the yard.

Jack breathed a sigh of relief. So far, so good.

"How about some iced tea?" Wade asked. "I was just about to pour me a glass."

Jack nodded. "I'll take it. Thank you." As the two men ascended the steps to the porch, he added, "Sorry to bother you unannounced. I tried calling, but it wouldn't go through."

Wade gestured in the direction of the red cliffs to the side of the house. "Cell phones don't work here. It's the iron in the rock. Kills the signal. Come on in." He held the screen door open.

Wade spoke with a relaxed accent similar to Jack's own and had an easygoing manner inconsistent with how people had described him. Jack wondered if the criticisms of Wade were unwarranted, maybe a product of envy. Then again, Jack had met plenty of men who'd kill you with kindness before they stabbed you in the back. He decided to keep his guard up.

Jack turned and saw Crockett still romping in the yard with the hound.

"They'll be fine," Wade said. "Red will keep him close to the house."

Jack hesitated a moment, then took the screen door from Wade and stepped inside.

The house was old but meticulously maintained. An oval rag rug was laid over wood floors that were clean but had probably seen a century or more of wear. The walls were paneled in lap siding and painted a simple white. The heads of dead animals hung everywhere—deer, elk, javelina. A full-size bobcat was mounted over the fireplace. The furnishings looked antique but sturdy—not the fussy variety his grandmother had preferred.

Wade led him to the back of the house and into the kitchen. "Have a seat," he said, pointing to a round table.

Jack pulled out a chair and watched as Wade filled two glasses with ice and tea. He scanned the room.

The kitchen was compact with stainless countertops on two sides. The refrigerator in the corner was an old pot-bellied model with a curved front and pull handle that looked like it had come off a fifty-seven Chevy. An aged gas stove anchored the other side of the room. Next to it, set on the countertop, was a small microwave and a handheld radio similar to the walkie-talkies Jack had played with as a kid, only larger.

"So, what brings you all the way out here to ask me about Cliff?" Wade set one of the glasses down in front of Jack and took a seat. "His death was quite a shock. And a real tragedy. Cliff was one of the few good guys in government."

"Was he a friend of yours?" Jack watched his body language for a reaction.

Wade pursed his lips, then turned and looked out the window, nodding slowly. "As much as a politician could be, I guess."

"What do you mean?"

"I would consider us as having been more acquaintances than friends. We'd see each other at some of the same events—weddings, funerals, fundraisers."

"Political fundraisers?"

"I'm a regular donor if I like a guy's politics."

"Did you donate to Cliff's campaigns?"

Wade nodded, twisting his glass on the table between his hands. "Several of them over the years."

"What about the most recent one?"

"His reelection in November?" Wade shook his head. "Nah, I stayed out of it this time."

"Because of the land trade?"

"Could have been viewed as a conflict of interest."

"Probably would have been."

Wade held Jack's gaze for a moment. "Cliff saw the benefits of the trade. My other tract is larger and closer to town. Parts of it can be developed. If the forest service sells off the land, they could make taxpayers a lot of money."

"Why not do it yourself?"

"Develop it?"

Jack nodded.

"That's not the business I'm in," Wade said. "I'm a rancher."

"Why take the smaller tract?"

Wade shrugged. "Why not? It's adjacent to this ranch. I could add it to what I've already got. Consolidate my holdings."

Jack wasn't sure he understood. Then again, he'd never been a rancher or a businessman. But he suspected there was more to Wade's passion for the property than what he was letting on.

"It seems like a lot of trouble for fewer acres," Jack said. "What's the real reason you want the land?"

Wade stared hard without answering, and Jack was afraid he had insulted him. Just when he expected to be asked to leave, Wade's face relaxed.

"Land is the oldest asset in human history. I have a chance to assemble something truly great here. There will still be larger ranches, but none as spectacular. There won't be another place like it."

There it was. Hank Wade's motive. Ego.

"Seems like a lot of people are against the deal."

Wade frowned. "Aside from some environmental whackos, most people see the benefit of it." He shrugged, then lifted his glass to his mouth but stopped. "Cliff did."

"You worked with him directly on the deal?" Jack asked. "Aren't these things usually negotiated between attorneys?"

"We quit talking through intermediaries months ago. I've always believed that talking man-to-man, face-to-face is the best way of doing business. Not through a bunch of suits."

"Even business with the government?"

Wade smiled. "Especially business with the government."

"So, what happens now?"

Wade swallowed some tea and set the glass down heavy on the table. "Who knows."

Roberts's death was a problem for him. The committee vote would likely be postponed until Cliff's successor could be appointed. And with the snail's pace that the government moved, it was anyone's guess how long that would be.

Wade picked at a callus on one of his palms. His hands were rough. The hands of a workingman, Jack noted, not of a typical millionaire.

The back door swung open, and a tall, lanky fellow stepped inside.

"Mornin', boss. We've got the horses penned."

Wade stood up, pulled the kitchen curtain aside to look, and nodded his approval. "Thank you, Brody. I'll be out as soon as I'm finished talking with my guest."

The man named Brody scrutinized Jack. His eyes were dark slits in a long, thin face punctuated by a dark beard covered in a layer of dust. He wore jeans and work boots and held a well-worn straw cowboy hat in his hand. There was a handheld radio clipped to his belt identical to the one Wade had sitting on the counter. Jack remembered the lack of cell service. It made sense; the radios were how the men communicated.

Brody nodded once at Jack, acknowledging his presence. He seemed suspicious, almost protective of his boss. That would make sense, too, Jack decided. Hank Wade was highly successful, and successful men typically attracted their share of enemies.

Brody looked at Wade. "Yes, sir, boss." He stole another quick glance at Jack before he stepped outside.

Jack spent the next several minutes asking Wade questions about his relationship with Roberts. Wade talked openly and candidly and seemed to have genuinely liked the congressman.

Next they talked again about the land deal. Wade insisted he thought the trade was more than fair. He talked some about ranching in Texas, then having moved to Colorado as soon as he could afford to.

Jack thanked Wade for the iced tea and followed him back through the house to the front door.

The dogs lay side by side in the yard, their tongues lolling.

"They look worn out," Wade said with a laugh as the two men stepped off the porch. "What's your guy's name?"

"Crockett."

"Well, bring Crockett around again sometime. Red likes his company."

"Will do." Jack nodded. "Thank you for your time."

As he drove away, Jack glanced in the rearview mirror and saw Wade call the hound to him. He patted the dog, then held open the screen door and let him in the house.

Jack thought of all the unflattering stories he'd heard and read about Hank Wade—ruthless millionaire, greedy rancher. But there was something good in a man who treated his dog right.

CHAPTER 22

JACK DROVE BACK through the stacked-log entrance and out to the highway. It had been a successful trip.

Despite the negative stories about Hank Wade, Jack could see the man's point. He was offering the government a more valuable piece of property in exchange for a smaller tract of land that would, in his words, complete his *dream ranch*. Jack understood. The ranch was beautiful. And with the addition of the high-mountain tract, it would stretch from the grass-lands along the highway, past the foothills, to the rugged snow-capped peaks that lay in the distance behind the house and barns. If Wade could pull it off, the ranch would be spectacular.

Several miles down the road, Jack slowed to let a coyote lope across the highway. As he did, he noticed the simple entrance to a ranch adjacent to Wade's. A small wooden sign with the name "Scotsman" burnt into it hung over the entrance.

Lea Scotsman.

Jack turned off the highway and pulled through. The country was similar to Wade's. Rolling green foothills covered in grass and large clusters of aspen and pines.

He wanted to talk to Lea. Except for Eric Dale and his band of activists, Jack had gotten the impression that people had genuinely liked Cliff Roberts. He was curious to know what Lea's opinion would be. And with any luck, maybe he'd find out why Susan had refused to see her. There was a story behind what had happened, and Jack hoped to get it.

He followed the winding road for about a mile and a half and came upon a large log structure. It looked like an old resort lodge—long and low, a single story with an array of windows to either side of the front door. An elevated porch stretched from one end to the other. Giant pines flanked both sides of the building and covered parts of the mountain behind it.

Jack parked the truck and rolled down the window. "One more stop," he told Crockett and got out.

He took split-log stairs to the front door, his boots making scratching sounds on the porch's unfinished pine boards. It was like stepping back in time and into a Jack London story. He wondered if the lodge had electricity or running water.

Jack knocked on the door and waited, then glanced down both sides of the porch. He knocked a second time.

After another minute, he tried the door and found it unlocked. He pushed it open and took a step inside. "Hello?" he hollered, his voice echoing down a long pine-log corridor.

"In the kitchen, Percy." It was a woman's voice from somewhere at the back of the lodge.

Jack closed the door behind him. The entrance hall, and what he could see of the rest of the place, was a single story high, but the ceilings were tall. Like the outside, the interior walls were formed of stacked logs. A giant chandelier made of antlers hung in the center of the living room off to the side. A broad fireplace built of river rock anchored the far wall. The shoulder mount of a large elk hung over the hearth. And wool

Navajo blankets that looked like they'd come from Waggoner Mercantile in Telluride were set on the floor and laid over the backs of an assortment of leather sofas and chairs. The place was beautiful.

Jack followed the corridor to the back of the house. Unlike the porch, the pine boards inside were smooth and polished. His footsteps echoed as he walked.

"Hello?" Jack called out again as he neared what he hoped was the kitchen.

"Did you get the lion?" the woman asked, obviously still thinking he was Percy.

Jack didn't want to scare her. "It's Jack Martin," he called out. "I met you outside the Robertses' home in Telluride."

He stepped into the kitchen and saw Lea sitting at the end of a long table. There was an open laptop set in front of her.

When she saw him, she closed the computer and stood up. If she was upset that Jack had let himself in, she didn't show it.

She crossed the room and extended a small, soft hand. "Jack, this is a nice surprise." She smiled as if they were old friends.

"I'm sorry about showing up unannounced and letting myself in."

She waved him off. "Don't be. It's good to see you again. What can I do for you?"

Jack was relieved. She was making it much easier than he had expected. What was it with the locals who could kill you with kindness?

"I'd like to visit with you for a few minutes if I could."

"Of course. Are you hungry?"

Jack smelled something cooking and realized what time it was. "I'm sorry. I'm interrupting lunch."

"Not yet. And I wouldn't mind if you did. We don't get many visitors these days. I'd be glad if you stayed." She walked to one of two ovens and pulled open the door. "We're having brisket."

Jack felt his stomach rumble.

Lea took her seat at the table. "We've got a few minutes before lunch," she said. "Now, what would you like to talk about?"

"For starters, Cliff Roberts." He saw her take in and release a slow breath.

For the next few minutes, Lea explained how she and Cliff met after he moved to Telluride from Washington, DC. From the stories she told, it sounded like they had been close. Jack wondered how close. It would explain the cool reception Lea had received from Susan.

Jack asked next about Hank Wade, and her demeanor changed entirely.

"He's a greedy, land-grabbing, vile human being," she said.

"But Cliff liked him."

She shrugged and shook her head. "I'm not sure what their relationship was all about."

Jack thought of the rumors of Cliff taking bribes. "I understand he was going to vote for Wade's land trade."

Lea held his gaze before she answered. "It was a bone of contention between Cliff and me," she said. "I didn't agree with his decision."

"Why?" When she hesitated to answer, he added, "I've got Cliff's side of the argument from a friend of his. I'd like to hear yours."

"Hank has threatened to fence the entire property close to town if he doesn't get his way. Turn it into some kind of high-end hunting lodge for wealthy clients out of places like New York and Chicago. Get them to pay him a small fortune to come hunt the deer and elk that he'll stock on the property. It would be like shooting fish in a barrel."

Somewhere near the kitchen, a back door opened, and a few moments later, a man wearing work clothes and carrying a rifle entered the room. He pulled up when he saw Jack.

"Percy, this is Jack Martin," Lea said. "He's gonna have lunch with us."

Jack stood up and shook the man's hand. He was stout in stature, but from his handshake Jack could tell he was strong. He was around seventy, nearly bald, and weathered from decades spent working in the sun.

Percy propped the rifle against a kitchen cabinet. "Still haven't found the cat," he said, pulling a glass from a shelf and filling it with water.

"We've got a mountain lion problem," Lea told Jack. "It's killing livestock."

The time for any significant conversation was over. The three spent the next half hour talking about the weather and Jack's time in Colorado while they dined on brisket and beans.

Lea told him about growing up on the ranch, leaving for school, then coming back. Jack watched closely as she talked. It sounded like a lonely life for a child and then for, presumably, a single woman. But from the way she talked, it seemed Lea didn't see it that way.

Percy spoke fondly of Lea's father and explained how he'd come to be the largest landowner in Ouray County—until Hank Wade moved in and started buying up ranches.

Nothing was mentioned about Lea's mother, and Jack didn't ask.

When he tried steering the conversation back to Roberts, Lea resisted. He saw Percy glance at her out of the corner of his eye, and Jack knew.

There was more to the story of Lea Scotsman's relationship with the late congressman than what she was willing to say.

CHAPTER 23

BUCKLEY BAILEY SAT drumming his fingers on his desk in the study and staring out the large window toward the ridgeline above town. The uppermost rocky crags were still covered with snow. He let his gaze drift east, toward Savage Basin, and was glad it was blocked from view by Ajax Mountain in front of it.

Cliff's plane would be somewhere just out of sight. Buckley hadn't seen it but had learned enough to know that the crash had been devastating. As hard as he tried, he couldn't force the image from his mind.

He got up and pushed his chair back, strode across the study and out into the large living room. He stood for a moment, listening for Celeste, then remembered she had told him she had errands in Montrose.

"Thank God for small favors," he mumbled aloud as he made his way across the room to the bar, his boots clomping on the Oriental rug.

Glass shelves were set against the stacked-log wall. Buckley pulled a crystal glass down and filled it with whiskey. It was early, but he needed a drink. He started back across the room but stopped, then turned and grabbed the decanter.

In the study, he set the glass and decanter on his desk and sank down into his chair, then stared up at the mountains again. He pulled the glass toward him and took a long drink of the whiskey.

He had made plenty of mistakes in his life—starting with the bribery scandal that had nearly derailed his fledgling political career two decades earlier. But through sheer grit and determination, he had managed to pull himself out of the mud. He had been knocked down plenty in his sixty years but had never been down for the count.

Cliff's death hit him hard. Buckley felt his chest tighten when he thought of what his friend's last few moments alive must have been like. He took another drink of whiskey, then ran a hand through his salt-and-pepper hair.

He and Cliff had been roughly the same age, and the two had grown close over the years. He thought of the fly-fishing trips they'd been on together, the trips to places like Moab and Santa Fe, the dinners with their wives. There had been hours of political debates and discussions, most in agreement with each other. Buckley was going to miss his old friend something fierce. He felt a lump form in his throat.

"Damn it, Cliff," he said, dropping a fist on the desk.

Buckley thought of their last conversation and had plenty of regrets. But regrets were of no use now. He pushed the thoughts from his mind and lifted his glass for another drink, then dragged the back of his hand across his mouth and screwed his eyes shut.

He should have stayed out of it. He should have called Charlie Dungee, let Charlie handle it like he'd handled most of the "situations" before. Buckley shouldn't have confronted Ted Hawthorne himself. He should have let Charlie do the dirty work.

But there hadn't been enough time. Charlie was somewhere in California, and Cliff was leaving for DC. And now it was too late.

Buckley hadn't wanted it to end this way. It was bad enough that he had lost a friend, but now he had to deal with the repercussions of what he'd done.

Buckley hoped like hell Jack was going to be able to help.

CHAPTER 24

JACK SWUNG THE truck off the gravel road onto the highway and headed back to Telluride. As he did, his cell phone buzzed on the seat beside him. He picked it up and glanced at the caller ID.

"Archie," he answered. "What do you have for me?"

"And hello to you, too, old buddy," Archie Rochambeau replied. "How are the kids, Arch? Doing great. What about the weather? It's May in Houston. The temperature just went from sixty to ninety like it's running from a state trooper. How about coming out to see me in Colorado sometime to cool off? Well, I'd love to. Thank you for askin'."

Jack chuckled. He missed his old friend. "Sorry, Arch. How're you doing?"

"I'd be better if the refrigerator wasn't shrinkin' my clothes."

Jack started to say something, but Archie kept going. "Did you hear the one about the tortilla factory that had ties to the mob? Turns out it was a shell company."

"Arch—"

"All right, all right. But I wish I had more compelling info for you."

"What'd you find?"

Archie cleared his throat. "Cliff Roberts. Congressman from Colorado. Has several sizable investment accounts with a couple of the big firms on Wall Street—UBS and Merrill Lynch. No mortgages or other substantial debt of any kind. A handful of credit cards that get paid off monthly like clockwork. Banks locally there in Colorado. Hold on a minute..."

Jack heard Archie shuffling paper and waited for him to continue.

"Here it is. Has checking and savings accounts at one Telluride Bank & Trust. Minuscule compared to the Wall Street accounts, but nice chunks of change by yours and my standard..."

Jack thought of the small white building on Main Street with Telluride Bank & Trust on the sign. He remembered the man with a wide-eyed expression who looked like a college professor. Something about seeing Jack and Crockett had spooked him.

Archie was still talking. "The guy's got lots of dough, no doubt about that," he said, referring to Cliff.

"Nothing seems out of the ordinary?" Jack asked. "No suspicious activity?"

"Nothing that I can find."

Jack thought about it for a moment. If Roberts had taken a bribe, the money would have to be somewhere. "No unusually large deposits into any of the accounts?"

"I went back three years on all of them," Archie replied. "Nothing."

The highway curved, and Jack began the climb toward Dallas Divide, a high mountain pass that was the geological divide between the San Juan Mountains and the Uncompahgre Plateau. He knew that as soon as he dropped into the valley below, he'd lose cell service. He had to think fast.

There was no money showing up on the congressman's end. But if Cliff had been bribed, he could have been paid in cash. Or maybe he had it sent to an offshore account. But the money would have had to come from somewhere, someone else's account.

He had an idea. "Arch, I'm driving and about to lose you. But I need you to check out someone else. The guy's name is Hank Wade. He's got a couple of ranches outside Ridgway, Colorado, not far from Telluride."

"Got it."

"Check for any large withdrawals on accounts registered to him. Follow the money and see if you can find out where it went." It was time for an end-run play. If the late congressman was being bribed, from what Jack had been told, there was a good chance Wade was at the other end of the payoff.

Jack crested the divide and started the descent into the canyon. He would have only two or three minutes before the call went dead.

He slowed the truck. "What can you tell me about the bank in Telluride?"

"Just that it's privately owned." Archie shuffled papers again. "Owned by a guy named Theodore Hawthorne." He laughed. "Now, there's a moniker you wouldn't want to be saddled with as a kid. Probably picked on mercilessly... unless he was built like one of you lucky guys who— "

"Arch."

"Right. Sorry. Bank has one branch. Deposits around a hundred and fifty million. Want me to check it out further?"

It could be a waste of time, but Jack knew it was typically easier to launder money through a smaller bank than a larger one. It was a shot in the dark, and he knew he might be sending

Archie on a wild-goose chase, but until Cliff Roberts's plane crash was ruled an accident, he would keep digging.

The highway curved sharply to the west as it dropped deeper into the valley.

"Look into Hank Wade's finances first," Jack said. "Then dig a little deeper into Telluride Bank & Trust."

"Will do."

"And, Arch..."

"Yeah?"

"Be carefu—" Jack began.

But the line went dead.

CHAPTER 25

JACK WAS ALMOST back to Telluride when he saw the sign for Ilium Road. He veered off the highway at the last minute. The sheriff's office was at the bottom of the hill.

He pulled into the parking lot and shut off the ignition. He wanted to talk to the sheriff.

The lot was nearly full. Jack noticed a small fleet of black Suburbans. A news van from Denver with a satellite dish mounted to its roof was positioned at the far side of the lot. The feds, Jack thought. And the media. He should have expected it.

Inside, a woman sat behind a counter scrolling through her phone. A plexiglass wall separated her work area from the lobby. She looked up when Jack opened the door, flooding the small, windowless room with sunlight. She seemed uninterested and started to drop her gaze back to the phone, but something made her do a double take.

"Can I help you?" She smiled and smoothed a few errant strands of hair behind her ear.

She was young. . . and pretty. Inquisitive brown eyes bored into Jack like lasers.

"I need to speak with Sheriff Burns. I'm Ja—"

"I know who you are." She stood up, still smiling. "I'll let the sheriff know you're here," she said and quickly disappeared around the corner.

There were several plastic chairs set against the walls of the lobby, but Jack remained standing. A minute or two later, the pretty receptionist opened a door and gestured for Jack to follow her.

"The sheriff will see you now, Mr. Martin," she said, smiling again. "I'll show you the way."

Jack followed her down a long corridor. An assortment of offices and meeting rooms opened onto it on either side. As he passed a large conference room, Jack noticed several men in suits at work at a long table. There were maps posted on the wall. The flurry of activity had the place buzzing.

As they neared the end of the hallway, Jack could hear Tony Burns talking in a loud voice. The sheriff hung up the phone as Jack rounded the corner and stepped inside.

"Come in, Jack." Tony stood up to greet him, then reached across the desk and shook his hand. "Have a seat." He motioned to an empty chair, then settled back down.

The desk was strewn with documents. Several stacks of paper and an array of three-ring binders were placed on a credenza behind him. Tony appeared busy—and tired. He had a weary look on his face.

"Budgets," he said when he noticed Jack looking. "My least favorite part of the job."

"It would be mine, too." Jack wondered why Burns was working on administrative tasks after what had happened just two days before.

Tony folded his hands on the desk and leaned forward. "I've been expecting you," he said. "I'm surprised you haven't been in sooner."

Jack was relieved he didn't detect any resentment in his tone. "I was hoping to get the latest on the investigation into the crash."

"Of course you were." Tony rested back in his chair and took in a deep breath, the weary look back on his face. "*My* investigation or the feds'?"

"That bad?"

He raised an eyebrow and nodded once. "You could say that."

"What's going on?"

"They've pretty much squeezed us out. Said since it's a dead congressman, it's federal jurisdiction."

"Who's *they*?"

"Who *isn't* it, is more like it. We got the alphabet soup in town. NTSB, FBI, FAA. I even had Secret Service in here this morning. Hell, they've practically commandeered my offices. Did you see the damn parking lot? It's a circus!"

"I'm sorry to hear it," Jack said. He knew from experience that it wasn't unusual for federal law enforcement to muscle the local guys out of an investigation.

Tony leaned back in his chair and folded his arms. "At least they're still talking to us."

"What do you know?"

"Right now they're swarming the crash site, digging through snow. Nothing has been said outright, but I'm getting vibes they think it was a bomb. The plane's trajectory when it hit appears to have been near vertical. They're scouring the place—I'm sure looking for bomb fragments or evidence of explosives in the wreckage. It's got to be like looking for a needle in a haystack up there in all the snow, but that's what they're doing."

"And what about you guys? You drop the investigation?"

Tony came forward in his chair and lowered his voice. "We're not dropping anything. And we're not waiting around for the FAA to make a ruling on the cause of the crash; that could be months. I've got a deputy over at the airport interviewing employees right now."

"Have you found out anything?"

"We know that weather shouldn't have been a factor. The winds weren't an issue when the plane took off. They had time to get up and out of here before turbulence would have been a problem—maybe a few wind sheers here and there, but nothing pilots used to flying in and out of here couldn't handle."

Jack was far from an expert on aviation, but the information bolstered the theory that the crash had been caused by a bomb.

"Anything else?" Jack asked.

"Just that Cliff was supposed to fly out the morning before, but for some reason—at the last minute—the flight was pushed back a day. Not sure there's any importance to it, but we found it interesting."

It *was* interesting. Jack thought back to his conversations with Buckley and Susan Roberts. Neither had mentioned that Cliff was supposed to have flown out the day before. The fact he left a day late could be insignificant. Then again, it could be a clue. Had the delay given someone time to plant a bomb on the plane? Jack made a mental note to ask Buckley about it later.

"Anyone see anything suspicious?" Jack asked. "Any unusual luggage or someone hanging around the plane?"

Tony shook his head. "Unfortunately, nothing like that—not yet. Kim's still out there."

"Kim, the deputy on search and rescue?" Jack thought of the cute redhead he'd spent the day with trekking to the crash site.

"That's her. Kim O'Connor. Best deputy I've got. If there's something to be found, she's the one most likely to find it."

CHAPTER 26

ERIC DALE SAT picking at a chip on the metal desk in the dimly lit temporary office of Wilderness Keeper.

He'd sent the other guys home for the day—back to the campground. And now, with Roberts dead, he suspected some of them would pack up and head out of town—on to a more lucrative gig.

With Roberts out of the way, there wasn't much to do except wait and see what would happen with the house committee's vote. Eric hoped the vote would be delayed indefinitely. He could go home, spend a week or two in Oregon, keep his promise to his mother. He hadn't been home since Christmas. The year before, he'd only made it to Oregon to see her twice, each visit lasting only a few days before an environmental crisis had called him away.

But if anyone should understand his absence, it was his mother, Mona Dale, celebrity activist. Mona had spent a three-year stint in Bedford Hills Correctional Facility for Women for orchestrating the bombing of the corporate headquarters of a Pennsylvania oil and gas company in 1973. Afterward, she had been interviewed on television and radio talk shows. Some hack newspaper reporter had even written her biography. The media had loved her. She was articulate—a Berkley graduate—and pretty in that hippie sort of way. Activism ran deep in Eric's family; he had learned from the best.

Eric heard the screen door open and turned in time to see two men dressed in dark suits step into the office. For a second he was reminded of the movie *Men in Black*. Then it dawned on him—federal agents. After everything that had gone on, he should have expected them.

The two pulled sunglasses off and scanned the room.

Eric cringed when he saw them notice the Kick Out Cliff poster. They didn't need it anymore; they should have thrown it out. He picked up his laptop and set it down on top of the matching flyers, which were still stacked on his desk.

"How can I help you, gentlemen?" He drew in a deep breath, trying to steady his nerves.

"Are you Eric Dale?" The agent glanced at a small notepad. "Alias Eric Dawson, alias Frederic Delaware?"

He should have never used the third name. It sounded ridiculous. But he'd been young and impressionable. And fifteen years earlier at a sit-in, when a cute blonde leaned over and whispered in his ear not to give the police his real name, it had sounded like a good idea.

"I'm Eric Dale." He rose from the chair slowly.

"We understand your group threatened a sitting United States Congressman."

Eric swallowed and stuck his hands deep into his pockets to keep them from shaking. He told himself that he had nothing to worry about; these guys would be talking to just about everyone in town. Eric knew the drill. He also knew this wasn't going to be good.

The agent closest to him said they needed to ask him a few questions. Eric knew he couldn't refuse or he'd seem guilty of whatever it was they wanted to pin on him.

Thirty minutes later, the goons were gone, but the damage had been done. Eric was rattled. It wasn't a matter of *if* they'd come back; it was the matter of *when* that bothered him. And next time, they'd probably come armed with a search warrant.

He wouldn't wait around any longer than he had to. A few days at the most. There were a couple of things he needed to do first, but after that, nothing good would come from hanging around Telluride.

CHAPTER 27

WITH THE LUNCH rush over, the café was quiet. Jack glanced around the room but didn't see Judith. One of the girls who regularly waited on him noticed him searching for her.

"Judith decided to take the afternoon off," the girl named Casey said. "She's doing her spring planting."

The thought of Judith having a life outside of the café had never dawned on him. It was a shocking notion, like when you were a kid and ran into one of your teachers outside of school. You just assumed they lived where they worked. It was strange to think of them with lives beyond the job. Jack knew it was ridiculous, but he had never imagined Judith being anywhere except the café.

"Does she live here in Telluride?" he asked, knowing that a lot of locals weren't actually local at all but lived in nearby small towns like Rico and Placerville.

Casey smiled, probably amused by the stupid look on his face. Jack checked himself.

"Judith's lived here her whole life," Casey said. "Same house, as far as I know."

"Close by?"

The girl nodded, sending her blond hair bobbing. "Just down the street. Purple house by the cemetery."

Purple?

A few minutes later, Jack stood on the sidewalk just off Main Street next to the town cemetery. Casey hadn't been lying.

The small Victorian house, probably built sometime around the turn of the last century, was painted a vivid shade of purple. The trim around the doors and windows and the gingerbread details on the porch were done in a stark white. It reminded him of something out of *Willy Wonka* or *The Wizard of Oz*.

There were raised flowerbeds on either side of the porch steps. A stack of empty pots sat just below one of the beds on the grass of the small front yard. Jack noticed an assortment of brightly colored flowers planted in the box above it. The other box was still bare.

The place looked happy, and Jack decided that only someone who loved life would live in a purple house.

Just then Judith rounded the corner holding two pots of flowers, one in each hand. She pulled up when she saw Jack.

"Well, this is a nice surprise," she said. "You out for a walk and get lost?"

Jack stepped forward and took one of the pots from her. "Let me help you."

"How much time do you have?"

Jack didn't know what to say. He knew nothing about gardening, and the last thing he wanted to do was spend the afternoon planting flowers.

Judith saw the look on his face and laughed. "You can set it down next to those," she said, pointing to the empty pots on the ground. "These will finish out the first bed."

She wore red gardening gloves and a bright green apron. Her shirtsleeves were rolled up, and her arms were smudged with dirt. A thin sheen of sweat sparkled on her upper lip. But she looked happy.

Jack set the flowers on the ground and took the second pot from her. He wasn't sure what to do next.

Judith gestured with her chin. "Right next to the other one." Jack placed the pot down. "Now, let's go inside," she said, pulling off a glove and wiping her brow with the back of her hand. "I've got a jar of sun tea on the back porch, and I could use a break."

The inside of Judith Hadley's house was like stepping back in time. The walls were painted a light shade of pink. Antique furniture was upholstered in bright, flowery prints. A large blanket, crocheted in matching colors, was draped neatly over the back of a small sofa, and lace doilies covered the tops of small tables set to either side.

Jack followed her into the tiny kitchen, not much larger than the inside of his trailer. The walls were papered in a sunflower print. A round table for two was pushed into a corner, and Judith gestured for him to have a seat.

There were sugar cookies under a glass dome set in the center of the table.

She must have seen him looking. "Are you hungry? I made them last night when I couldn't sleep. Help yourself."

They were tempting, but Jack declined.

Judith opened the back door and stepped outside onto a tiny porch. She came back in holding a glass jar filled with tea. She poured it over ice into a couple of glasses and set them on the table, then took a seat.

"I'm glad you came to see me, Jack," she said, watching him, her face etched with concern. "But I know you're not here for the tea."

"I'd like to ask you a few questions."

They spent the next several minutes talking about Cliff Roberts and his relationship with Lea Scotsman.

"They were always close," Judith said. "She would come into the café with him from time to time when they were still in school. She went to school in Ridgway, but the kids around here all know each other. I don't think they ever dated, but it wasn't for Lea not wanting to. You could see it in her eyes." Judith leaned back in her chair, remembering. "*I* could see it anyway. Cliff never had much intuition for those sorts of things."

"And recently? What was their relationship like before Cliff died?"

"They were still close. Well. . . as close as two adults of the opposite sex can be when one is married."

"Did Susan have a problem with their friendship?"

Judith took a sip of tea before she answered. Jack could tell the direction of the conversation made her uncomfortable.

"She probably *would* have had a problem if she knew they were still close."

"Were they involved romantically?"

Judith immediately shook her head. "Oh, no, nothing like that. Just close friends, really—confidants."

She might believe that nothing had been going on between Cliff and Lea, but Jack still wasn't convinced. He decided to let the topic drop. . . for now.

"I understand they were on opposite sides of Hank Wade's land deal with the government."

"They were. Cliff felt it would be a good trade for the forest service, but Lea didn't agree. Of course, her ranch butts right up next to Wade's, and although he's not bad to look at, his reputation makes you think he wouldn't be a great neighbor. I know that was a source of tension between Cliff and Lea recently. He stopped in one morning last week before he went out to discuss it with her. I think he was hoping that being on opposite sides of the issue wouldn't damage their friendship."

"Cliff went to see Lea?"

"He did," Judith replied. "It was probably the last time he saw her."

Jack was surprised by the revelation. Lea hadn't mentioned Cliff coming to see her. She'd made it sound like they talked only on occasion. Why would she keep his visit a secret?

"Did he mention how the trip to see her went?"

Judith's expression turned sad. "I didn't get the chance to ask him. That morning was the last time I saw him—except for the town hall that night, but I was just one of the crowd. I didn't talk to him."

"Was Lea at the town hall?"

"No. I would have seen her if she were."

"What about Hank Wade? Was he there?"

"No. And I'm glad he wasn't."

"You don't like him?"

"Not many people do."

"But Cliff did."

She drew in and released a long breath. "For some reason they got along. I wouldn't say they were friends or anything, but, yes, Cliff seemed to like him."

Jack thought about the bribery rumors and knew that money often made for strange bedfellows.

"What can you tell me about Hank Wade?" he asked.

"That he's a looker. Broken up more than one marriage, but you didn't hear that from me." Judith's answer came quick and dripped with scorn.

Jack wasn't interested in Wade's love life. "I heard he's not from Colorado. Do you know where he's from?" From talking to Wade, Jack already knew, but he wanted to hear what Judith had to say.

Judith pursed her lips before answering. "Texas. From what I hear, he was left a little family land around Pecos. Sold it off but managed to keep all the mineral rights. People say he cheated the buyers to keep them, but I don't know how they'd know that. Anyway, an oil company comes along and punches some gushers. That's how he got rich. Came here years ago and started buying up ranches in the San Juans. Some think he wants to make his headquarters ranch one of the largest in the country. If he gets his way, it might not be one of the largest, but it'll darn sure be one of the prettiest and most expensive."

"Why here?" Jack asked, thinking aloud. "Why Ridgway?"

She shrugged. "Prettier than Pecos, I guess."

Jack agreed. He'd been to Pecos.

Judith continued. "My two cents is that Hank has a chip on his shoulder about growing up poor and now thinks he has to prove himself. I've seen the type before."

Jack suspected she was right.

Next, he thought of his visit with Lea. She had made it clear how much she disliked Hank Wade. And the congressman's decision to vote *for* the land deal with Wade had her upset enough for Roberts to make a trip out to see her. Jack wanted to know why.

The visit with Judith had paid off. He now had new questions to ask—holes in the story of Cliff Roberts that needed to be filled.

CHAPTER 28

Saturday, May 14

EARLY THE NEXT MORNING, Jack was back on the highway to Ridgway. He had spent the previous evening researching Lea Scotsman, and from what he could tell, she kept a low profile. There were no social media accounts, no interviews in area newspapers. Yet he knew from the size of her landholdings that she was a very wealthy woman.

When Jack arrived at the lodge, Lea was outside talking to Percy. The look of surprise on her face was quickly replaced by a smile.

Jack got out of the truck, and she walked toward him.

"What a nice surprise," she said, and looked like she meant it. "But if you've come for breakfast, I'm afraid you're too late. Percy and I get started early."

"I was hoping to ask you a few more questions."

"Of course. Come inside." She turned to Percy. "Good luck finding the lion. Let's hope today's the day. I'll see you at lunch."

Percy nodded at Lea, then told Jack, "Good morning." There was a guarded expression on his face. He was suspicious—or nervous—Jack wasn't sure which.

Jack followed Lea into the lodge, where she ushered him into the living room and gestured for him to have a seat on a large leather sofa facing the fireplace.

"What can I help you with?" she asked, sinking into a chair.

There was no sense in beating around the bush. Jack got right to the point. "You didn't tell me about Cliff's visit to see you last week. I'd like to know why."

If she was surprised or offended by the question, she didn't show it. "There's not much to tell. Cliff drove out to explain his position on the land trade. He knew I didn't agree with him, but he didn't want there to be any hard feelings between us before he left for Washington."

She said it matter-of-factly, as if it wasn't a difficult question to answer, but Jack knew there was more. She was holding something back.

"You didn't mention his visit yesterday when I asked you about him."

Lea shrugged. "I didn't think it mattered."

Jack studied her a moment. She was beautiful. . . and evasive. Getting the truth out of her wasn't going to be easy.

He settled back onto the sofa. "Why keep his visit a secret, Lea?"

She stared back without answering, and Jack knew she was debating whether or not to trust him with the truth. He wasn't sure how much he trusted *her* yet, but it was no secret he'd been a detective.

"Look," he said, leaning forward. "I've been hired to find out what happened to Cliff."

"Hired by who?"

"That doesn't matter."

"It matters to *me*. Was it Susan?" She was on the edge of the chair. "Did Susan send you out to talk to me?"

Jack didn't want to tell her who'd hired him, but he wanted to settle her down. "It wasn't Susan."

The muscles in her face relaxed, and she eased back into the chair.

"Did Susan know about Cliff's visit?" Jack asked.

"Probably not," Lea replied. "I don't think Cliff would have told her."

"Why the secrecy?" When she didn't answer, Jack added, "Look... the sheriff seems to think Cliff's crash wasn't an accident. And I'm beginning to think the same thing. I'm just trying—"

"What do you mean not an accident?"

She was frowning. The revelation had caught her by surprise.

Jack lowered his voice. "Lea, the evidence is pointing to a bomb." She drew in a sharp breath, and Jack held up a hand. "It hasn't been officially determined yet—it'll probably take months. But that's the way it's looking."

"Someone *murdered* Cliff?"

"We don't know for sure yet. But that's what I've been hired to look into."

Lea took a moment to process the information. "Why you? I mean, I know you're a detective, but isn't the government investigating this?"

Jack nodded. "A slew of agencies is already in town, but I've been asked to look into it, too. The person who hired me thought maybe I'd be able to help get to the bottom of it faster."

She nodded slowly. Jack gave her a moment.

"Lea, I need to know more about Cliff to find out what happened to him. And reconstructing his last few days is a start. I need you to be honest with me... Lea?"

She was mindlessly studying her hands, and Jack waited for her to look up.

"Okay." Her voice was faint, almost inaudible.

Jack held her gaze. "Were you having an affair with Cliff?"

She pulled back as if repulsed by the question. "No," she said, shaking her head. "Cliff and I were friends."

"Then why keep his visit a secret? Is it because of Susan?"

"Yes—I mean, no." She looked confused.

"Which is it, Lea?"

"It's both. Susan never understood our relationship. I guess if I were in her position, I probably wouldn't, either. But Cliff kept his visits to himself to save me from any negative publicity—especially after he became embroiled in the land controversy. It was to protect me."

"How often did he visit you?"

"Almost never. He would send me an occasional birthday or Christmas card, and he used to send an email every now and then to check on me, but that stopped after he was elected to Congress. I think he was afraid his account was monitored. But that's it. That's all there was."

Jack was skeptical. When he didn't reply, she continued.

"I'm telling you the truth. Before last week, he hadn't been out here in almost ten years. We were close when we were young, but then we went our separate ways. We kept in touch now and then, but that was all."

She looked as if she was telling the truth. Jack decided to accept her version of events—for now.

"What was Cliff's relationship like with Susan?" he asked.

"I can't say. He didn't speak of her much. I've only met her on a handful of occasions over the years."

"Can you tell me about her?" Jack wanted Lea's impression of the dead congressman's wife.

She thought about the question a moment. "I know she and Cliff met when he went to Washington. She was working for another congressman at the time. But when they married, she quit. Cliff said she never liked the city—she's from Kansas or Missouri or somewhere."

"I've heard she lives mostly in Telluride now."

"She does, but not by choice. I think she'd go back home if she could. Doesn't like the city, but Telluride's too remote."

"But as far as you know, she and Cliff got along? No marital problems?"

Lea nodded. "I think they were fine," she said. "I've never heard otherwise. I know she helped him with his congressional duties—writing speeches and press releases. That's what she did for the congressman she worked for before. But their relationship is really none of my business, so I've never given much thought to it."

She blinked a couple of times, and Jack didn't believe her last statement.

"Being at odds over the land deal with Hank Wade must have made Cliff's last visit difficult."

She studied her hands again. "I made my case, and he made his. We didn't agree. I told him I was going to fight the land trade tooth and nail and that I'd already sent letters to the other members on the committee. I let him know that I was going to do everything in my power to see that it didn't happen." She was quiet a moment. "I wish now that I hadn't gotten so angry with him."

"How did Cliff take it?"

"He said to do whatever I felt I needed to." She looked up from her hands, and he saw the pain in her eyes. "I reminded him that these mountains are what turned his life around. He was a mess when he got here. But there was a group of us kids that hiked all over the San Juans back then—here in Ridgway, around Telluride, and as far south as Ophir and Trout Lake. We had quite the adventures back then."

As she remembered, her eyes softened. They were beautiful, a hazel green that seemed to dance as she spoke. Jack shook his head, bringing himself back to the conversation.

She was still talking. "It's been thirty years since any of us have been up in the country Wade wants. It's an ambitious hike, but I told Cliff he needed to see it again before he gave it away. There's nothing like it. High-mountain lakes the same color blue as an Alaskan glacier. Did I tell you hikers have reported spotting moose up there? That would be a sight to see. I was just telling Percy. . . "

Jack watched her as she talked, recalling past camping trips into the high country, stories about growing up on the ranch and hiking the hills and mountains around it. She was animated, smiling and gesturing with her hands. It was almost hypnotic.

Jack sat quiet, listening. But her words soon faded away, and he found himself watching her, no longer listening. He wished he'd met her sooner—before the feud with Hank Wade had made her angry and before Cliff Roberts's plane crash.

And especially before he suspected that she could, in some way, be a party to murder.

CHAPTER 29

ON THE WAY to Telluride, Jack ran back through his conversation with Lea in his head. There were several things she had said that bothered him. He didn't think for a minute that she hadn't had feelings for her old friend before he died.

Jack thought about Cliff and remembered that Tony had told him the flight to Washington had been delayed a day. He wondered why Cliff had pushed back the flight and whether the delay had provided time for someone to plant a bomb on the plane. Who would have known about Cliff's last-minute schedule change besides his wife, Susan?

A few miles outside of Telluride, Jack regained cell service and called Buckley, but there was no answer.

He drove slowly through town and stopped at an intersection for a group of teenagers to cross the street. He went on but slowed as he approached Telluride Bank & Trust. He glanced through the windows as he passed and was disappointed that there was no sign of the nervous man who'd been unlocking the door the morning before, when Crockett barked.

At the campground, he pulled next to the trailer and got out. There was a sheet of paper attached to the door, fluttering in the wind. Jack read it before he reached the door: Kick Out Cliff.

It was identical to the flyer thrown through Susan Roberts's window, the same as the ones stacked on Eric Dale's desk. But Cliff's name had been scratched out, and his photograph had been replaced by one of Jack.

He jerked the flyer off the door and glanced through the trees toward the tent circle in the distance. There was no sign of the rowdy activists, nobody posturing for a fight. The campsite was quiet. Where were they?

Jack crumpled the flyer and stuffed it into a pocket, then let Crockett out of the trailer. The dog jumped and panted at his feet.

Jack reached down to pet him. "Who was our visitor?" he asked, glancing over his shoulder.

There was a rustling noise through the trees in the direction of Otto's tent. Jack stood up and listened. Crockett tensed and stared toward the adjacent campsite.

"Let's go see what it is," Jack told him, and the dog bolted.

By the time Jack cleared the trees, Crockett was nowhere to be found, but within a few seconds, he emerged from Otto's tent, panting and wagging his tail. Otto followed close behind and looked up when he noticed Jack coming toward him.

"Howdy, neighbor," the old man said, shuffling in the direction of the picnic table.

Jack noticed a brown paper bag sitting on top of it. The dark green logo identified it as a bag from the local market. Otto had been shopping.

Otto lifted the bag from the table. His hands shook, causing the rustling noise Jack and Crockett had heard through the trees.

"Have a seat," Otto said, turning toward the tent. "This is the last one. I'll be right back."

When the old man returned, he sank down into the folding chair at the end of the table.

Jack straddled the bench. "Did you happen to see anyone at the trailer earlier?"

Otto shook his head, sending his gray beard swaying. "Can't say that I did, but I've been to town. Just got back not five minutes ago. Why do you ask?"

"I had a visitor sometime this morning."

Otto frowned. "What was it about?"

"I think someone was trying to send me a message." Jack didn't feel the need to elaborate.

"Anything broken?"

Jack shook his head.

Otto narrowed his eyes, studying him, and knew that Jack was holding something back. He swiveled his head in the direction of the group of tents pitched in a circle, then glanced at his own. The door flap was zipped open and laid to the side. His rusted bicycle was propped next to it. Nothing appeared amiss.

"Whoever it was must not have thought I needed the same message," he said, pursing his lips, thinking about it. "Their mistake. From now on, I'll take extra care in watchin' for you."

The old man probably didn't have more than a high school education. Maybe not even that. But he was as intuitive as anyone Jack had ever known, and he had grown fond of the old guy.

"Can I ask you a favor?"

Otto's blue eyes lit up, and he reached over the side of the chair for Crockett. "Want me to watch him for ya?" he asked, petting the dog.

"I'll probably be an hour or so. I've had him cooped up all morning."

"No need to explain," Otto said, pushing himself to a standing position. "I told you I'd be happy to have his company anytime—isn't that right, Crockett? I'm going to get my pole. Crockett and I are going to do a little fishin'. He likes that. You go on," he said, throwing up a hand and heading in the direction of the tent. "Come on, Crockett."

Jack watched him disappear into the tent, Crockett following on his heels.

As he walked back to the trailer, he heard the old man mumbling something to the dog about a fishing lure, and Jack smiled. He locked the trailer door and started for town, glancing at his phone. Buckley hadn't returned his call, but there was someone else who could give him the answers he was looking for.

Susan Roberts.

As Jack made his way up Main Street, he passed a real estate office and caught a glimpse of Congressman Roberts's photograph. It was on the front of the local newspaper. Copies were set in a small wire stand next to magazines showing local houses for sale.

Jack pulled the paper from the rack and unfolded it. The photograph showed Cliff giving his speech at the Opera House during the town hall. The story included a second photo of Cliff standing with a small group of people that included Buckley Bailey. According to the caption, it had been taken the following night at a fundraising dinner at Allred's, the fancy restaurant at the top of the gondola line, midway between Telluride and Mountain Village.

Jack folded the paper and took it with him.

A few minutes later he climbed the steps to Susan Roberts's porch and rang the bell.

"Hello, Detective." She seemed surprised to see him.

"I'd like to ask you a few questions."

"Of course." She ushered him inside and into the living room. "Have a seat."

Jack set the newspaper on a side table and took the chair he'd sat in only two days before. There was a framed black-and-white photograph of an older couple on the small table beside him. The man looked familiar.

"They're my in-laws," Susan said, noticing him studying it. "In fact, almost all the furniture and art in the house belonged to them."

Jack scanned the room. Everything looked expensive but old. There were other black-and-white photos, along with a color one of a baby that Jack suspected was Cliff.

"The portrait over the fireplace is also of the senator," she said. "It used to hang in their family home in Denver. But Cliff was devastated when his father died, and his mother gave it to him. He brought it here." There was sadness in her eyes.

Jack glanced at the painting and was struck by the likeness. It was a large portrait. Edward Roberts looked to have been in his fifties or sixties when it was painted. He was dressed in a dark suit and tie and sat in an antique chair similar to the one Jack was sitting in. He held a lit cigar; a thin plume of smoke trailed above his hand, which was rested on the arm of the chair. It was a formal-looking portrait, and one that gave the impression the senator still lorded over the small living room.

"Cliff looked so much like his father, don't you think?"

Jack was about to answer when a man walked in studying a sheet of paper.

"Suze, you're sure this was the final draft of the press release?" He saw Jack and pulled up. "Oh, I'm sorry. I didn't realize you had company."

"Gerald, this is Jack Martin," Susan said. "Jack—Gerald Purvis, Cliff's chief of staff."

Gerald was around Jack's age. He had a thin build, a full head of brown hair that was starting to gray at the temples, and fair skin that could use some time in the sun.

Jack stood up to shake Gerald's hand and was surprised to find that, despite the man's soft appearance, his handshake was firm.

"Jack is helping the sheriff look into the crash," Susan told him.

Gerald looked as if he was about to reply, then simply nodded. It was an unusual response. He cleared his throat. "I'll let the two of you talk. Susan, I'll be in the study."

"Thank you, Gerald."

Jack took his seat again.

Susan eased down onto the sofa, slipped her shoes off, and pulled her feet up under her. She was attempting to appear relaxed, but Jack wasn't buying it. Something had her nervous. He watched the muscles in her neck tense before she spoke.

"Have you found out anything more about the crash?" she asked.

"Nothing that you probably haven't already heard from the sheriff's office."

"I haven't heard much of anything from Tony or his people," she said, sounding perturbed. "In fact, I was going to give him a call later." She eyed Jack skeptically. "So, why have you come?"

Jack lifted the newspaper from the side table. "I'd like to find out about the days leading up to the crash. I picked this up on the way over and was hoping you could answer a few questions."

"Of course. What would you like to know?"

Jack unfolded the paper and pointed to the photograph taken at the fundraising dinner. "This was the night following the town hall."

"That's correct. It was a dinner at Allred's."

Jack started with an easy question. From experience, he knew if he could get someone to answer a few quick questions, the better chance he had of keeping them talking when he asked the more difficult ones.

"Were you at the dinner?"

"I was."

"Can you tell me who these people are with Cliff?" Jack asked, rising from the chair and handing her the newspaper.

"You already know Buckley, but this is Ted Hawthorne," she said, pointing at the thin man to Cliff's left. "He lives here in Telluride and is an old friend of Cliff's—"

"He's a banker?"

Susan seemed surprised that he knew. "Yes, he is."

Jack remembered the name from his conversation with Archie Rochambeau. He hadn't recognized him in the picture but realized it was the same nervous little man he'd seen in front of Telluride Bank & Trust the morning before.

Susan turned her attention back to the photograph. "This is Bart and Vera Whitestone from Denver," she said, pointing at an elderly couple. "Bart was a friend of Cliff's father, Edward, and has been a strong supporter of Cliff."

"And the woman standing to Cliff's right?" The woman was the last person in the photograph.

"That's Elizabeth Mayweather. She lives in Mountain Village."

The easy questions aside, Jack was ready to get to the point of his visit. "My understanding is that Cliff was supposed to fly out the following morning but didn't."

"That's right."

"Do you know why he delayed leaving?"

Susan shook her head. "I have no idea. He didn't say."

"Do you know when he decided to delay the trip? Was it after the town hall or the fundraising dinner?"

She thought about the question. "It was a last-minute decision, I think. He didn't tell me he was staying another night until we were on our way home after the dinner at Allred's."

"Did he mention *why* he was staying?"

"He didn't." Susan didn't elaborate further, and Jack knew it was going to be more difficult to get information from her than he'd hoped.

"What did he do that next day?"

"I'm afraid I don't know," she said. "He left early that morning before I got up. He said something had come up, and he had a couple of things to take care of. I assumed it was related to his reelection campaign."

"Did he mention going anywhere in particular?"

Susan shook her head. "He didn't. He was gone most of the day. I'm sure he stopped by Pandora Café at some point for something to eat."

Jack already knew from Judith that Cliff hadn't been to the café, but he kept the information to himself.

"Did he happen to mention any names that you can think of? Someone that he might have been going to meet?"

"No. I'm sorry." Susan turned and stared through a window. She was looking toward Savage Basin in the mountains above town. When she turned back, her expression was sad.

Jack felt sorry for her and stood to go. "I won't take up any more of your time."

Susan rose from the couch. "I'm happy to do what I can to help. Come by anytime." She led him to the front door and opened it. "Can I ask you something?"

The look on her face made him uncomfortable. "Of course."

"Have they found anything of my husband's at the crash site? Any personal belongings?"

Jack thought it was an unusual question. He remembered Buckley asking about Cliff's luggage. "I haven't heard. Is there something in particular you want them to find?"

She seemed disappointed and gave a quick shake of her head. "I was just hoping to get something back—his wallet, his wedding ring, anything." She swallowed and looked on the verge of tears.

Jack understood. He wished he had more to tell her. But as Buckley had predicted, the government's investigation seemed to be moving at a snail's pace.

"If I find out anything," he said, "I'll let you know."

She held his gaze, and Jack knew she was disappointed with his answer. But it was the best he could offer, and it frustrated him.

He took the steps to the sidewalk and started for the campground.

Susan had kept the newspaper. As Jack passed the real estate office, he grabbed another. He wanted to know more about the fundraiser.

He checked his cell phone. Buckley still hadn't returned his call, and Jack was growing impatient. He needed to talk to the former governor. After his visit with Susan Roberts, he had a few more questions to ask him.

He hoped Buckley knew why Cliff had delayed his trip to Washington and what he'd done or who he'd gone to see the extra day he was in town. He also hoped Buckley could fill him in on Gerald Purvis, Cliff's chief of staff.

Jack wanted to know more about the man who called his dead boss's wife "Suze."

CHAPTER 30

SUSAN WATCHED THROUGH open blinds as Jack Martin crossed the road, headed down the hill, and finally disappeared around the corner at Main Street. His visit had been unexpected, and she hoped he couldn't tell it had rattled her.

It was ridiculous that she let him get her flustered. He was a detective—and a very handsome one at that—but she was the wife of a congressman. She had graduated at the top of her class at the University of Missouri and had been a valued member of Missouri's congressional staff until she married Cliff. Jack might be a well-known detective who'd solved a few high-profile cases, but she was successful in her own right. He was friendly enough, but she vowed not to let him intimidate her again.

Buckley should have never gotten him involved; it wasn't his place. He should have consulted her first. But what was done was done, and she was more than capable of dealing with the consequences.

Susan turned from the window and started for the living room. The newspaper that Jack had brought was still lying on the sofa. She picked it up and glanced at it, then felt the familiar sinking feeling as she stared down at Cliff's photograph. She felt tears sting her eyes.

Cliff had looked so handsome that night, standing onstage at the Opera House. He was dressed in dark jeans and the green flannel shirt she had given him the previous Christmas. Susan ran a finger over the shirt on the news page, remembering Cliff's expression when he'd opened the gift. He had flashed his best politician's smile and insisted that he loved it, but she knew instantly that he didn't.

Despite growing up in the mountains, Cliff's tastes had been more sophisticated. Susan knew he secretly preferred the business suits he wore in Washington to the jeans and loafers he wore when he was in Telluride. Unlike Cliff, Susan hoped she never had to put on another power suit.

It had been a bone of contention between them since not long after they were married. Susan had been born into a working-class family in Cape Girardeau, Missouri. But as a college graduate fresh out of the Missouri School of Journalism in Columbia, the job in DC working for her local congressman had seemed like a dream come true. But she soon detested her daily schedule, which was orchestrated to the half hour and felt as rigid as a straitjacket. And she never liked the city.

She had spent nearly a decade toiling in the capital when she met the dashing junior congressman from Telluride. Their romance had been a whirlwind of political dinners, events, and intimate dates to many of the most exclusive restaurants in Washington.

After only a few months together, Cliff had flown her to Denver on his family's plane to meet his mother. An extravagant luxury not lost on the small-town girl from Missouri.

While dating, she and Cliff often spent holidays and long weekends at the family home in Telluride. Susan enjoyed escaping the city, and after they married, she spent more of her time alone in the mountains, leaving the hustle and bustle of government work to her politician husband, who had thrived on chaos.

She set the newspaper on a table, crossed the room to a window facing east, and looked toward the high-mountain basin where Cliff's plane was lodged somewhere in the snow. She folded her arms tight against herself, trying to ward off the pit in her stomach that she'd felt since Tony Burns's visit the morning of the accident.

"Is he gone?" Gerald Purvis had entered the room.

Susan wiped her eyes, then turned to face him. "He is."

Gerald was holding a sheet of paper. He studied her and frowned. "Are you all right?"

Susan waved off the question. "I'm fine. It's just been a horrible last few days."

"Why don't you lie down and rest. This can wait," he said, holding up the paper.

"No." She wiped her nose with a tissue and forced a smile. "There's too much we need to do. You didn't fly all the way out here for me to sleep. Now, what is it?"

Gerald hesitated a moment, then held up the paper again. "Is this the final press release Cliff was going to issue?"

She took it from him and glanced over it. "It is."

"So, Cliff was still going to vote to *approve* the land trade?"

"Yes. That was *always* going to be his vote."

"It's just that he called me the morning after the fundraiser. He'd emailed me this release the day before but told me to hold off on sending it to the media. I thought maybe he wanted to go over it—maybe make a few changes."

"Why would he do that?" Susan asked, growing impatient.

"I don't know, but I was hoping you did."

"Well, I don't."

Gerald held her gaze for a moment, making her uncomfortable. He nodded. "As soon as we know when the committee intends to hold the vote, I'll see that it's released to the media."

"When will that be?"

Gerald shook his head. "We probably won't know until next week."

"Well, as soon as you find out, get this out there so everyone knows where Cliff stood on the issue," she said, handing back the press release.

"Right."

She sensed hesitancy in his voice. "I need to call the sheriff's office. Would you mind getting me a glass of water?"

"Of course."

After he left the room, Susan pulled her cell phone from the coffee table. She knew Gerald sensed that she wanted to be alone, but she didn't care. His presence in the house had become suffocating. When she called and told him about the accident, he had immediately arranged a flight to be with her. Susan knew his intentions were good, but she was ready to be rid of him.

After he arrived, Gerald had helped her draft an official statement regarding Cliff's death and had patiently weeded through Cliff's portraits and chosen one to include with it. He had also helped her write a personal response, which she posted to her Facebook and Instagram accounts and had been quickly picked up and broadcasted by the media.

Gerald had been a lot of help, but Susan needed time alone. She wanted time to think—time to figure out what she would do next. Her world had been turned upside down, and she needed to find a way to right it.

There was still so much to do. There were requests for interviews she needed to decline and loose ends to tie up with pending legislation. The governor of Colorado would appoint a replacement to complete Cliff's current term in office, and as a native of Colorado, Gerald was on the short list of candidates. The governor's office had wasted no time contacting her to schedule a Zoom call. The appointment would only be temporary. Whoever inherited Cliff's seat would be immediately embroiled in the upcoming election. And the last thing Susan wanted was to get tangled up in another campaign.

There were funeral arrangements to be made. But how was she supposed to plan anything without a body? She was frustrated that nobody had called her to let her know what was happening with the investigation.

Susan scrolled through the contacts on her phone and found Tony's cell number. She wanted answers. Most of all, she wanted to know what they had found in the wreckage. Thinking about it made her stomach roll.

There was too much at stake.

CHAPTER 31

SHERIFF TONY BURNS replaced the receiver on his desk phone and leaned back in the chair. An agent with the FAA had just informed him that they'd found evidence of an explosive in the wreckage of Cliff Roberts's plane.

A bomb had brought the plane down. They had suspected as much, but now it had been confirmed.

Trenchrite. Tony had never heard of it. The agent explained it was a water-gel explosive that had almost entirely replaced traditional dynamite. "Safer to manufacture, transport, and store," she had said.

Someone had placed a bomb on Cliff's plane. The more Tony thought about it, the angrier he became.

He'd met Cliff sixteen years earlier, soon after moving to Telluride. And although Tony never thought of him as a typical local, certainly not *one of the guys*, Tony had liked him.

Cliff had always been friendly and outgoing and had even sought out Tony's opinion on several legislative issues over the years. Tony knew Cliff's family was wealthy, but he had never mentioned it. And, more importantly, he had never acted like it. In fact, Tony thought Cliff had played *down* his family's money, wanting to be a politician *of* the people as well as for them.

Cliff had been a decent, stand-up guy. Not one Tony had ever sat and had a beer with, but one who had shown him nothing but respect. And Tony had respected him in turn—which was more than he could say about other politicians he'd met.

Tony laced his fingers behind his head and stared at the ceiling, wondering who would want to kill him. He racked his brain, but the only name he could come up with was Eric Dale. Wilderness Keepers. But Tony couldn't see it. Although the group had made threats, Dale didn't seem the type to carry through with them. Tony had dealt with violent extremists hell-bent on violence before, but Dale never struck him as one of them.

He brought his weight forward, booted up his computer, and googled *trenchrite*. Within a few minutes, he'd learned it was a popular explosive used in avalanche control, as well as for blasting in road construction and mining.

He shoved his computer mouse aside and pinched his nose, massaging it. With all the highway projects and mining in the area, probably a quarter of the population would have access to the stuff. What he'd learned did nothing to help narrow the suspect pool.

Tony reached for the intercom on his phone. "Kim, do me a favor and find out what kind of dynamite was used in the Montana bombings—the ones Eric Dale's group is suspected of setting."

He sat drumming his fingers on his desk when the intercom on his phone buzzed.

"Sheriff, Susan Roberts is on line three for you."

"Thank you." Tony exhaled a deep sigh. He told himself that informing Susan of Cliff's death had been the hardest thing he'd have to do. But now he would have to tell her it was murder.

CHAPTER 32

AFTER VISITING SUSAN ROBERTS, Jack returned to the campground for his truck. He wasn't going to wait for Buckley any longer. He would catch him at home or find out where he was from his wife, Celeste. Jack was taking Judith's instruction to heart; he wasn't going to trust Buckley any farther than he could throw him. And he wanted to know why Buckley had gone AWOL.

As Jack pulled off the highway into Mountain Village, Buckley finally returned his call. His timing was uncanny. Jack glanced in his rearview mirror to make sure he wasn't being followed.

"Jack." Buckley's voice boomed through the line. "Sorry I'm just getting back to you. I've spent the day on the phone."

Jack wasn't sure he believed him, but it didn't matter. There were questions he wanted to ask him in person. "I'm just down the road. I thought I'd come by."

"Well, come on! I was just about to have a drink."

Buckley's tone was friendly, but Jack wasn't buying it. Something had him nervous, and Jack was going to do his darnedest to find out what it was.

166

He parked in the Baileys' driveway and pulled the newspaper from the seat of the truck.

Buckley had been watching and opened the front door as Jack climbed the steps to the porch.

"You're just in time," Buckley said, holding a crystal glass aloft. It was filled with a caramel-colored liquid Jack suspected was whiskey.

Jack didn't care much for liquor but figured the tradition of friendly imbibing might help him pry the information he wanted out of the former governor.

"Don't mind if I do," Jack replied, stepping inside.

Buckley shut the door and immediately started across the room for the bar, his boots clomping on the slate floor and then across the rug. He pulled a crystal glass from a shelf and reached for a bottle. "Whiskey good for you?"

"Fine. Thank you."

Buckley dropped in a few ice cubes and poured the drink. "Have a seat," he said, gesturing at the living room sofas and then handing Jack the glass. "Got any news for me? How's the investigation going?"

"That's why I'm here. I need to ask you a few questions."

The two men sat facing each other.

"Ask away."

"What can you tell me about Gerald Purvis?"

"Purvis?" There was a look of disgust on Buckley's face. "Why do you ask?"

"I just met him."

"He's in town?"

Jack nodded. "I went to see Susan."

"Well, that didn't take long." He narrowed his eyes and shook his head. "Purvis is Cliff's chief of staff. The scuttlebutt is that he's already lobbying the governor to appoint him to serve out the rest of Cliff's term in office. He's a slippery one."

"Why would he come to town?"

"To help Susan handle the fallout." Buckley threw an arm over the back of the sofa. "There's got to be a million things to do now with Cliff dead—press releases, running interference with the media. I'm sure there's outstanding business to address or tie up. Susan has been staying in Telluride mostly, avoiding Washington, but she did a lot to help Cliff. I'm sure she and Purvis have worked closely together."

It made sense that Susan would need help. But did it explain the intimacy of him calling her "Suze"?

"What do you have there?" Buckley asked, indicating the newspaper.

Jack unfolded it and laid it on the coffee table between them. "I was hoping you could tell me about the people in this photograph."

Buckley spun the paper around and squinted. "That was taken at Allred's. It was a fundraising dinner."

Susan had already told him, but Jack kept quiet and let Buckley talk. He took a sip of whiskey.

"Let's see here." Buckley pulled reading glasses from his shirt pocket and leaned over the table. "This is Bart and Vera Whitestone," he said, pointing at the photo. "Big donors to the party. Longtime friends of Edward and Margaret, Cliff's parents. They've got a place here in Mountain Village but rarely use it anymore. Too old, I guess. Their kids come.

"This here's Ted Hawthorne," he said, sliding his finger across the photo. "Local banker and an old friend of Cliff. And that's Elizabeth Mayweather. Wealthy widow always good for a sizable donation. And you've already met this handsome fella," he said, pointing to himself in the photo, then spinning the newspaper back around.

"Cliff was supposed to fly out the morning after the dinner but didn't," Jack said. "Do you know why he changed his plans?" He watched Buckley closely, knowing his body language could reveal more than what he said.

Buckley rested back on the sofa and crossed an ankle over the opposite knee. He looked relaxed. "That's a good question. I don't know why he put off leaving."

"He didn't mention anything about it at the dinner?"

"He didn't."

Jack was growing frustrated. *Someone* had to know why Cliff Roberts stayed in town an extra day—long enough for somebody to plant a bomb on his plane.

Jack pulled the newspaper toward him and studied the photograph. According to Susan, Cliff hadn't told her that he was staying another day until they were on their way home that night. It was possible something at the fundraiser had prompted him to change his plans.

"How many people were at the dinner?" Jack asked.

Buckley set the glass down. "Oh, I don't know, maybe thirty or so."

Too big for intimate conversation, Jack thought. "What goes on at an event like that?"

Buckley shrugged. "Same thing that goes on at most any political dinner. Lots of glad-handing—you know, shaking hands and shooting the bull—trying to get folks to open their wallets. We had cocktails early, Cliff gave a short speech thanking everyone for their support, and then we sat down to eat."

"Who did Cliff sit next to during dinner?"

"Let me see," Buckley said, thinking about the question. "Susan was on his right. And if I remember correctly, it was Vera Whitestone to his left."

Jack wondered if there was anything the elderly donor from Denver could have said to prompt Cliff to change his travel plans. It wasn't a promising lead.

"Was there anyone Cliff spoke with before or after you ate? One-on-one, maybe?"

"I can't say that I noticed anyone in particular." Buckley started to shake his head, then stopped. "Come to think of it, he did talk to Elizabeth alone for a while."

"The woman in the photograph?"

"Yeah. Elizabeth. They had their heads together powwowing about something after we ate. I saw Susan pull him away when the Whitestones were leaving. I'm sure to say goodbye, thanks for the support, something like that. Bart and Vera were the first ones to leave."

"Do you have any idea what Cliff and Elizabeth could have been talking about?"

"No clue," Buckley replied. "Could have been a million different things—politics, donations, the weather." He raised and then dropped his hands. "Who knows?"

"Was Hank Wade there?"

"No. He used to donate to Cliff's campaigns, but not anymore. Not since he started talking about the land swap. I'm sure he figures it wouldn't look good."

Jack had to agree. He thought about Elizabeth Mayweather and decided it wouldn't hurt to ask the wealthy widow a few questions. Although she looked older than Cliff, there could have been more to their relationship than politician and political donor.

"Do you know Elizabeth Mayweather?"

"Well, sure. Practically everyone in town does. She's donated to one or two of my own campaigns. Nice woman. A little high-octane for my taste, but nice." He took a drink of whiskey.

"What do you mean 'high-octane'?"

"You meet her, you'll understand." Buckley rose from the sofa and started for the bar. "You need another one?" he asked, raising his empty glass.

"I'm good. Thank you. So, tell me more about her."

Buckley replenished his whiskey and returned to the couch. "Elizabeth? She's a piece of work. Not like any other woman I know—always hunting, fishing, or hiking. Rich as hell though. And a man can put up with a lot when a woman's got that much money." He took another drink, and Jack noticed his words were beginning to slur.

"Do you think she'd talk to me?"

Buckley raised an eyebrow, and a sly smile lifted the corners of his mouth. "You lonely for a wealthy widow?"

Jack set his glass down on the coffee table, ignoring the comment. He was finished drinking. "Something caused Cliff to change his plans after the dinner that night, and I'm hoping she can shed some light on what that might've been."

Buckley's smile dropped. He looked disappointed. "I'm sure she'd talk to you." He pulled his cell phone from a side table. "Let's call her and find out."

Buckley spent a few minutes on the phone talking about the plane crash and saying what a tragedy it was. Then he got to the point of the call. Jack listened quietly, hoping Elizabeth Mayweather would agree to speak with him.

"Thank you, Elizabeth," Buckley said a while later. "I appreciate it." He was silent a moment. "Yep, I'll give him directions. He'll be over shortly."

Buckley ended the call. "Done. I'll get you her address." He rose from the couch and walked to the bar, then pulled a notepad and pen from a drawer.

Jack got up and walked toward him.

Buckley scribbled something on the pad, then tore the sheet off and handed it to him. "Elizabeth's address."

Jack thanked him and followed him to the front door.

There was no easy way of asking the last question he had for the former governor. But Jack hoped that, with liquor in him, Buckley would tell the truth.

"One last thing," Jack said, stepping outside. "I've heard rumors about Cliff taking bribes."

Buckley stood erect, holding the door.

"Is there any chance those rumors could be true?"

Buckley stared at him. For a moment, Jack was afraid he would shut the door in his face. A crow screeched loudly overhead, shattering the awkward silence.

Buckley blew out air and cuffed Jack on the shoulder. "Hell, son, if a politician is worth his salt, he's eventually accused of taking bribes. It's inevitable. It's practically a national sport." He shook his head and smiled. "But Cliff was one of the good guys. And you know what?"

Jack waited for the answer.

Buckley's expression was grave. "That might just be what got him killed."

CHAPTER 33

GERALD PURVIS SAT at Cliff's desk in the study watching a hummingbird through an adjacent window. It buzzed furiously around a flowering plant with tall purple blooms. His to-do list sat half-finished in front of him.

"Catmint," he said aloud, almost in a daze, as he mindlessly threaded a pen through his fingers.

It was as if his life had come full circle. He thought back to the small basement bedroom from his childhood. A single long window ran nearly the room's length and sat high near the ceiling, a row of catmint planted just below. Throughout his childhood, he'd spent countless hours staring at it, daydreaming about life beyond the screen of gray-green foliage and purple flowers, life beyond Wheat Ridge, Colorado. His room had been both his sanctuary and his prison.

And now here he was decades later, staring out through the glass at the world beyond. So much had happened in the forty-two years he'd spent on the planet, yet so much had remained the same.

It had been a wild ride after he'd finally escaped the clutches of a priggish family that never understood him. Gerald thanked God daily for the scholarship to Ohio State, or it would have been four more years living at home and commuting to Colorado Boulder. Instead, he had found freedom at OSU, and a new peer group—friends who understood him. For the first time in his life, he felt part of something, no longer an outsider.

Then came the whirlwind of being a single man in DC. The nightlife and parties threatened to derail him shortly after he arrived. He had quickly depleted his meager savings and had been forced to live within the frugal confines of a congressional aide's salary. It was what saved him. Gerald knew that now.

What had started out as an entry-level position working for Colorado's longest-serving congressman had morphed into a love affair with the whirlwind of activity and proximity to power.

His big break had come some years later, when Cliff Roberts arrived in DC. The junior congressman had tapped Gerald early to head up staffing his new office. Gerald had thrived in the position and over multiple reelection cycles had been promoted several times until he'd reached the pinnacle of legislative staffing positions—chief of staff.

Working with Cliff had been exhilarating. Gerald was going to miss Cliff but hoped he could springboard himself into the late congressman's seat. He knew that some would think he was crass or an opportunist, but he'd been called worse, and he didn't care. It was finally *his* time to shine.

Gerald had taken Susan a glass of water nearly an hour earlier. He needed her help with a pile of work. There was correspondence to respond to, outstanding legislative issues to deal with, and press inquiries. But Susan was still a wreck. He had suggested she lie down for a while, and she'd agreed.

He glanced at the brass clock set on the fireplace mantel and saw that it was already past four. The afternoon was quickly getting away from him.

A few minutes later, Susan entered the room. "I'm sorry," she said. "I fell asleep and just now woke up. I had no idea I was so tired."

She looked rested. The dark circles under her eyes were gone. She pulled a file of pending legislation from the top of the desk and sat down in a chair by the fireplace.

"Hank Wade called while you were asleep," Gerald told her.

She was rifling through the contents of the folder but stopped. There was an odd, almost panicked look on her face. "Did you talk to him?"

It was more of an accusation than a question, and it surprised him. "No. He left a message."

"What did he say?"

"He asked if we were going to make a statement about Cliff's position on the land deal."

"Of course he did." She said it with disgust.

"Should I call him back?"

"No. I'll do it later." She turned her attention back to the contents of the folder.

Gerald watched her out of the corner of his eye. It didn't seem Susan liked Hank Wade, and he wondered why. Sure, he was an abrasive millionaire used to getting his way, but in politics, people like that were a dime a dozen. Plus, he wasn't hard on the eyes.

Cliff had been friendly with Wade before he died. Gerald knew that he had met with him on several occasions regarding the land deal and that Wade had even donated to several of Cliff's earlier campaigns. But Gerald had heard that, after Wade proposed the trade, to avoid conflict of interest, he had turned the money spigot off. Or had he?

Like most politicians, Cliff was no stranger to accusations of bribery. The only politicians Gerald could think of who *hadn't* been accused of taking bribes for political favors were weak and irrelevant.

The accusations almost always came from members of the other party. Gerald had never believed their claims against Cliff, but something had been gnawing at him, and he now wondered if the rumors could be true. Things had seemed *off* since he'd arrived the day before. Gerald wanted to probe, but he knew he had to tread lightly.

"Are you going to stay in Telluride?" he asked Susan.

Her answer came quickly. "Not any longer than I have to."

"Where will you go?" he asked, tapping the pen on the desk.

Susan still rifled through the folder, seeming unfazed by the question. "Somewhere warm," she answered. "With a beach."

It surprised him. He thought Susan loved the mountains. Although she often assisted the staff in DC, they hadn't seen her inside the Capitol in years. He decided to let the subject go.

"Who was the cowboy earlier?" he asked.

"Jack Martin?"

"Something about him seemed familiar. You said he was helping the sheriff?"

"He's a detective. I'm sure you heard about the author who was murdered here a few months ago. Jack solved the case."

Of course. Gerald remembered the cases—first Aspen, another in Vail, then the last one in Telluride. He had seen Martin's photograph in the media. Most of the staff in Cliff's office was from Colorado, and they had followed each investigation closely.

Susan pulled several pages from the folder. "This is the only pending legislation that Cliff was opposed to," she said, fumbling with the papers, then abruptly handing them to him. "I'm still not feeling well. I think I'll lie down again."

Her demeanor had changed. She seemed nervous, almost jumpy. Gerald watched her disappear down the hall. He had plenty of other questions for her, but they would have to wait. He wanted to know more about Martin. Why was the celebrated detective helping the local sheriff? And why had he come to see Susan? Was it about the plane crash?

Then it dawned on him. The only reason Jack Martin would be involved was if Cliff's death hadn't been an accident.

Gerald felt his palms grow sweaty, and he laid the pen down on the desk. The realization changed everything.

CHAPTER 34

BEFORE HE LEFT Buckley's, Jack put Elizabeth Mayweather's address into his phone. It was a long shot that she would know why Cliff had stayed in town an extra day, but so far, long shots were all he had.

He followed the GPS directions, winding and twisting his way up the mountain, passing condominiums, then houses of varying sizes.

His cell phone buzzed. It was the sheriff.

"Tony, what's going on?"

"Real quick, Jack. I don't have much time." He sounded frustrated. "The feds have doubled their efforts and are trying to take over my office."

"It was a bomb, wasn't it?" Jack asked.

"How did you know?"

"Something hasn't smelled right from the beginning."

"Yeah, I kinda figured as much, too. I just hoped I was wrong." He sighed. "I wanted you to know, but I gotta go."

"Hey, Tony?"

"Yeah?"

"Thanks for the call." Jack knew Tony didn't have to let him know about the bomb and that he would be in violation of his own office's policies by doing so.

Jack wasn't surprised by the news, but it cemented his determination. He was being paid for this case and needed the money, but that wasn't the reason behind the growing fire inside him. He remembered the sound of Susan Roberts crying and the sight of Buckley angry and upset over the death of his friend. He thought of how fondly Judith had talked about Cliff. But most of all, Jack wanted to know who had been brazen enough to plant a bomb on a congressman's plane.

Elizabeth Mayweather's house was high up the mountain. A pair of rock columns flanking both sides of a driveway came into view just before the road ended in a cul-de-sac. Jack pulled through the columns and onto a cobblestone driveway. It was narrow and wound through a thick stand of pine; early-spring wildflowers bordered both the sides and were beginning to bloom.

The driveway opened onto a small clearing. A large log home with gingerbread moldings that looked like it had been plucked from the Alps was nestled in a thick grove of trees. Flowers and ivy draped from a dozen brightly colored window boxes.

Jack parked the truck and got out, then took a flagstone path toward the front porch. Spring grass and more wildflowers blanketed small lawns on either side of the walkway.

It was like he'd driven through some mysterious portal and emerged into a dream. It was a weird cross between *The Sound of Music* and Narnia.

A large bronze knocker fashioned in the shape of a wolf's head was fixed to the front door. As he raised it, the door opened.

"Hello. You must be Jack Martin," she said. "I'm Elizabeth."

She was short, with an athletic build and shoulder-length auburn and gray hair. She was attractive, without a stitch of makeup that Jack could see, and wore cargo pants and hiking boots.

Jack shook her hand. "Thank you for letting me come on short notice."

Elizabeth waved him off. "It's no problem," she said, ushering him into the house and shutting the door. "Your timing is perfect. I had just gotten back from my afternoon walk when Buckley called. Come in."

Jack followed her through the foyer, then down a side hall to the kitchen. It was open to an adjacent sitting room with a large picture window that looked out onto a small yard framed by a wall of pines. There was no view of the mountains, only forest.

"Have a seat," she said, pointing to a sofa covered in a floral fabric. She took a facing chair. "Buckley said you wanted to ask me about Cliff."

"He delayed leaving Telluride after the fundraiser at Allred's, but nobody seems to know why."

"I thought he was supposed to leave the next morning, too," Elizabeth said, untying the laces of her boots. "I didn't know until I heard about the crash that he hadn't."

"Buckley mentioned he saw the two of you talking alone after the dinner."

"And you were hoping I would know why he didn't fly out the next day as planned." She pulled off a boot and rubbed the bottom of her foot. "Cliff asked me about my hiking guide," she said, remembering. "I'm not sure why, but he asked for his name."

"You regularly use a guide?"

"I always do on longer hikes," she said. "It's foolish to go alone. You flirt with disaster when you do."

Since moving to Colorado, Jack had heard countless stories of accidents when people had hiked solo, people who had gotten lost or fallen from extreme heights. Some had sustained injuries preventing a hike out. Others had succumbed to unexpected weather conditions—lightning or snow. It seemed the possibilities for tragedy while hiking alone were endless.

"Did Cliff contact him?" Jack asked.

"I don't know. The fundraiser was the last time I talked to him."

Jack thought about it for a moment. "Did you happen to discuss the land trade between the government and Hank Wade with Cliff?"

"Oh, heavens no," she said. "I donate to candidates if they're friends of mine, but I have a policy about staying out of government affairs. Politics is an ugly business that I don't want to be bothered with."

Jack understood. "Do you remember anything else that you and Cliff talked about?"

Elizabeth shook her head. "No. That's all I remember. Susan interrupted us when some friends of his from Denver were leaving. I didn't talk to him after that except to say goodbye."

"And the guide? Have you talked to him since that night?" Jack was curious about whether Cliff had contacted him. It wasn't much to go on, but he needed to follow the lead and see it through.

"I haven't. Would you like his name and number?"

"Please."

Elizabeth pulled off the second boot, then rose from the chair and crossed the room to the kitchen. A few seconds later, she returned with a sticky note and handed it to him. "His name is Turner Biggs. He's the best in the business; grew up in these mountains and knows them inside and out—literally. If you're crazy enough to want to see some of the old mines, he's your guy."

Jack stuck the number in his pocket. "Do you hike often?"

"As often as I can. Around the house most days—up the ski slopes and anywhere this side of Palmyra Peak. But I occasionally do longer ones with Turner."

A long hike sounded like a dream. It had been months since Jack had been able to spend any length of time on the trail. As soon as the snow melted in the high country, he would take Crockett and go.

But first, there was a murder to solve.

CHAPTER 35

AS SOON AS Jack left Elizabeth's, he pulled the phone number of the hiking guide from his pocket. The call went straight to voice mail without ringing, and Jack knew he was probably somewhere off the grid.

He left a message and hung up.

Next, he called the sheriff.

"Sorry to bother you, Tony, but I've got a question."

"What is it?" He sounded tired. Since it had been determined a bomb had caused the crash, Jack knew an alphabet soup of federal agencies was probably running him ragged.

"You mentioned Deputy O'Connor was interviewing employees at the airport."

"Yeah."

"I was wondering if she found out anything." Jack thought there was a good chance an employee or someone with access to the airport had planted the bomb.

"She talked to all of them. Nobody claims to have seen or heard anything."

Jack could hear the frustration in his voice. He knew the perimeter of the airport was fenced, probably with security wiring of some kind or electrified. Somehow, someone got access to Cliff Roberts's plane. "Somebody's not talking," he said.

Tony agreed. "But what can I do about it? Can't force the truth out of them at gunpoint."

Jack had an idea. "What about people with access who aren't employees?"

"Like who?"

"There's a hangar out there. I assume a few Telluride residents store their private planes in them."

Tony was quiet, so Jack continued. "Can you get a list of names of people who park their planes out there?"

"I'm sure we can," Tony replied. "Any name in particular you're looking for?"

It was another long shot, but Jack decided to throw it out there. He knew Tony would be discreet.

"Let me know if there's one owned by Buckley Bailey or his wife, Celeste," he said, then paused a moment. "Or Hank Wade."

CHAPTER 36

SHERIFF BURNS HUNG up the phone and leaned back in his chair. The call from Jack had him thinking.

Once again, Martin was right. Someone had planted a bomb on Cliff's airplane, and if it wasn't an employee, it was somebody who had access to the plane while it was at the airport.

He pushed the intercom button on the phone. "Kim, can you come in here?"

Deputy O'Connor showed up a few seconds later with a notepad and pen. "Yeah, Sheriff?"

"Call the airport. Get a list of planes that were parked there the morning Cliff Roberts's went down." He thought about it a moment. "And the day before. Once you have a list, find out who owns them."

She scribbled on the notepad. "Yes, sir. Anything else?"

"Yeah, ask them who has access to the hangar who *aren't* employees. Contractors, local pilots, et cetera. See if you can get a list of names."

"Yes, sir." She made a couple more notes. "I'll get right on it."

She had been gone only a few seconds when Deputy Travis Barry poked his head around the corner.

"Sheriff, I just heard on the radio there's a fire burning outside Ridgway." His voice was tense.

"Wildfire?"

"No, sir. It's a structure. Sounds like a barn, but they didn't say exactly."

"Arson?"

"They're not saying yet, but it sounds like it could be. It's on Hank Wade's place."

Tony took a second to process the information. "Wade has two ranches. Which one?"

The deputy shrugged. "Report said 'near Ridgway.' That's all I heard."

"All right, thank you, Travis."

Tony took a pencil from his desk and tapped it. Barns didn't light themselves. And he knew that area ranchers took extra precautions to avoid sparking an accidental blaze—fires in the mountains could be devastating.

Controversy had surrounded Hank Wade ever since he'd moved into the area almost ten years earlier and started buying up land. Tony found him friendly enough and didn't have anything against him, but he knew others did.

One name came to mind. Eric Dale.

Tony reached for the phone, but as he did, the intercom buzzed.

"Sheriff, Norm Johnson is on line one for you."

Norm Johnson was the longtime sheriff of Ouray County where both of Wade's properties were located.

"Norm," Tony answered. "I was just about to call you."

"You've heard?"

"I was just told. Is it arson?"

"Don't know for sure, but it appears so. The damage is significant and looks to have multiple points of origin."

They were classic signs of arson. Tony leaned back in his chair. "Which property?"

"The one closest to town. It was a barn. Fire's nearly out, but it's going to be a total loss. And Wade's fit to be tied."

"I can imagine." Tony would be the same if he were in Wade's shoes. He knew Norm wasn't calling just to give him an update. "How can I help?"

"Eric Dale."

The answer sent a cool chill up Tony's spine. "What about him?"

"Wade swears he saw Dale on the highway headed in the direction of Telluride. We want to bring Dale for questioning, and I was hoping you'd have your guys on the lookout, and if they see him, pick him up."

"What time did Wade see him?"

"An hour ago. He was on 62, headed your way. Wade saw the smoke from the highway not long after and found the barn burning when he got there."

"And Wade's sure it was Dale?"

"Says he's positive. He was in Placerville to pick up supplies and saw Dale just before he noticed the smoke on his way back."

Tony was silent a moment. "He could have been headed to Norwood," he said, knowing it wasn't likely. "Or Durango."

"Could have," Norm replied. "But I'd heard he's been staying in Telluride."

Tony ran a hand down his face. "Yeah, he has." Dale had been a headache ever since he had arrived in town with his band of hoodlums. Tony came forward in his chair. "Al right. I'll put the word out to pick him up."

"Thank you," Norm said. "And, Tony, let me know as soon as you have him. I'll send someone over. I'm at the barn now, and Wade's been on my case to arrest Dale since I got here. I need him off my back."

"Will do."

Tony hung up the phone and immediately instructed dispatch to put out an APB on Dale.

He picked up the pencil and began tapping it on the desk again. Eric Dale had made threats against Cliff, and then his plane had gone down. Had he also made threats against Hank Wade? Tony hadn't heard of any but would find out. He sat for a while longer, thinking. Now that the congressman was out of the way, had Dale set his sights on Wade?

Tony got up and walked around his desk, then stood in the doorway listening. He could hear the flurry of activity of the feds working down the hall. He wasn't even sure which agencies were still using his office. His patience had worn thin, and he was ready for them to leave. But if word got out about arson on Wade's property, he was worried their efforts would only intensify.

Tony returned to his desk and called Deputy Barry into his office.

"I just heard the APB on Eric Dale," Barry said, stepping around the corner.

Tony dropped his voice so that no one passing in the hallway could hear. "Dale drives a beat-up navy truck."

"Yes, sir. I've seen him in it."

"Get out there and find him."

CHAPTER 37

THE SUN HUNG low on the horizon as Jack made his way from Mountain Village back to Telluride. He stuck the transmission in manual and downshifted when the highway began its steep descent toward the valley floor. Next, he wound down the driver's-side window, letting in a rush of chilled evening air. It felt good. It had been a long day, and he was beat.

He wanted to get back to the trailer, maybe have something to eat, then sit beside the river with Otto and Crockett and let the day's problems drain away—at least for a little while.

His cell phone buzzed beside him on the seat. He pulled it toward him and glanced at the caller ID.

"Hey, Arch."

"Well, hello and howdy doo to you, too. You sound completely tuckered out, old buddy." There was a hint of concern in his lighthearted tone.

"Just a long day," Jack replied. "Whatcha got?"

"I've got a cross-eyed wife, but we're getting a divorce. I found out she was seeing someone on the side."

"Arch."

"Have you heard the one about—"

"Arch."

"All right, all right. Man, you're a tough crowd." Archie Rochambeau sighed. "Here's what I got. Hank Wade of Ridgway, Colorado, formerly of Pecos, Texas. Big bucks—and I'm talking *big*. Keeps his money spread around. Has accounts with several of the large Wall Street firms and a local bank in Midland."

"Anything unusual about them?"

"Hold your horses, Batman. Let me finish." Archie cleared his throat. "Accounts look legit. *However*, a large withdrawal was recently made from one registered to him in said local bank—the one in Midland. I compiled a list of withdrawals for the past three years for all the accounts. Nothing else appears fishy except this one withdr—"

"Where'd the money go?" Jack interrupted. His gut was screaming it had been to pay a bribe, and he wanted to know if it had gone to Cliff Roberts.

"It was transferred to a bank in the Caymans."

"The Caymans?" Jack thought about it. "Whose account?"

"Well, see, that's the problem. The Caymans are über-secretive. Getting info out of them is harder than selling a Ford to Elon Musk. I don't know who's behind the account, but I *did* find out it's registered to a Bridal Veil Limited. Mean anything to you?"

Jack thought about it. *Bridal Veil Limited.* "No," he said, gripping the steering wheel harder. "It doesn't mean a damn thing."

"Well, here's an interesting note. The money was transferred into the account *after* your congressman died. Makes it seem he wasn't the one behind Bridal Veil. Why would Wade send it to him if he was dead?"

"He wouldn't."

"I'll keep fishing for a name," Archie said. "But there's something else. I found out a large sum was immediately transferred *out* of the same Caymans account. It went in—it went out."

"Where did it go?"

"Don't know that, either." Archie sighed. "Man, I'm telling you, those island bankers are tight-lipped. I can't even tell you what *country* the money was transferred to, much less whose account. But I'll keep digging. I still need to look into that Telluride bank for you. Give me another day or two."

Jack let out a frustrated breath. "Thank you. Let me know as soon as you find out anything else."

"Will do, boss."

Jack pulled into Telluride. The call from Archie had him thinking. The money Hank Wade transferred to the Caymans could have been a bribe to someone else on the congressional committee. Jack decided to research who the members were later and send Archie the names. More than likely, it wouldn't help him discover who had planted the bomb on Roberts's plane, but it would out a crooked politician. Jack would keep his and Archie's names out of it but send the information anonymously to one of his old colleagues at the FBI. Jack didn't care who got credit for it, as long as another DC scumbag was drained from the swamp.

He drove slowly through town, letting a group of pedestrians cross the street. Then, as he neared the New Sheridan Hotel, two people on the sidewalk caught his eye. From the back, something about the woman seemed familiar—her blond hair, which hung loosely to just below her shoulders, her sexy figure in designer jeans. As he passed, Jack turned to look, and his suspicions were confirmed. It was Susan Roberts. She said something and smiled at the man following close behind her. Jack saw him lay his hand gently on her back as she stepped inside the hotel. It was Gerald Purvis, Cliff's chief of staff, the man who had called her "Suze."

It was dinnertime. They would probably be dining at Chop House, the fancy restaurant inside. Jack's stomach growled as he remembered the charbroiled steak he had watched Alice Fremont's literary agent consume there months earlier. The restaurant was too pricey for Jack's budget, and he knew he would probably never get to eat there, but that wasn't what bothered him.

What had Jack suspicious was how friendly the congressman's wife and former chief of staff had looked as they stepped inside.

CHAPTER 38

BACK AT THE CAMPGROUND, Jack grabbed a clean set of clothes and headed to the public bathroom. He was hungry and wanted the easy company of Crockett and Otto, but first he needed a shower.

He shut his eyes and turned his face toward the spray of warm water, letting it relax the tension in his jaw and neck. Steam collected and swirled around him. He turned and let the water run over his shoulders and back, then drew in and released several slow breaths, allowing the little he knew about what had happened to Roberts wash through his mind.

The information was splintered.

Jack thought about Eric Dale and the group Wilderness Keepers, the threats made over the land deal with Hank Wade. Wade's ranch was beautiful. Jack understood his desire to add the last piece; he would want to do the same if he were in Wade's position. It was already one of the most beautiful ranches in the country. But Dale and his band of activists stood in the way. Environmental groups were passionate about their causes—sometimes even violent—but was a small plot of land worth killing someone for?

Jack watched the warm water swirl at his feet and disappear down the drain and thought of Lea Scotsman's ranch. It was smaller than Wade's but still large—and just as beautiful. Lea loved the land, but had she also loved Cliff Roberts? Jack knew that jealousy was a strong motive for murder.

Next, the image of Susan Roberts and Gerald Purvis entering the hotel flashed in his mind. Jack remembered Gerald calling her "Suze" and the hand laid gently on her back. They were obviously close—but how close? When Susan tired of life in DC had she also tired of her husband?

There were others to consider. Buckley Bailey. And maybe someone else Jack hadn't thought of yet. He turned off the water and stepped out of the shower, pulled the towel from the rack where he'd hung it, and dried off.

Back at the trailer, Jack took the Telluride newspaper from the table and studied the photograph from the dinner at Allred's. He looked first at Cliff, then at Buckley, and wondered if there was more to the relationship between the two than Buckley was letting on. Murder among friends was not unheard of.

Jack glanced at the elderly couple from Denver. They looked frail and immobile.

Next, his gaze slid across the page to Elizabeth Mayweather, then to the man he knew was the nervous local banker, and he made a mental note to pay Hawthorne a visit soon.

There were still too many moving parts. The information Jack had gathered was fragmented, and he couldn't tell how all the pieces fit together. He would keep asking questions—keep digging. Somewhere in the jumble of clues was the answer to who killed the congressman.

Jack tossed the paper down, turned to the mini fridge, and pulled out a block of cheddar cheese. He cut a chunk from it, then sat down at the table with a bag of beef jerky and a Shiner Bock. It wasn't a rib eye at Chop House, but it would do.

When he was finished eating, he stepped out of the trailer and crossed to where Otto was sitting with Crockett on a blanket by the riverbank. Daylight was nearly gone, but Jack could see that he was whittling on an aspen branch. Although the temperature had dropped, there wasn't any wind. The sound of the river rushing over the rocks was soothing.

As Jack got closer, he noticed several pairs of socks hanging from the limb of a tree.

Crockett jumped up to greet him.

"Have you been good?" Jack asked.

Otto turned slightly. "He's always good." He pointed to an empty spot on the blanket with the knife, and Jack sat, stretching his long legs out in front of him.

Crockett settled down next to him, and Jack stroked the dog's brown coat as he talked. "What's up with the socks?"

"Washed 'em in the river this morning. I'll be leaving in a few days."

It was then Jack noticed the old man was barefoot. He glanced at Otto's mismatched boots, which were set nearby, leaned over, and picked one up. He turned it over and examined the worn-out bottom. The boot was falling apart, the rubber sole curling away from the leather at the toe and nearly worn completely through in places.

"You going to wear these?" Jack asked.

Otto didn't look up. "They've lasted me this long. I figure they'll last me another summer."

Jack watched the old man whittle for a while longer, then set the boot down next to the other. The second one was a different color but was in the same poor shape. Jack couldn't imagine how they would last through the summer.

An easy silence settled between the men as they sat by the river. Jack watched the sky grow an inky black, a halo of light over Ballard Mountain promising the eventual appearance of a full moon.

Otto was the first to break the silence. "You seem hungry."

"I just ate."

"Not that kind of hungry," Otto said, closing the knife. He tossed the nub of stick into the water.

Jack thought about it for a moment. It was true; he had never met Cliff Roberts but was preoccupied with finding the man's killer. Buckley was paying him to investigate this case, but Jack knew that wasn't why he cared. It was never the reason.

He thought back to the cases through the years that had wrecked him emotionally. The first had been the murder of his grandparents in Baton Rouge. He quickly blocked the images from his mind and moved on to the others. There was the federal judge, a mother of three gunned down outside the courthouse in downtown Houston. The girls who had been kidnapped along Interstate 10 and likely taken to Louisiana that he'd never found. The mass shooting at the diner that had gotten him fired from the FBI. There were even cases that he had solved that still haunted him, ones he couldn't shake from his mind. There were so many.

Jack sucked cold air redolent of pine deep into his lungs and held it there before letting it out slowly, trying to let go of the memories. At least for a while.

The old man struggled to stand, and Jack helped him up. As Jack folded the blanket, Otto brought a kerosene lamp from the tent and set it on the picnic table. The two men sat down together.

Crockett noticed something in the trees and darted away. Jack didn't worry; he always came back.

Otto pulled a pack of Camels from a pocket, shook out a cigarette, lit it with a plastic lighter, then put it to his lips and drew in air. He let the smoke out slowly, then turned the cigarette over in his calloused hand, studying it. "Silence is the sleep that nourishes wisdom."

Jack was confused. "What was that?"

"Silence is the sleep that nourishes wisdom," Otto repeated. "Francis Bacon. English philosopher."

Jack thought about it for a moment. His friend, the old drifter, was wise. He studied Otto's face in the glow of the lamp. His skin was weathered, creased by decades of living in the mountains, but the kerosene flame had his blue eyes dancing. The old man was complex yet simple and asked no more from the world than what he needed to get by. Jack watched him as he smoked, content with an uncomplicated life. If only the rest of the world were as honest and kind.

The question of what happened to the congressman began churning again in Jack's mind. "Otto, can I ask you something?"

"It's a free country."

Crockett had reemerged from the dark and settled at Jack's feet.

"What do you know about Telluride Bank & Trust?"

"Not much. Don't trust banks. Never have."

"You don't have an account somewhere?"

Otto blew out smoke. "Nope. But I got one of those safe-deposit boxes, over at the Alpine Bank. Can't leave stuff lying around the campground while I'm away in the mountains. Used to could, but not anymore. Not with the way things are today." He shook his head. "Some people would steal the gold right out of your teeth if they knew you had it."

He leaned in close to the lamp, opened his mouth, and pointed to the back with a thick index finger. Jack caught a glimmer of gold when the light hit it. Otto laughed at the surprised look on his face, then coughed a few times.

He cleared his throat. "I have one of them security boxes, but I'm not comfortable havin' even that. They say I've got the only two keys, but I don't believe 'em. I expect one of these days, I'll come back to town, and the whole thing'll be cleared out. And that'll be it." He lifted his hands from his lap, then let them fall.

"So, you don't know Ted Hawthorne?" Jack asked. "At the Bank & Trust?"

"Nope. Can't say that I do." He puffed again on the cigarette.

Jack hadn't expected Otto to know Hawthorne, but then again, the web of connections weaved in small towns often surprised him.

He remembered the look on Hawthorne's face when Crockett barked as they'd driven by. Hawthorne had appeared startled, then nervous, and had quickly disappeared inside the bank.

Jack remembered the image of Hawthorne in the photograph taken the night at Allred's. He had been standing just to Cliff's left. Judith had said he and Cliff were friends. But just how close were they?

Otto didn't know Hawthorne, but there was someone better to ask. Jack pulled his cell phone from the pocket of his jeans and squinted at the bright light from the screen, then scrolled through his contacts for the number.

CHAPTER 39

Sunday, May 15

BUCKLEY BAILEY SAT alone in his study, resting his forearms on his desk and drumming his fingers. He needed to call Jack, but part of him was afraid to. He worried that bringing the famous detective into Cliff's mess had been a mistake.

Buckley had intended for Jack to investigate Eric Dale, but there were too many secrets the famous detective could inadvertently uncover. The moments immediately following Cliff's crash had been a blur that required quick decision making. Buckley hoped he wouldn't regret what he'd done.

He stared down at his iPhone lying on the desk. He placed his fingers on it and slid it side to side, thinking.

"Oh, to hell with it," he said, finally picking it up. He scrolled for Jack's number, but the phone buzzed in his hand.

"Jack," Buckley answered. "I was just about to call you. Sorry I didn't answer last night. Had a late dinner with the missus and then turned in early. It's hell getting old. What do you know?"

Buckley leaned back in his chair and kicked his boots up onto the desk, then listened as Jack told him about his visit with Elizabeth.

"Why in the world would Cliff care about a hiking guide?" Buckley asked, confused. "I know he used to roam the mountains as a kid—he's told me stories. But as far as I know, he hasn't hiked in years."

"So you don't have any idea why he would ask her about the guide?"

"None." Buckley rubbed the stubble on his chin. "What's the guy's name?" he asked. "Maybe it'll ring a bell."

"Turner Biggs."

The name meant nothing to Buckley. "Don't know him. Did you call him?"

"I left a message last night. He didn't answer."

"Probably in the mountains somewhere. I hear some of these crazy locals will go off the grid for days at a time."

"That's what I was thinking. I'll try him again today if he doesn't call me back by lunch."

"You think he'll be able to tell you why Cliff stayed around another day?"

Jack sighed through the phone. It sounded distant, like he was driving. "I hope so."

Buckley wasn't a detective, but he sure as hell hoped Jack had a more promising lead than a hiking guide. Then again, maybe the guide was a member of the wacko activist group.

"What else you got working?" Buckley asked.

"Tony Burns told me they're interviewing airport employees to find out if anyone saw or heard something. I'll check back with him later and see if anything turned up. In the meantime, I asked him to compile a list of people who had access to the planes parked out there."

"Good." It wasn't much information, but at least it seemed Martin was asking the right people the right questions and not asking the wrong people the wrong ones. He cleared his throat.

"What about the crash? Have they found anything yet?" Buckley swallowed, waiting for Jack's answer.

"I haven't heard anything about the crash site in a couple of days," Jack said. "I'm sure the feds are still up there and not letting anyone in. But I can ask the sheriff if you want me to."

"Do that," Buckley replied. "Let me know what he says. So, what's next? Sounds like you're driving."

"I'm on my way to see Hank Wade. He had a barn burn down yesterday."

Buckley came forward in his chair. "Well, that's interesting news." He was suspicious. Barns didn't catch fire on their own. "Arson?"

"I haven't had a chance to ask him yet," Jack replied. "I heard it from a friend who's got a scanner. But the barn was in Ouray County, not San Miguel. Not Tony's jurisdiction."

"But he'll know about it," Buckley said. "You call him. My money is on that greenie son of a buck Eric Dale. You let me know when you find out. Ask Wade about it."

"I'll call you after I talk to him."

"Good. Anything else?"

"Yeah, I've got a question for you."

"Shoot."

"What do you know about Ted Hawthorne?"

Buckley felt his chest clench. "Why?"

"I've heard he was a friend of Cliff's. I was thinking of paying him a visit."

Buckley's brain was swimming. He had to think fast. "Cliff didn't talk to Ted that night. . . at the fundraiser. Not like he did with Elizabeth."

"I'd like to find out if—"

Buckley cut him off. "I think you'd be barking up the wrong tree. It would be a waste of your time. You talk to Wade. Find out more about that fire, and let me know what he says. And let me know what that guide says when you get ahold of him, too. That's where you're going to find the answers we're looking for. That crazy tree hugger burned down that barn. And I'd put money on him being the one who took down Cliff's plane. You just need to find the evidence."

Jack tried to tell him the FBI and the NTSB were all over the crash site and would likely be the ones to break the case, but Buckley didn't care.

"They won't get it done fast enough," Buckley told him. "You can do things behind the scenes, put some pressure on people—the right people—and find out sooner." When Jack didn't reply, he added, "At least help them out, Jack. Keep looking into those activists. You know I'm right about the wheels of government turning at a snail's pace. Cliff deserves better."

Jack was silent a moment. "I'll see what I can find out."

Buckley let out the breath he'd been holding. "You do that," he said. He could hear the sound of a truck passing in the distance. "And, Jack?"

"Yeah."

"Thank you."

After he ended the call, Buckley went back over the conversation. Eric Dale had burned down Hank Wade's barn—he was sure of it. Just because Cliff was no longer around didn't mean the land swap was dead. But Buckley hoped Dale had overplayed his hand this time, that Jack could somehow find evidence he was behind the fire. He wanted Dale behind bars until someone could pin Cliff's death on him.

He thought of Elizabeth Mayweather's hunting guide. For some reason Jack seemed hell-bent on talking to him. Buckley didn't hold out much hope that it would help, but decided that, as long as Jack didn't waste too much time with the guy, it wouldn't hurt.

What *would* hurt was if Jack decided to focus his attention on Ted. Damn banker.

Buckley grew agitated thinking about it. He pushed himself up from the desk and stomped toward the bar. It was early, but he needed whiskey.

Ted Hawthorne was a problem he should have taken care of long ago.

CHAPTER 40

JACK TOSSED THE cell phone onto the seat beside him. For some reason, Buckley had no interest in talking about Ted Hawthorne—even seeming to steer the conversation away from the banker. Buckley was hiding something.

Crockett sat on the passenger seat, staring ahead. When Jack hit the roundabout outside of town, he continued west. They were on their way to pay Hank Wade another visit. Jack hoped he could talk Wade into letting him take a look at the barn that had caught fire the day before.

Jack had seen businesses looted and burned by activists. But something about Wade's barn didn't sit right, and he hoped a trip to see it would help him figure out what it was that bothered him. If the scene was still being investigated, there was no way the sheriff would allow him on the property. But if Jack could convince Wade to accompany him, he might stand a chance.

But finding who set the barn on fire wasn't the only answer Jack was looking for. He wanted to know who was behind the account in the Cayman Islands. Wade had transferred a large sum of money to someone, and Jack wanted to know who it was and what the money was for.

Cliff Roberts had died before Wade sent the money, so he wouldn't be the person behind Bridal Veil Limited. And since Archie hadn't been able to uncover any suspicious activity associated with *any* of Roberts's financial accounts, Jack was beginning to think the accusations of bribery against the dead congressman weren't true.

Wade had probably sent the money to pay off someone else on the committee. The night before, Jack had printed a list of their names and was sure at least one was a crooked politician.

He thumped his fingers on the steering wheel, wondering who could be behind the Bridal Veil account and racking his brain, trying to think of a way to approach the subject with Wade. Wade wouldn't offer up the information freely. It had to be handled carefully, a simple question that could lead to more complex ones, then hopefully, to an answer. Jack hoped that somewhere in the half-truths and lies that Wade would tell, he would find the kernel of a clue.

A half hour later, Jack pulled through the log entrance onto Wade's ranch. He scanned the rolling pastures for men on horseback but didn't see any. Several minutes passed before the compound came into view. A handful of cattle were divided among the livestock pens, and two pickups were parked near the barn. Another, the latest Ford model—a truck Jack could only dream about—sat close to the house. He figured it belonged to Wade.

The red hound lay on the grass just off the front porch and lifted its head as Jack pulled closer. He parked the truck and got out. Crockett, not waiting for permission, leapt from the seat and loped toward Red. The two dogs greeted each other like long-lost friends.

"They look like a couple of littermates," Wade said, stepping off the porch into the morning sun. He extended his hand, and Jack shook it.

"Sorry to bother you again—" Jack began.

"No apologies necessary," Wade said. "Red likes the company. I do, too. Come on in."

They left the dogs playing in the yard. Jack followed Wade inside. In the living room, Wade gestured toward a couch and lowered himself into a facing chair.

"I heard about your barn," Jack said and saw Wade's face go hard.

"I should have had someone over there watching. I would have given anything if one of my guys could have caught the SOB before he got the thing lit."

"What do you think happened?"

"Eric Dale burned it down," he said without hesitation.

"What does the sheriff think?"

"It doesn't matter what he thinks. Dale is responsible. I figure I'll give the locals a few more days to pin this on him. If they don't, I'll hire someone of my own." He stared at Jack a moment and raised an eyebrow. "Maybe I'll hire you, Martin."

Jack bristled at the arrogant way he had said it, not asking but *assuming* Jack would take the case. Hank Wade was friendly but could be a bully with a sense of entitlement, a character flaw not uncommon among successful men used to getting their way. Although Jack wanted to find out who was behind the fire, he'd rather investigate it without being paid than work for a man like Wade.

"What was in the barn?" Jack asked, changing the subject.

"Luckily, just some ranching equipment and horses. Thank God whoever did it at least had the decency to let my horses out first. But the equipment and the building are a total loss."

"I'm sorry to hear it," Jack replied. "Why do you think they did it?"

"Because they're lunatics!" Wade came forward in his chair. "They don't want me trading the land to the government. You know how these groups are—they'll bomb anything to get their way. Logging companies, pipelines, abortion clinics. Left, right—it doesn't matter. They all do it."

Wade checked himself and settled back in his chair, smoothing his jeans over the tops of his thighs.

Jack gave him a moment before he continued. "Any idea why they chose the property closer to Ridgway and not this one?" Jack assumed the risk of being seen would have been greater on the ranch near town.

"Nobody lives on that ranch," Wade replied. "There's no house out there. Everyone knows I live on this one."

"Have you been there since it happened?"

"To see what was left?"

Jack nodded.

"No. They let my guys move the horses that night, but they won't let us back on the property yet."

Jack knew he wouldn't be able to see the ranch if law enforcement wasn't letting Wade back on it yet. He decided to wait a few days, see what else he could find out. If he still needed to see the barn, he would ask Tony for help.

"Will it affect the land trade now that the barn is gone?" Jack asked.

"It shouldn't. The forestry service would've probably taken it down anyway."

"What about Cliff Roberts's death?"

"What about it?"

"How will it affect the vote?"

Wade shrugged. "As far as I know, it doesn't change anything. There might be a delay while they sort things out—stick someone else on the committee. But government business isn't going to grind to a halt because one congressman gets blown out of the sky."

The statement was crass. Wade waited for a response, but Jack remained silent.

"They'll hold the vote as planned," Wade continued. "I'll get the land I want, and the taxpayers will get a good deal."

Jack knew he was glossing over the ramifications of the congressman's death and was more worried than he was letting on. He thought of the large sum of money that had been transferred from Wade's account. It was time to start asking harder questions.

"You spoke with Cliff about the deal before he died. Were you in contact with any of the other members on the committee?"

Jack saw Wade blink and knew immediately he'd hit a nerve.

"Early on, I sent all the committee members a letter explaining the benefits of the trade." Wade talked slowly—almost methodically—choosing his words carefully. "I've had no further contact with any of them except for Cliff. He was chairman of the committee, but more important, he was the congressman for this district."

Jack suspected he was lying about talking to the other members. Someone had a small fortune transferred to their account in the Caymans, and it wasn't Roberts—he was already dead. Someone else was behind Bridal Veil Limited.

But had Wade bribed the congressman in the past? Was Eric Dale right? Was that why he was voting to approve the trade?

Jack watched Wade closely. "There are rumors that Cliff Roberts took bribes for political favors."

Hank Wade held his gaze without flinching. "If he did, they didn't come from me."

CHAPTER 41

JACK PULLED ONTO the highway and squeezed the steering wheel as he hit the gas. His conversation with Hank Wade had him frustrated.

Jack had interrogated hundreds of people over the years, from bumbling delinquents to savvy career criminals. He put Wade near the top of the list of the hardest ones to crack. Wade was shrewd—and cagey. Jack was sure the millionaire rancher was hiding secrets that, no matter how hard Jack had tried, he couldn't get him to reveal.

Jack went over the details of their conversation in his head as he drove the twists and turns on the way back to Telluride.

With Roberts dead, Wade must have bribed someone else on the committee. And Jack was sure that one of them was behind the Bridal Veil account in the Caymans. As much as Jack hated to ask Archie for another favor, when he got back to the trailer, he would give him the list of names of the other politicians on the committee.

When Jack had pressed Wade about Eric Dale, Wade wasn't able to give a definitive answer for why he believed Dale had set fire to his barn. Wade kept insisting that he'd seen Dale on the highway not long after the fire had started. It wasn't much of an indictment. Jack suspected the rancher's hatred for anyone standing in the way of him getting what he wanted had clouded his judgment.

It was a stretch to assume Dale had gone from soliciting signatures for his petitions to burning down private property. But if Dale was an official suspect, the sheriff in Ouray would have contacted Tony Burns. As far as Jack knew, Dale was still living in Telluride—Tony's jurisdiction. He made a mental note to ask him about it and find out.

As he neared Telluride, Jack eased the truck to a stop, letting a herd of elk cross the highway toward the open field that ran along the valley floor. Crockett sat erect, watching the elk from the passenger seat beside him.

As he waited, Jack glanced up at Savage Basin, perched high in the distance at the far end of the canyon. The reflection from the noon sun had the snow on fire.

To the south, Ingram Falls—frozen blue only three months earlier—was a white ribbon snaking its way from Ingram Basin to the valley below. The sight was as beautiful as anything Jack had ever seen.

Crockett stared at the elk still crossing the highway, and Jack laid a hand on him. "When the snow melts," Jack said to the dog, "we'll hike above the canyon. How about it?"

As Jack drove through town, he noticed two Tahoes from the sheriff's office double-parked outside of Waggoner Mercantile. A truck from the marshal's office was parked directly in front of them.

Jack was curious what the law enforcement powwow was about. He slowed to look as he passed, but the large plate-glass windows reflected the parked cars and buildings across the street. He couldn't see inside.

He had met Opal and Ivy Waggoner while investigating the disappearance—then murder—of author Alice Fremont. They were eccentric old sisters—one nicer than the other. It had been months since he'd seen either one.

Jack took a right at the next corner and pulled the truck into an empty parking spot. He rolled the windows down for Crockett and got out.

"Stay here, boy. I'll be right back."

It was a good time to do a little shopping. At least, that's what he'd let the Waggoner sisters believe. He hoped that whoever the officers were inside, they wouldn't recognize him. Repeatedly poking around in their business was a quick way to be told to get lost.

Jack walked back to Main Street, then rounded the corner and dodged a handful of tourists as he made his way up the hill. As he neared the store, he could see through the window and noticed multiple people standing inside—several in uniform. They were standing in a circle, and from their body language, the discussion looked heated.

A bell jingled above the door as he opened it, and a stout man in uniform turned in his direction. The sheriff. Jack knew immediately that he'd been busted. Tony would never believe he was there to buy a rug or turquoise jewelry.

Burns rolled his eyes and turned back to the group. Jack wasn't sure if he was irritated with the ongoing discussion or frustrated to see Jack. Probably both.

The others hadn't seemed to notice him, so Jack made a feeble attempt to look like he was shopping for a Navajo blanket, letting them talk. He rifled through several blankets stacked on a shelf along a wall. Tony wouldn't fall for it; after all, the expensive rugs would hardly fit the Airstream's decor. The gesture was ridiculous, but looking busy was the only thing Jack could think of doing. He stole occasional glances at the group as they talked.

Jack recognized Kim O'Connor. She stood next to another deputy—a young guy, tall and thin and armed to the hilt. He had several clips attached to his belt and looked ready to take on a small army. Jack had seen him before but couldn't recall his name.

Harlan Croix from the marshal's office stood between the Waggoner sisters.

Opal Waggoner was talking. "Fascist tyrants won't be satisfied until they burn the whole town down."

"It was just a flyer," Ivy reprimanded her sister softly.

"That's how it starts," Opal said, stabbing her cane on the wood plank floor. She shook a crooked finger at Ivy with her free hand. "And if there's one thing I know about, it's tyrants."

"And that doesn't surprise *any* of us, does it, Sheriff?" Ivy replied, her voice still sweet, but rolling her eyes.

Jack noticed Harlan suppress a smile.

Tony cleared his throat, but Opal kept talking. "If I've told those vandals once, I've told them a dozen times that I don't want any of their hateful propaganda littering the outside of my store."

"It's my fault, Sheriff," Ivy said. "I told them they could put it on the window. I've seen their flyers around town, and I happen to agree with them." She turned to Opal as if daring her sister to respond. Opal harrumphed, but Ivy continued. "I don't like that man. And I agree with them that he *shouldn't* have the land he wants."

Jack realized she was talking about Hank Wade.

Opal looked over and noticed Jack standing along the wall. "Well, well, well, if it isn't Telluride's very own Lone Ranger.

Maybe *he* can do something about this," she said, looking at the sheriff but pointing her cane at Jack.

Jack had the sudden urge to turn and run, but it was too late.

"Hello again, Detective," Ivy Waggoner said in a kind voice. "What a nice surprise. Can we help you with something?"

Opal grabbed a sheet of paper lying on the display case next to her and hobbled in Jack's direction. "No, Ivy," she said, shaking the paper at him. "Maybe he can help *us*."

Jack took it from her and recognized the new flyer Eric Dale's group had been putting up across town. Since Roberts's death, they had taken down the old flyers and put up ones with a likeness of Hank Wade behind bars. With the death of the congressman, they had transferred their focus to the evil millionaire rancher.

"If the local law won't protect us from being harassed," Opal said, turning in the direction of the sheriff and deputies, "then maybe Lone Ranger, here, could at least provide us with some security."

Tony sighed, came forward, and took the flyer from Jack. "I'll talk to them, Opal."

"I'll do the same, Ms. Waggoner," Harlan Croix said. "I'll instruct them to refrain from attaching anything to your windows in the future. Unless you give them permission first."

"Which I'll do over my dead body."

Tony sighed again. "In the meantime, Opal, I'll advise you not to initiate further contact with anyone in the group."

"I have no problem with that as long as they keep their litter *off* my windows." Her cane hit the floor again.

"They're my windows, too," Ivy insisted.

The sisters were still bickering when Jack and the officers stepped outside.

Harlan Croix nodded at him. "Jack."

"Deputy Croix," Jack replied.

Croix turned to Tony. "I'll take it from here," he told the sheriff. "Sorry she felt the need to drag you guys into this, too."

"It's fine, Harlan. See you later." Tony turned to Jack and dragged his hand down his face. "Well, that was fun," he said. "What are you doing here, Martin?"

"I wanted to ask you a few questions."

Kim opened the door to one of the Tahoes. "Need anything else, Sheriff?"

"No. I'll see you guys back at the office." Tony turned his attention to Jack and eyed him skeptically. "So, you saw all the commotion and just happened to guess that I'd be inside?"

"I figured there was a good chance you would be."

"And your questions couldn't wait?"

Jack remained silent, hoping the moment would pass. The last thing he wanted was for the sheriff to freeze him out now.

"Uh-huh." Tony checked his watch and opened the driver's-side door of the Tahoe. "All right, but I can't talk now. I'm late for something I've put off twice already. Be at my office in an hour."

Jack watched him pull down the street, then started for his truck. He saw something out of the corner of his eye and turned to look. Telluride Bank & Trust was across Main Street from Waggoner Mercantile. There was movement in a window, and Jack noticed the nervous banker he'd seen unlocking the door two days earlier staring at him.

Ted Hawthorne.

When they made eye contact, Hawthorne quickly turned away.

Something had the banker spooked, and Jack was determined to find out what it was.

CHAPTER 42

JACK TOOK HIS regular seat in Pandora Café, and Crockett settled on the floor at his feet.

"Well, aren't you a handsome boy," Judith said, handing Crockett a biscuit. She wiped her hands on her apron. "They're left over from breakfast. I hope it's all right I gave him one."

"I'm starving," Jack said. "Leftover biscuits sound like heaven."

"I've got something better," she said, wagging a finger. "I'm trying out a chili recipe today. And you're from Texas—I want your opinion. It's on the house."

Before Jack could protest, she turned and disappeared into the kitchen. A few seconds later, she returned carrying a large bowl and set it down in front of him.

"Try this and let me know what you think."

Steam rose from the chili and carried a scent Jack hadn't realized he'd missed. He leaned in and drew in a breath.

"I haven't had chili since I've been in Colorado," he said. "This looks great."

Judith set a plate of grated cheese and corn chips next to the bowl. "I'll be back in a second to see if you like it."

Jack sprinkled cheese over the chili and noticed Crockett watching him. "Sorry, boy. This isn't for you." He snuck a sideways glance and saw that no one was looking, so he took a pinch of the cheese and set it on the floor, where Crockett gobbled it up.

A few minutes later, as he shoveled the last of the chili into his mouth, Judith reappeared. She glanced at the empty bowl. "Well, I guess it was all right."

Jack wiped his mouth with a napkin and leaned back in his chair. "Judith, I think you've outdone yourself. That was fantastic."

She picked up the empty bowl and smiled. "Now, that's a compliment coming from a Texan."

"Technically, I'm from Louisiana."

"Close enough." She started for the kitchen but turned back. "You just gave me an idea," she said. "I think I'll try gumbo next."

Jack watched the lunch crowd thin as he finished his iced tea. The clientele was still mainly locals, but the days were warming fast, and he knew more tourists would show up soon. He hadn't yet spent a summer in Telluride but imagined it would be the same as in Aspen. The crowds would get bigger until they practically exploded over the July 4th weekend. It would remain crowded until schools started back in the fall.

Jack would investigate the crash for Buckley and, depending on how much money he made, would decide how long he could afford to stay in Telluride. But there was no sense in thinking about that now.

As he finished the last of his tea, Judith set a generous slice of cherry pie down on the table. Jack glanced up, thinking she'd brought it to him by mistake.

"You look like a man who could use a piece of pie."

"Is it that obvious?"

Judith untied her apron, laid it over the back of a chair, and sat. "How's the investigation going? Have they found out what happened to Cliff?"

"Not yet." Jack took a bite of pie. The press hadn't yet gotten wind that the feds had found evidence of a bomb. Jack couldn't bring himself to tell Judith that Cliff had been murdered.

"You still looking into it for Buckley?"

"I'm trying." Jack finished his bite. "Let me ask you something. What can you tell me about Ted Hawthorne?"

"A lot. What do you want to know?"

Jack wasn't sure. "I've heard he was a friend of Cliff's."

"He was. They went to school together."

"And Lea Scotsman?"

Judith nodded. "The three were pretty tight back in the day. Ted and Lea are still friends, as far as I know. She comes into town now and then to go to the bank—usually stops in here for a bite afterward."

"Tell me about Ted. I haven't met him yet, but I'm going to."

Judith took her time answering. "Ted's. . . an interesting sort of fellow. Quirky personality. Nothing like Cliff. Cliff drew people like bees to honey. But for whatever reason, the two were friends. Then again, I don't remember Cliff having a negative word to say about anyone."

What was it about Hawthorne? Nobody wanted to talk about him. First Buckley, now Judith. Whether she knew it or not, she was steering the conversation back to Cliff.

"Has Ted lived here long?"

Judith nodded. "Grew up here. Inherited the bank from his father when he died. It was the *only* thing left that he inherited."

"What do you mean?"

"The bank has been owned by Hawthornes for over a hundred years. The family was well-to-do until Ted's grandfather died and his dad inherited the family fortune. He was a gambler. Eventually lost it all at the casino outside of Cortez. Everything except the bank." Judith shook her head in disgust. "Even the old Hawthorne home that had been in the family for generations was sold to pay off his debts. Cliff's father, Edward, bought it years ago."

"The house Susan is living in?"

"That's the one. Famous old house in town. It's on the museum's walking tour. I think it about killed Ted when Cliff and Susan moved into it."

Jack wondered what it would do to a friendship. For Hawthorne, Cliff and Susan moving into his ancestral home had to be humiliating. He thought of the photograph in the newspaper, the one of Ted standing with Cliff at Allred's.

"But Ted still owns the bank?"

"He does. It didn't amount to much when he took it over after his father died, but Ted's smart—and shrewd. He turned it around. From what I hear, the bank may be small, but it's a moneymaker. Lots of wealthy depositors. Lea Scotsman for one. And probably Buckley and Celeste Bailey. Loads of second home owners—millionaires from Texas and Florida. I bank there, too, but my balance is probably less than the interest Ted pays on most of the other accounts." She said it without a hint of resentment and laughed.

"So where does Ted live now?" Jack was intrigued by Cliff displacing Ted from his ancestral home.

"He's got a condo along the river. Nice, from what I hear. But I've never seen it."

They sat in silence, Jack processing the information, knowing Hawthorne would have resented his old friend living in the house he'd grown up in. The house he would have expected to one day inherit and live in himself.

Judith fidgeted in her chair.

Jack could tell she wanted to say something. "What is it?" he asked.

"It's not my business, and you can tell me so if you want to." She paused a moment. "But what about *your* family, Jack? After you solved Alice's murder, there were things written in the paper. I was just wondering..."

Her voice trailed off, but Jack knew what she was asking. The look on her face was one of concern, not morbid curiosity.

He offered Judith an easy smile, reassuring her that he wasn't offended by the question. "I'll tell you about my grandparents sometime," he said. "But not today."

Judith held his gaze for a while, then let the subject drop.

CHAPTER 43

JACK STOPPED AT the threshold of the Sheriff's office. Tony was on the phone, and by the look on his face, something had him frustrated.

Tony pointed to a chair in front of his desk, and Jack sat.

"Call me the second you find out," Tony said into the receiver, then hung up. He laid his forearms on the desk and looked at Jack. "You want to know what I think?"

Jack wasn't sure he did and remained silent.

"I think some people have a knack for meddling," Tony continued. "And lately, you always seem to be at the center of things after they've gone haywire. I don't know whether to be grateful you're here or suspicious."

There wasn't any animosity in how he'd said it, only weariness. It was then Jack noticed the dark circles under his eyes. Tony looked like he hadn't slept in days.

"I want to help," Jack said. He wanted to ask about Ted Hawthorne and Hank Wade but felt it could wait. "Tell me what I can do."

Tony stared at him for a long minute before he replied. "All right. Here's the latest. And it's a lot." He leaned back in his chair. "Deputy O'Connor interviewed everyone at the airport who had access to the tarmac the night before and the morning that Cliff's plane went down. Nothing turned up. Nobody saw, heard, knew, or even suspected a thing. Until this morning.

"There's a kid that works there early—before school. When Kim talked to him, she said he seemed nervous but didn't think anything of it. After all, what kid *wouldn't* be nervous having to talk to law enforcement after a couple of people died."

"How old is he?" Jack asked.

Tony came forward in his chair and picked up a sheet of paper on his desk. "Sixteen. Name's Ronnie Bugler. Anyway, his mom hears about the crash later that day, asks him about it when he gets home from school, but the kid is *jumpy*." Tony made air quotes with his fingers. "Her description. She said she knew something was wrong. Gave it another day, then dragged him in here this morning after she got the truth out of him."

"Which was?"

Tony heaved a sigh. "Someone paid the kid a hundred bucks to slip a small package onto Cliff's plane."

Jack sat erect on the edge of the chair. "Who?"

"Kid didn't know. Couldn't even give us a decent description. The guy was wearing a long coat and a cowboy hat."

"Height? Weight?"

Tony shook his head. "He couldn't tell—said it was still dark. The guy called him over to the fence that surrounds the airport, handed him a package the size of a shoe box and a hundred-dollar bill, and told him which plane to put it on. The guy said it was a surprise for a friend of his."

"And the kid put it on the plane not knowing it was a bomb." Jack was thinking out loud.

"He said he stowed it in the luggage compartment at the rear of the plane. It fits with the location of where the feds are saying the explosion likely occurred."

"Have you let them know?"

Tony nodded. "Brought in the FBI's lead investigator while the kid was still here. They talked to him, too. But as far as I know, they didn't get anything more out of him than we did. The kid's mom grounded him, but I'm afraid there's not much more we can do but hope he remembers something else."

Jack remembered being sixteen and broke and understood the kid being more interested in the cash than the guy in the dark handing it to him. As much as he hated to admit it, Jack thought he would have probably done the same thing.

Tony was still talking. "According to the FAA, there are no planes parked at Telluride registered to Buckley or Celeste Bailey, or any companies associated with them. But if the bomb was passed through the fence and the kid put it on Cliff's plane, I don't think it matters anymore."

Jack didn't think it mattered any longer, either, but he still wanted to know who would have had access just in case. "What about Hank Wade? Does he have a plane out there?"

Tony shook his head. "He *has* a plane—a couple of them, as a matter of fact—but he keeps them in Montrose. And as far as we can tell, he's never even flown in or out of Telluride."

"What about Eric Dale?" Jack asked. "Could he have been the guy who paid the kid?"

Tony lifted a pencil from his desk and rolled it back and forth between his hands. "We showed the kid a picture of Dale, but he couldn't identify him. Of course, Dale probably would have sent one of his minions to do his dirty work, or maybe been in disguise."

Jack looked past Tony and through the window behind him. There were dark clouds that looked similar to smoke boiling in the distance.

"What about Wade's barn? Did anyone question Dale about it?"

"We brought him in." Tony clenched the pencil firmly with both hands, no longer rolling it. "He claims that at the time the fire started, he was changing a flat tire somewhere on Last Dollar Road."

"Where's that?"

"Last Dollar is a dirt road that runs above the airport, if you can believe it. But it winds its way through the mountains until it finally meets the highway just outside Ridgway."

"And do you believe him?"

"I have to," Tony said, looking unhappy about it. "We don't have any proof otherwise. He claims some idiot lost a load of nails; he saw them just before he ran over them."

"Any witnesses?"

"No. But we found nails in the bed of his truck. He said he picked them up after he changed the tire so the next guy to come along wouldn't have the same problem."

"You think he's telling the truth?"

Tony shrugged. "There was no gas can or lighting fluid of any kind in his truck. Not even a match."

The intercom on the desk buzzed, and a woman's voice came over the line. "Sheriff, a car's gone off 145 about a quarter mile west of Silver Pick Road. A bystander called it in. EMS is already en route."

"Ah, hell. What next?" Tony threw the pencil into a desk drawer and slammed it shut. "This is going to be a bloody mess." He dragged his free hand down his face, then pressed the button. "Get Deputy Barry out there to see what happened."

The intercom was silent for a moment.

"Tony," the woman finally said. She sounded nervous. "The car is registered to Susan Roberts."

CHAPTER 44

As Tony had rushed out of his office on the way to the crash, he had ordered Jack not to follow. "This has nothing to do with you, Martin," he'd said, jumping into a Tahoe with Deputy O'Connor.

Jack had given them a head start, then pulled out of the parking lot and turned west toward the crash.

"Hang in there, Crockett," Jack told the dog sitting next to him on the seat. "Change of plans again."

Highway 145 had been chiseled from the mountain, tall red cliffs on one side, a sheer drop to the San Miguel River on the other, most of it without guardrails. A rollover out here, Jack thought, would be deadly, plunging a vehicle and its occupants nearly a hundred feet, in parts, to the valley floor and river below.

Jack drove the tilts and curves slowly and thought of Susan Roberts. He wondered if her crash had been an accident—a tire blowout, maybe a careless mistake as she'd made one of the hairpin turns. But she would have driven the roads around Telluride for years. And, although dark clouds were threatening an afternoon storm, the highway pavement was dry. Something in Jack's gut told him it hadn't been an accident.

He wondered if she had driven off the road on purpose. She didn't have children; maybe the death of her husband had sent her over the edge—literally. But she didn't seem the type.

An accident only days after Cliff Roberts's crash seemed odd. Had whoever killed the congressman also wanted his wife out of the way? It was a stretch, but Jack had to consider the possibility.

He saw flashing lights in the distance and slowed the truck. A cluster of Tahoes from the sheriff's office and an ambulance were blocking both lanes. A uniformed officer stood in the middle of the road, turning traffic around, sending vehicles back toward Telluride.

As he got closer, he recognized the officer on the road as one of Tony's deputies. Jack held his breath and gestured that he wanted to park, and the deputy waved him through. Past the Tahoes and ambulance, another deputy was turning traffic around in the opposite direction, sending it back toward Placerville.

Jack pulled to the side of the road and stopped, the mountain's red cliffs only inches from the passenger-side window. He left Crockett in the truck and got out, then glanced across the highway, where only a few feet from the edge of the pavement, the ground dropped away. His stomach lurched, imagining the carnage below. He decided not to look.

Instead, he focused on the group that had gathered some distance away, several people looking down where Susan Roberts's car would be. Tony and Deputy O'Connor were talking with a couple of paramedics. A man holding a helmet stood nearby. That's when Jack noticed the motorcycle parked behind one of the Tahoes.

As Jack walked toward the group, he saw a man in jeans and a flannel shirt measuring skid marks that ended at the cliff's edge.

Tony noticed Jack and came toward him, frowning. "Why am I not surprised?" He stuck his hands on his hips. "I should charge you with interfering with an investigation."

"You should," Jack replied.

They both knew it wouldn't happen.

Tony stared at him a moment, still frowning, then shook his head. "All right, come on."

He turned, and Jack followed him to the edge of the highway. It was then that Jack caught his first glimpse of the mangled wreckage below. There were two guys combing through what was left of some kind of SUV.

Jack looked back at Tony. "What happened?"

"According to the guy on the motorcycle, he passed the Range Rover and a dark pickup headed in the opposite direction. Both were traveling at a high rate of speed, the truck right on the Rover's tail. He looked in his rearview mirror after they passed and thought he saw the Rover go over the edge. The pickup was behind it but didn't stop. The guy thought maybe he'd seen wrong, but he turned around to take a look. That's when he called us."

Jack looked back at the wreckage and noticed a small trail of smoke still coming from what he assumed was the engine. One of the men looked like he was trying to reach something inside.

"The license plate?" Jack asked.

"Still intact." Tony exhaled. "Registered to Susan Roberts. I was just told that it looks like one of the tires could have been shot out, but they're not sure yet."

Jack wondered who would intentionally run Susan off the road. It was what he had expected but what he'd also hoped wouldn't be true.

"Survivors?"

Tony shook his head. "One deceased. The body's in bad shape. Mike Greenwald is down there assessing it now so we can get things cleared out of here and get the road back open."

"So, it was murder?"

"Looks like it."

From his vantage point on the cliff overlooking the wreckage, Jack hadn't recognized the county coroner. He had met Mike Greenwald months earlier while investigating the murder of Alice Fremont.

Jack watched as Greenwald emerged from the twisted metal and pulled something from his pocket, then held it to his ear.

Tony's cell phone rang.

"What is it, Mike?" Tony had the call on speaker.

"The deceased doesn't appear to be female."

"Well, who in the hell is it?"

"I pulled a wallet from his pocket. The name on the driver's license is Gerald Purvis."

CHAPTER 45

SHERIFF BURNS SPENT the drive to Telluride glancing in his rearview mirror. Before he left the accident, he made Martin promise he wouldn't follow him to Susan Roberts's home, but Tony was watching for Martin's truck just in case.

He had left O'Connor in charge of the scene. And although he knew it would take at least another hour, Tony had instructed her to wrap things up as quickly as possible and get traffic moving again.

Tony had been relieved when they discovered Susan wasn't in the Range Rover, but when he tried her cell phone and couldn't reach her, he grew nervous. Where was she? He thought of the report from the motorcyclist. Had the person in the dark truck sought Susan out after the crash? Had he already gotten to her? Tony couldn't help imagining Susan lying dead on the floor of her Telluride home.

He knew he was letting his imagination run away from him, but his mind was wandering. Had Susan been the intended victim, or had it been Gerald Purvis? There was probably a logical explanation for why Purvis was driving her car. Tony knew that Purvis was Cliff's chief of staff; he'd met Purvis once before.

He had seemed like a nice fellow, competent, from what Tony could tell.

Tony hoped the crash had been an accident but suspected it hadn't been. But why would someone shoot out the tire, running Purvis off the road intentionally? He hoped Susan could provide some answers.

The guy on the motorcycle had mentioned a dark truck. It gave Tony an idea.

He used the radio to call Deputy Barry. "Travis, I need you to locate Eric Dale. Find out where he was at the time of the crash on Highway 145. And get a photograph of his truck. I want to see if the guy who called in the crash can identify it as the one following Purvis before he went off the road."

Tony ended the call as he pulled into town and glanced in the rearview mirror one last time, making sure Martin wasn't following him before he turned the corner off Main Street and headed to the Robertses' home.

He parked along the curb and got out. And as he made his way up the sidewalk, he looked back over his shoulder. Damn Jack Martin for making him so paranoid.

Part of him was grateful that Martin was in town—Tony liked being able to bounce ideas off the experienced detective. But the other part of him was annoyed as hell. Every time he turned around, Martin was there.

He wiped his boots on the mat and knocked, relieved when Susan opened the door only a few seconds later.

"Tony?" There was a look of concern on her face.

"I'm sorry. I tried calling."

"It's fine."

"Can I come in a minute?"

"Of course." She led him into the living room.

"Susan, there's been another accident."

"What? What kind of an accident?"

"Your Range Rover. It went off the highway between here and Placerville."

"*My* Range Rover? How do you know?"

"The license plate is registered in your name."

She stared at him a moment, and then her eyes grew wide. "Where's Gerald?"

"They're pulling a body from the wreckage now. They found a driver's license on the deceased that belongs to Gerald Purvis."

Susan brought her hand to her throat and dropped onto the sofa. "Oh, no."

Tony saw her eyes start to well. "I'm sorry, Susan."

She shook her head. "No, no. Not Gerald, too." She started to cry.

Tony took a seat on the couch beside her and gave her a moment. "I need to ask you a few questions."

"Of course," she replied, wiping her eyes.

"Why was Gerald driving your car?"

"He borrowed it to go to Montrose. Someone was flying in from the governor's office to interview him. We were trying to get him appointed to serve out the remainder of Cliff's term. But now. . . " Her voice trailed off, and she began to cry again.

Tony pulled a tissue from a box on a side table and handed it to her.

"Thank you," she said, dabbing at her eyes. "This is just so horrible."

"I'm sorry, Susan. But I wanted to tell you myself."

She laid a hand on his arm. "Thank you for coming."

"There's something else I need to ask you. It could help us find out what happened." He took in a deep breath. "Can you think of anyone who would want Gerald dead?"

Susan looked up at him with an expression of horror. "What are you saying?"

"There's a possibility Gerald was run off the road intentionally."

She stared at him, then shook her head, her face contorted with disbelief and fear. "What are you saying?" she asked again. "First Cliff, now Gerald?"

He remained silent, and Susan grew visibly frustrated.

"Tell me the truth, Tony. Are you saying Gerald was *murdered*?"

CHAPTER 46

TONY HAD INSISTED Jack stay away from Susan Roberts's home, saying he would be in the way of law enforcement if he tried to interfere. He also made it clear that, even though Buckley had hired him to find out what had happened to Roberts, Gerald Purvis's accident was none of his business. So Jack gave him a head start.

He waited until Tony's Tahoe was out of sight, then turned his truck around and headed for Telluride, careful to keep his distance. Although he'd give anything to be there when Tony informed Susan of the crash, the last thing he wanted was for the sheriff to think he was a nuisance and freeze him out.

He played out the scene in his head. Tony would tell her about the accident, then ask why Purvis had been driving her car. If he was smart, he would also ask who stood to benefit by having Purvis out of the way. Jack's gut told him the same person who had taken down Cliff's plane had a hand in running Purvis off the road. The two deaths so close together was too coincidental, and Jack didn't believe in coincidences. He was sure Purvis had been murdered.

It was late afternoon. The skies still threatened rain, casting the town in an eerie darkness. Jack glanced up the side street toward the Robertses' home and saw the Tahoe parked at the curb. He would give Tony until the following day. Then, if Jack hadn't heard from him, he would pay the sheriff another visit.

As he passed Pandora Café, his stomach growled, reminding him of the chili he'd had for lunch. He swung the truck into an empty spot along the curb and got out.

"Let's go, Crockett."

The dog leapt from the truck, and the two crossed the road to the café.

Judith was setting plates of food down on a table in front of a couple of tourists in designer hiking clothes. Shiny expensive backpacks were draped over the backs of their chairs. The longer Jack stayed in Telluride, the easier it was to detect the tourists.

Judith turned in his direction and smiled, then disappeared through the swinging door into the kitchen.

Jack took his table next to the fireplace, and Crockett laid at his feet. Jack scanned the café. It was a small dinner crowd that, despite the couple of tourists, was mostly locals.

Jack heard Cliff Roberts's name mentioned at a nearby table but couldn't hear what was said. The congressman's death would still be news. He remembered what Judith had said about gossip spreading like wildfire in a small town and wondered how long it would take for them to find out about Gerald Purvis.

Judith approached his table and set a menu and a glass of iced tea down in front of him. "Back already?"

"I was hoping you still had some of that chili I had for lunch."

She beamed as if he'd paid her the highest of compliments. Jack suspected, when it came to her food, it was.

"As a matter of fact," she said, "I do have some left. Will you take some to Otto for me? I think he'll like it, too."

"I know he will."

Several minutes later, Judith reappeared with a bowl of chili for Jack and a plate of chopped hamburger for Crockett.

She set the plate on the floor. "I hope it's all right," she said, straightening up. "I figured he was hungry, too."

Judith was an angel. Jack didn't know what he'd done to deserve a friend like her.

Crockett finished the hamburger in a few seconds.

"Lie back down," Jack told him. "It's going to take me a while longer." The dog obeyed, and Jack smiled at him. *Two* angels that had come into his life in just over a year. He was a lucky man.

As he ate, Jack watched customers come and go. The tourists in designer duds paid and left. They were replaced by a woman in tight-fitting jeans and a T-shirt. She was a little heavy-handed with the makeup, but attractive, and had a sullen-looking teenager in tow who was nearly the spitting image of her.

The kid stared down at his phone, but the woman looked in Jack's direction and caught him watching her. She flipped her brunette hair over a shoulder and smiled. Jack knew he'd been caught and hoped the lighting in the café hid the flush he felt warm his cheeks. He nodded to the woman, then turned his attention back to the chili.

Several minutes later, Judith reappeared with a paper bag. "Looks like you enjoyed it as much the second time," she said, smiling. "This is for Otto."

"He'll love it."

Judith set the bag in front of him, then pulled out an empty chair and sat, her smile gone. "I heard Cliff's crash wasn't an accident."

Jack stared at her a moment, wondering how much he should tell her and how much she already knew. "There was a package placed on the plane before it took off. It's looking like it was a bomb."

She grimaced. "Who would do such a thing?"

"A kid did it. But he had no idea what it was. Someone paid him to put it on the plane."

"Who?"

"That's the million-dollar question," Jack replied. "The kid couldn't give them a good description."

Judith thought about it. "What was a kid doing at the airport?"

"He works there."

"What's his name? I might know him."

Jack shook his head, trying to remember. "Ronnie something or other."

"Ronnie Bugler?"

"Yeah, that's it. Do you know him?"

Judith inclined her head toward the teenager sitting with the woman in tight clothes. "He's right over there."

"That's Ronnie Bugler?"

Judith nodded.

Jack couldn't believe his luck. But then again, it *was* a small town. There were a dozen questions he wanted to ask the kid. He watched as the teenager worked his cell phone furiously with both thumbs, probably playing a video game.

Jack glanced at the woman sitting with him and saw her finish off the last of a sandwich. They would be leaving soon.

"Is that his mother?"

Judith nodded again. "Her name's Candy. Candy Bugler."

Jack remembered Tony mentioning that the kid had clammed up when he was questioned. But what teenager wouldn't get scared being interviewed by law enforcement? And then his mother had hauled him into the sheriff's office. If Ronnie Bugler had been nervous being questioned by Kim O'Connor, how terrified had he been being hauled into the sheriff's office?

Jack looked back at Judith. "Do you think she would let me talk to him? I'd like to ask him a couple of questions."

Judith snickered, raising an eyebrow. "From the stars in her eyes, I would guess yes."

Jack frowned, confused.

Judith sighed. "When I took her order, she asked me about the new stranger in town." When Jack didn't reply, she added, "She was talking about *you*, silly. I think 'bona fide hunk' were her exact words." Judith was grinning at him, and Jack felt his face flush for the second time in under an hour.

When Jack approached the table, Candy's eyes lit up.

"Excuse me," Jack said. "Would you mind if I asked Ronnie a couple of questions?"

"Ronnie?" Her smile was replaced by a look of disappointment.

The kid glanced up from his phone and shifted nervously in his seat.

"I'd like to ask him about the package he put on the plane," Jack said.

There was panic in the boy's eyes, and he turned to his mother for help. She started to speak, but Jack held up a hand.

"I'm not law enforcement. Just a friend of a friend. Please, just a couple of quick questions."

Jack waited, holding his breath, while Candy considered the request. Finally, her face softened, and she gestured toward one of the empty chairs. Jack saw Ronnie shoot her a look of angry disbelief.

"Thank you," Jack said, pulling out the chair and taking a seat.

Ronnie fidgeted nervously with his phone. Jack knew he would have to take it slowly, or the kid would clam up. He needed the kid to trust him.

"Sheriff Burns said you were very brave to tell them about putting the package on the plane." Ronnie glanced at Jack briefly, then back to the phone in his lap.

Jack cleared his throat. "Is there anything you remember about the guy who gave it to you?"

The kid shook his head without looking up.

"Speak up, Ronnie," his mother scolded him.

"I mean, no, sir." He shifted in his seat. "Like I told the sheriff, it was dark. I didn't pay no attention."

"I probably wouldn't have, either," Jack said. "If someone had offered me a hundred dollars when I was your age, I would have done the same thing—I'd've put that package on the plane and not thought anything of it."

Ronnie stopped fidgeting and looked at Jack with something resembling relief.

"Is there anything else you can tell me about that morning?" Jack asked. "Did you notice anyone else around the congressman's plane before it took off?"

The kid set his phone on the table and shook his head slowly. "Only Jerry."

"Who's Jerry?"

"He drives the fuel truck. He fills up the planes."

"Jerry didn't mess with the plane at all? Just gassed it up?"

Ronnie nodded.

"Anything else?" Jack asked. "Anything that seemed unusual or out of place that morning?"

Ronnie Bugler chewed on his fingernails as he thought about the question. "No. Only that the flight was the first one scheduled that day. It was late getting off, and some of the guys were complaining that it was going to back them up early. But there wasn't any more traffic that morning because of the wind, so it didn't really matter."

"Why was the plane late getting off?"

Ronnie smiled for the first time since he'd entered the café. "There was a fight. The congressman and some guy. Well, not really a fight—there weren't punches thrown or anything like that. But it was still pretty funny. The tall guy was throwing his hands up in the air, talking real loud."

This was news to Jack. He wondered why Tony hadn't mentioned it. "Did anyone else see the argument?"

Ronnie shook his head. "Nah. Probably just me. I wish the guys could have seen it, though. It was hilarious—the guy stomping and waving his arms around."

"Where was the pilot?"

"I don't know," Ronnie replied. "Inside filing his flight plan, I guess."

"Could you describe the guy?"

Ronnie thought about it a moment. "He was tall... and old." He started to chuckle. "Looked like some angry old dude from the Wild West."

"How so?"

"He was wearing cowboy boots and a cowboy hat. After he gave the guy the envelope, he was waving the hat around and talking real loud, hollering about something. I tried to hear but couldn't. But, man, the guy looked off."

"He handed the congressman an envelope?"

Ronnie's head bobbed. "Yeah."

Cliff Roberts had been handed something just before the crash. Jack's mind raced. Who was the other guy? Ronnie had said it was a tall, loudmouthed cowboy. Why had he been arguing with the congressman? Could it have had something to do with what was in the envelope? But an envelope wouldn't have been large enough to contain a bomb.

"How big was the package you put on the plane, Ronnie? Could you tell what was in it?" The kid had stopped smiling, and Jack knew he was nervous again. Too many questions too fast. Damn it.

"I—I don't know," Ronnie stuttered. "I'm sorry."

"That's all right, son. Did you mention the argument when you were questioned by the sheriff?"

"Nah. Forgot about it till just now."

Jack got to his feet and dug his wallet from his pocket. He tossed three twenties on the table, more than enough to cover his chili and the Buglers' meals.

"Thank you, Ronnie. You've been a huge help."

Candy opened her mouth to say something, but Jack tipped his head at her and spoke first. "Thank you, Candy. I'll see you around."

"I hope so," she replied.

Jack called Crockett to him, and the two left.

Jack knew darn well who had argued with the congressman the morning his plane was blown out of the sky. And now Jack wanted nothing more than to find out what games the loudmouth cowboy was playing.

CHAPTER 47

CELESTE BAILEY OPENED the front door and quickly replaced her smile with a frown. "Jack? Is everything all right?"

Jack chastised himself for wearing his emotions on his sleeve. Buckley had lied to him, but he should have expected it. He had never known a politician who wasn't a liar. Some were just worse than others. And although Jack had figured Buckley for one of the better ones, now he wasn't so sure.

Jack wanted to know what the argument on the morning the plane had gone down had been about. And he wanted to know why Buckley had kept it a secret.

Celeste stood in the doorway, waiting for an answer. Jack resisted telling her that everything *wasn't* all right, that her husband was a liar.

"I'm sorry I didn't call, Celeste. But I need to talk to Buckley."

The look of concern was still on her face, but she stepped back and pulled the door open. "Come in."

Jack followed her to the study, where Buckley was on the telephone. He waved to one of two club chairs set in front of a large window, but Jack remained standing.

A few seconds later, Buckley ended his call. "Jack! I was just about to call you. Have a seat."

"I'd prefer to stand."

The air in the room quickly grew tense.

"What's this all about?" Buckley asked. "Did you find out something?"

"I did," Jack replied. "And that's the problem."

There was an awkward silence.

"Well, out with it," Buckley finally said. "I'm not paying you to keep secrets."

"They're not my secrets."

Buckley's face grew hard. "All right, Jack. Enough games. What's got the burr under your saddle?"

Jack watched him closely, ready for a lie. "What was your argument with Cliff about before he took off that morning?"

Buckley was surprised, but he quickly regained his composure. He stared at Jack a moment, then let his face relax.

"All right." He pointed to the chair again, then got up and dropped into the other. "Sit down, and I'll tell you about it."

Jack took a seat.

For a while Buckley stared through the window at the snow-capped peaks of the San Sophia Ridge above town. The view was spectacular, but Buckley didn't seem to notice. He turned back with a look of resignation, and Jack braced for what he hoped would finally be the truth.

"There was a detective in Telluride trying to dig up dirt on Cliff. . . or Susan. Or both."

"Politics of personal destruction."

"Exactly." Buckley rested an ankle across the other knee and picked at his boot. "Anyway, the guy tried posing as a tourist and was dropping Cliff's name around town, fishing for something on him—something that could be used against him in the election. But Telluride's a small town. Word got out, and I knew immediately what was going on."

"Who hired the guy?"

"As far as we can tell, it was Cliff's opponent in the upcoming election."

"What do you know about the opponent?"

"He's a jerk state senator from Boulder trying to make a name for himself. But it doesn't matter," he said, waving a hand dismissively. "This shit happens all the time. If it wasn't this guy, it'd be somebody else. The only problem is, this detective they hired got lucky. He found a live one."

"What do you mean?"

"He found someone in town who'd talk."

"Who?" Jack saw Buckley's jaw clench.

"A pipsqueak, good-for-nothing banker."

A banker?

"Ted Hawthorne?" Jack asked.

Buckley looked like he was about to spit. "That's the one."

"What did he have on Cliff?" Jack's mind was racing. Did Hawthorne have proof of financial misconduct? Something proving Roberts had taken bribes for political favors?

"It's personal," Buckley said. "And I don't see the need to sully a good man's name."

"Cliff's dead." Jack was frustrated by all the secrets. "And I'm trying to find out who killed him. I need to know what Hawthorne told the detective."

Buckley stared at him without responding, but Jack held his gaze. He wouldn't relent this time and wouldn't tolerate any more secrets.

Buckley shifted in his seat, then finally spoke. "Ah, hell. I guess it doesn't matter now." He paused, searching for the right words. "Ted put the guy on Susan's trail, gave him some gossip. He ended up getting photographs of Susan with a man that wasn't Cliff."

Jack took a second to digest the information. The detective hired by Roberts's political opposition found out Susan was having an affair, and the information would have likely been used against him in the reelection. Jack hated politics.

"Who was she with?" he asked.

Buckley remained silent, still picking at the sole of his boot.

"You?" Jack asked.

Buckley dropped his foot to the floor as he came forward in his chair. "No, Martin. It sure as hell wasn't me. What kind of man do you think I am?" His voice was raised. "It doesn't matter *who* the guy was. The whole damn thing doesn't matter now that Cliff's dead—"

"I need to know."

"And I want to save Susan the embarrassment."

Jack wasn't sure, but Buckley seemed to be telling the truth. He decided to let the matter of Susan Roberts's affair drop. There were other, more pressing, questions he wanted the former governor to answer.

"What does this have to do with your argument with Cliff?"

"Everything." Buckley physically deflated and let his gaze drift out through the window again. "I gave Cliff a set of the photographs that morning."

"Of Susan and the other man?"

He nodded. "Cliff was upset—I expected him to be. First he tried making excuses for her—*the photos didn't mean anything, they were just friends*, things like that. Then he escalated it by accusing *me* of being behind it all, blaming *me* for hiring the damn detective. He was upset and said some stuff I knew he didn't mean."

"But you got angry with him," Jack said. "You argued back."

"I did." Buckley slumped back in his chair. "I regret it now. But how in the hell was I supposed to know it would be the last time I'd see him?"

Jack couldn't help but feel sorry for him, but there were a few things that still didn't add up. "How did you get ahold of the photographs?"

Buckley's eyes had fire in them again. "I heard that detective was seen coming out of the Bank & Trust, and I knew immediately that that no-good SOB had given him something. Ted's an old friend of Cliff's, but I never trusted him, and I was right not to. I could tell that little Napoleon was pea-green with envy and resented Cliff ever since I met him. Cliff didn't see it, but I did. Anyway, after I heard about that detective, I went to the bank early the next morning, before any of his employees showed up, and confronted him."

"And Hawthorne just handed over the photos?"

"Of course not. He didn't have them. But I got it out of him what he'd done—that he'd gone and run his mouth to that detective about rumors of Susan's affair. I got the guy's contact info before I left the bank. Then I stole. . . er, removed the camera and a few files from the guy's hotel room in Montrose."

"And where was the guy when you broke into his hotel room?"

"*I* didn't break into the guy's room. I'm not an idiot, Martin. I've got people for that."

Jack didn't want to know anything more about Buckley's *people*. "So you gave Cliff the photographs?"

Buckley nodded slowly. "We had the film in the camera developed. When I saw what they were, I went ballistic. I thought Cliff would, too, but I was wrong." He shook his head and looked sad. "Misstep on my part, I guess. But I thought he needed to know. *I* would have wanted to know. It could have wrecked his reelection. I never guessed that I would have been more concerned about it than Cliff was. Maybe he just needed time to think about it. Anyway, it tears me up knowing his wife's infidelity was the last thing I talked to him about. He was my friend."

Jack asked about Roberts's opponent in the upcoming election, but Buckley quickly dismissed the theory that he could have been behind the plane crash.

"The guy's a nutjob, an old hippie. Peace and love and all that. He's not behind this." Buckley seemed convinced, and Jack let the matter drop.

Maybe it wasn't the political opponent, but who *had* murdered the congressman?

Jack still had a slew of suspects.

The two men talked for a while longer, and Jack left the Baileys' house finally knowing why he'd been hired. Buckley's guilt over Roberts's death was palpable. He was struggling with the loss of his friend. But his struggle was with more than just guilt and grief. It was more complicated than that. Buckley was also wrestling with the dangerous combination of regret and anger.

Jack had watched him closely, studying his body language as he talked about Susan and about his argument with Cliff. Jack knew politicians were adept liars, but he was confident Buckley was finally telling the truth.

When Jack pulled out of Mountain Village onto the highway, he noticed the sun had dropped close to the horizon, casting Wilson Peak in a shadowy silhouette. The day was waning, and it had been a long one.

As he drove toward Telluride, he ran through the events in his head. The day had started with his visit with Hank Wade but had quickly gone downhill after Gerald Purvis had been run off the road. Jack resisted the urge to call Burns and find out how Susan Roberts had reacted to the news. He wanted to know why Purvis had been driving her car and where he'd been before the crash.

Jack remembered the familiar way Purvis had referred to her as "Suze." His thoughts turned to Susan and her affair with the mystery man Buckley had refused to reveal. Jack was confident it hadn't been the ex-governor but wondered why he felt the need to hide the man's identity. Had Susan been having an affair with Purvis, as Jack suspected? And what did it mean now that Purvis was dead?

How did Hawthorne figure into all of it? Why would he give information about Susan and Purvis to a detective hired by Cliff's political opponent?

There were a lot of questions Jack needed answered. But they would have to wait until the next day. He was exhausted and felt like he'd been hit by a Mack truck. He wanted to get back to the trailer and pull off his boots. Maybe sit awhile with Otto and listen to the river as the sun finished dropping below the horizon. And there was the Cormac McCarthy novel he was just getting into. Maybe he would read a few more chapters before bed.

Jack lifted a hand from the steering wheel and rubbed the tension from the back of his neck. What he really wanted was a night of sound sleep, the kind that had eluded him for days.

Things weren't going as planned. The case was a jumble of puzzle pieces that still didn't fit, and he was frustrated. He hoped talking to Tony the next day would help fit some of the pieces together.

The fire in Jack was lit. He was determined to find out who had killed Cliff Roberts and Gerald Purvis.

But first he wanted rest. Something in his gut told him he was going to need it.

CHAPTER 48

Monday, May 16

THE TRAILER WAS cold and dark. Jack pulled his cell phone from the floor and glanced at the time. Five thirty, exactly an hour since he'd last checked, and still too early to get up.

Crockett was asleep, curled at his feet. Jack had long ago given up trying to coax the dog to sleep on the floor and was surprised when he found he'd grown used to the warmth against his feet and that he now took some odd comfort in the dog's presence that he couldn't explain. Growing up, he never had a dog, and now he couldn't imagine life without one. But they needed a bigger bed.

Jack lay on his back, his hands clasped behind his head, and tried to fall back asleep. But after several minutes, he threw the blanket off and swung his feet to the floor. Sleep had evaded him all night. It was futile to keep trying.

Crockett lifted his head, yawned once, and laid it back down.

Jack pushed the window shade to one side and glanced at the mountains to the east. They were outlined in a faint pink hue. No one that he needed to talk to would be up yet. He let the shade drop and dragged his hands down his face, trying to come fully awake.

Jack was exhausted and running on adrenaline. And although it had been another sleepless night, he was anxious to start the day. There were people to see, questions that needed answering. And something in his gut—something he couldn't explain—told him the next twenty-four hours would be significant.

He switched on a light and grabbed a Red Bull from the mini fridge, then spread his notes on the table—everything he'd learned about the case. Which, so far, wasn't enough.

For the next hour and a half, he pored through the pages one by one, racking his brain, wondering what he was missing.

At seven, he gave up, stepped outside into the cold, pine-scented air, and drew in a deep breath, steeling himself for the day ahead.

The campground was quiet.

He glanced in the direction of the tent circle and noticed that only one tent remained. The activists were gone—at least, most of them were. He hadn't noticed the night before.

He wondered if Eric Dale was still in town. If he was smart, Jack thought, he'd be far from Telluride. But something about Dale made him believe he'd still be around. Jack intended to find out.

By seven thirty, Jack had showered and dressed and left Crockett with Otto. On his way to town, he took a different route through the campground, purposefully passing by the activists' campsite. The single tent was quiet, and Jack resisted the urge to check if anyone was inside.

He passed out of the campground, crossed Main Street, and headed uphill to town. As he pulled open the door to Pandora

Café, a woman up the street caught his eye, and he let the door close.

The woman was slim and pretty, with dark hair. She was wearing jeans and boots and a Navajo-patterned wool coat that looked like it could have come from Waggoner Mercantile. Jack watched as she stepped off the curb in front of Telluride Bank & Trust and walked toward a tan Tahoe. He recognized her instantly.

What was Lea Scotsman doing in Telluride? And why had she been at the bank hours before it opened?

Jack walked quickly in her direction. He was a block away but closing the distance fast.

As she reached for the door handle of the Tahoe, he called out, "Lea!" and quickened his pace.

She glanced briefly in his direction but opened the door and got in.

"Lea!" Jack called a second time, jogging toward her. He saw her pull the Tahoe from the curb, heading out of town.

Jack stood on the sidewalk with his hands on his hips and watched as she disappeared over the rise just past the courthouse. He was sure she had seen him, yet she had driven away. She was avoiding him. But why?

He turned in the direction of Pandora Café but stopped when he caught a glimpse of movement inside the bank. Hawthorne.

Breakfast could wait. It was time to finally meet the mysterious banker.

A brass plaque fixed to the outside of the building read: Site of Butch Cassidy's first bank robbery, June 24, 1889.

"Well, I'll be damned," Jack said aloud. He wiped his boots on the mat at the entrance, pulled open the door, and stepped inside.

"We're not open," a high-pitched male voice called from somewhere at the back of the bank.

Jack glanced around, taking note of the lack of security. There was no thick plexiglass separating the bank's inner sanctum from the lobby. No heavy doors with keypads to keep unwanted guests out of the interior offices; only a set of short swinging doors that looked like they had been pulled from a saloon.

Two cameras that looked decades old were mounted near the ceiling in different corners. One pointed down at the bank's entrance. The other covered the interior of the building, including a small teller's counter. An ornate walk-in vault, its double doors etched with elaborate scroll designs, appeared to be securely fastened shut—the only effective security Jack could see.

He scanned the architecture. The ceiling above the cameras was pressed-tin panels painted white to match the walls. Thick plaster molding that looked original to the building ran between the walls and ceiling. Jack couldn't imagine that much had changed since Butch Cassidy had robbed the place. Intrigued, he made a note to ask Judith and find out more.

Hawthorne appeared around a corner, wearing glasses and reading a set of papers. He pulled up when he realized he wasn't alone.

"I thought you left," he said. "I'm sorry, but the lobby doesn't open until ten. There's an ATM down the street at Chase." He stepped forward, saw Jack more clearly, and his eyes widened.

"I'm new in town," Jack said, "and I was thinking of opening an account."

Hawthorne stared at him a moment, unable to speak. Seeing Jack had him rattled.

"We're not open. But if you would like to come back later."

"Of course." Jack took a step closer. "I'll come back. But was that Lea Scotsman I just saw walking out of here?"

Hawthorne hesitated.

"I'm a friend of Lea's," Jack added, hoping to ease his tension and get him to talk.

He eyed Jack skeptically. "I know most of Lea's friends," he said. "But I don't know you." He stood erect with his chin up, squeezing out every quarter inch of height he could. It was a feeble attempt to gain the upper hand. Jack recognized the tactic immediately. It wasn't going to work.

"I've only been in town since January, but I met Lea a while back. And I swear, the woman I saw coming out of here a few minutes ago looked just like her."

Hawthorne stared at him for a while longer, then removed his glasses and rubbed the lenses with a cloth he'd pulled from his pocket. "I'm bound by fiduciary laws not to disclose the business of my customers."

Cleaning the glasses was a ploy to appear unfazed, but Jack knew the truth. Hawthorne was nervous. Was it the question about Lea Scotsman? Or was it Jack's presence that had him on edge? Jack wasn't sure, but he wanted to find out.

He changed the subject. "I understand from Lea that you were friends with Congressman Roberts."

Hawthorne looked up abruptly, and Jack saw his eyes twitch. He'd hit a nerve.

"It was a terrible thing about the crash," Jack continued, treading lightly. "I didn't know him, but I hear he was well liked in Telluride. It'll be a big loss for the community."

"It will."

"I understand y'all grew up together."

"We did." He spoke almost robotically; his words were short and clipped.

"Then his death must be a big loss for you, too," Jack said. "I'm sorry."

Hawthorne simply nodded. He was a hard one to crack.

Jack cleared his throat. "Being an old friend, I guess Cliff banked here."

Hawthorne's eyes narrowed. "Did Buckley send you?"

The question surprised Jack. He knew immediately their conversation had hit a dead end and fished for a response.

"Buckley?"

Damn. It was all he could come up with. He knew the banker would never believe that he didn't know who Buckley Bailey was.

"Buckley...Bailey," Hawthorne replied, his face growing hard. He was posturing, trying to play the tough guy, which was an admirable feat at 140 pounds or so.

For several minutes, Jack tried making small talk, asking questions about the bank and its history. But it was no use. Hawthorne's answers were short and spoken in a tense, high-pitched voice. And no matter what Jack tried, he wasn't going to talk.

The skinny man swelled with self-importance, but Jack knew the truth. The rapid rise and fall of his chest gave him away. Under his tough-guy veneer, Ted Hawthorne was scared. But scared of what?

Jack thanked him for his time. "I'd still like to open that account," he said, reaching for the door. "I'll come back when you're open."

He stepped outside and heard Hawthorne lock the door behind him. Jack turned and saw him scurry behind the teller counter and pick up a phone. Jack stepped to the side, out of Hawthorne's view, then peered around the corner through the window and watched.

Hawthorne gestured wildly as he talked. Something about Jack's visit had the banker in a panic.

Two women in hiking clothes and carrying walking sticks passed Jack on the sidewalk and turned and looked back at him.

He glanced at the brass plaque that told of Butch Cassidy's robbery and realized how suspicious he must look staring through the window of the bank. Jack cleared his throat and nodded at the women, then turned and started up the sidewalk in the opposite direction.

He was frustrated. The visit to Hawthorne had raised more questions than it had answered. He still didn't know what Lea was doing at the bank that morning. Or why she had avoided him.

He also didn't know why Hawthorne was reluctant to talk about Cliff Roberts. Was it because he'd talked to the detective hired by Cliff's political opponent? Jack figured it was.

He thought about the photograph from the fundraiser, then the ones of Susan and her mystery man that Buckley had given to Cliff.

He stopped and glanced back at the bank. Roberts might have thought Hawthorne was his friend, but Jack knew that he wasn't.

Ted Hawthorne was obviously holding a grudge. But was he guilty of murder?

CHAPTER 49

IN CASE THE women who had seen him staring into the bank were still watching, Jack walked half a block in the opposite direction before he doubled back. They had been heading in the direction he wanted to go—toward Pandora Café. And Jack was hungry.

As he passed Telluride Bank & Trust, he glanced through the window and saw Hawthorne still on the phone. Jack saw him slam the receiver down and turn toward the back of the building and wondered who the nervous banker had called. Had it been Lea? Or Buckley? Maybe the detective Hawthorne had put on Susan Roberts's tail?

Jack curled his hands into fists as he walked. It was another piece of the puzzle that didn't fit.

He stopped at an intersection, waved a truck past, then stepped off the curb. He glanced across Main Street and noticed Eric Dale standing on the far corner, watching him. Dale was leaned up against the brick wall and looked as if he'd been there awhile. Jack wondered how long.

Jack held up a hand. "Dale!" He had a few questions for the activist.

But Dale turned and headed quickly in the opposite direction.

Jack was tempted to run after him but stood in the middle of the street and watched him go. What was going on? First Lea, now Eric Dale. Why was everyone suddenly avoiding him?

CHAPTER 50

JACK PULLED OPEN the door to Pandora Café and stepped inside. He stood a moment, letting his eyes adjust, and was disappointed when he saw that his usual table next to the rock fireplace was already taken.

A stout man with a broad back sat facing the rear of the café. His shirt was stretched taut between his shoulders; he was hunched over the table, eating.

Jack walked toward him, the plank floor creaking with each step, and cuffed the man on the shoulder. "Mind if I join you?"

Tony Burns looked up, startled. "Shit, Martin. It's a wonder I didn't choke on my eggs." Jack pointed to the chair across the table, and Tony nodded. "Have a seat."

Jack dropped into the chair—his usual.

"How's it going this morning?" Tony asked and shoveled another bite of egg into his mouth.

"Except for suddenly being *persona non grata*, it's going swell."

Tony frowned. "What do you mean?"

"It's nothing," Jack said and cleared his throat. There was no sense in beating around the bush. "Did Susan Roberts have anything interesting to say yesterday when you told her about Purvis?"

Tony was raising a slice of bacon but stopped and narrowed his eyes, giving Jack the same look he would a petulant child. Tony took a bite of bacon and chewed, making Jack wait. When he was finished, he pulled a napkin from his lap and wiped his mouth, then glanced around the café. The early-morning crowd was still light.

He leaned across the table and dropped his voice. "You're out of line asking me about an ongoing investigation." He took another bite of bacon and frowned at Jack while he chewed, considering the question. "All right," he said, wiping his mouth with a napkin. "But I don't have to remind you that anything I tell you is confidential."

"You never do."

"Purvis borrowed her car to go to Montrose. He was supposedly meeting someone from the governor's office about being appointed to Cliff's vacant seat."

"Have you contacted the governor's office to confirm it?"

"We did. There was no meeting. Purvis was on his way back to Telluride, but we have no idea where he'd been before the crash."

Jack thought about it for a moment. Either Purvis had lied to Susan about where he was going and why he needed her car, or Susan was the one lying.

"Do you believe her story?" Jack asked.

"Susan's?" Tony pursed his lips, taking a moment to think about it. "I do. She seemed genuinely upset when I told her Purvis was dead."

"Did you tell her there wasn't a meeting?" Jack was curious to know how she had reacted when confronted with the truth.

"Not yet. But I plan to."

Jack wanted to be there when Tony told her that Purvis's meeting was a lie. "Can I—"

"No, you can't. I'll talk to her alone."

It wasn't an argument Jack was going to win, so he let the subject drop. "Any updates from the feds on the crash?"

"They found more bomb components, including a timer. It was simple. The device seems to have been crude but effective."

"Not the work of a pro," Jack said, thinking aloud.

Tony finished his eggs. "Doesn't appear so."

Judith lifted Tony's empty plate from the table. "Morning, Jack. What can I get you?"

After she had taken his order and left, Jack turned back to Tony. "There's something I need to tell you."

Tony leaned back in his chair. "Is this something I'm going to regret hearing?"

Jack suspected it probably was. "I talked to the kid from the airport."

"What kid?"

"The kid who put the package on Roberts's plane."

"Ah, hell, Martin." Tony let out a hissing breath. "Ronnie Bugler?"

"Yes." Jack gave him a moment. "Do you have a problem with that?"

"Would it matter if I did?"

"No."

"Then I don't have a problem with it." Tony sighed. "What'd he say?"

"He told me the same thing he told you guys. That a man he couldn't identify gave him a hundred bucks to put the package on the plane."

Tony waited for more information, then eyed him skeptically. "That's it?"

Jack wasn't ready to disclose the argument between Buckley and Cliff. He shrugged. "That's it. I just wanted you to know. In case you heard."

Tony stared at him, then crumpled his napkin and laid it on the table. "All right, Martin," he said, standing up. "If you say so." He took several bills from his wallet and set them next to the napkin.

Jack's phone vibrated from a text, and he pulled it from his pocket.

"I'll see you." Tony started to leave.

"Tony," Jack said, staring at the text.

"Yeah, what is it?"

"You mentioned Last Dollar Road once?"

"Yeah?"

"Where is it?"

"Outside of town, above the airport. It's a dirt road between here and Ridgway. Why?"

"I got a text to meet someone there. It says to take Last Dollar Road six miles out of town."

Tony frowned. "That would be in the middle of nowhere— well *past* the airport. Who wants to meet you out there?"

"It doesn't say." Jack handed the phone to him so he could read it.

I have the information you're looking for. Take Last Dollar Road off 145. Go six miles. I'll be waiting. Come alone.

Tony handed back the phone. "I don't like it."

"It could be about the plane crash," Jack said. "Maybe it's about Purvis."

"You're not actually considering going, are you?" He looked at Jack like he was crazy. "You have no idea who this is."

"If I don't go, we'll never find out."

"Let me ask you something," Tony said, sitting back down. "How many people in town know you've been asking about Cliff?"

Jack watched Judith refill coffee for a local. The guy said something that made her laugh. Jack was sure the guy then glanced in his direction. Or was he being paranoid?

"How many people know, Jack?" Tony repeated.

Faces flashed through Jack's mind: Lea Scotsman... Eric Dale... Ted Hawthorne... Susan Roberts... and Buckley Bailey. There was also Hank Wade, Candy and Ronnie Bugler, Elizabeth Mayweather, and Turner Biggs, Elizabeth's hiking guide.

He looked at Tony. "I'm not sure."

Tony shook his head. "I don't like it," he said again.

Jack didn't either.

CHAPTER 51

LAST DOLLAR ROAD was exactly as Tony had described it. The first few miles were paved and wound through a high-alpine meadow dotted with houses and a few barns. Not far past the airport, the asphalt ended and the road narrowed to a single gravel lane that made its way into the mountains.

Jack checked the odometer. When he reached the six-mile mark, he pulled the truck to the side of the road, killed the engine, and got out. It was quiet—too quiet. For the first time since he'd left Pandora Café, he was having second thoughts and wondered if he should have taken Tony's advice and not come.

It was a risky move meeting the sender of an anonymous text in the middle of nowhere. Jack didn't know who he was waiting for. Was it a man? A woman? Was it a Good Samaritan who knew Jack was investigating Roberts's murder and wanted to help? Someone who didn't want to be seen talking to him in town? Or was Jack waiting for Cliff's killer?

Tall, leafless aspens lined both sides of the road, their long, spindly branches swaying in the morning breeze like eerie skeletons. Last Dollar Road was remote. Jack hadn't seen a house—or even a car—for several miles.

He leaned against the driver's-side door and pretended to set his hands on his hips but reached around with his thumb and felt the steely comfort of the 9mm tucked in his waistband. He had grabbed the pistol when he'd gone back to the campground for his truck. Although curiosity about the anonymous text burned inside him, he wasn't stupid.

He leaned against the truck for several more minutes, then checked his watch. Whoever had sent the text was making him wait.

Two crows squawked loudly overhead, as if mocking him for his foolishness. Jack shielded his eyes from the sun and watched them light on a tall pine in the distance. He dropped his hand and looked down the road in both directions. He was growing impatient.

He kicked at the road with the toe of a boot, then shook off the dirt and rechecked his surroundings. The crows had gone, and it was quiet. He listened for the rustle of wildlife in the forest, knowing that elk, deer, bear, and even an occasional mountain lion lived in the woods around him. He heard nothing.

Ten minutes passed, and Jack started to think he was being stood up. Someone was playing a practical joke—or had wanted to waste his time by sending him on a wild-goose chase.

Jack pushed off the truck and took several steps into the road, the sun bearing down on him.

He turned again to look for a car and heard the shot a fraction of a second after he felt the impact. He went down, and the silent forest around him fell dark.

CHAPTER 52

TONY BURNS RUSHED to where Jack lay motionless on the gravel road. As he ran, he searched the surrounding mountains, expecting more gunfire. His adrenaline was racing.

When the two had parted ways outside the café, Tony hadn't told Jack that he had every intention of following him. The anonymous text had him smelling a rat.

Jack was lying faceup with his legs stretched out at odd angles. His eyes were closed.

Tony stole glances over each shoulder as he drew closer, then looked in the direction of the gun blast, searching for movement. But the mix of aspen and pines was thick between the road and the ledge above. There were a million places for someone to hide.

He crouched next to Jack and grabbed his wrist, feeling for a pulse. Then touched the mic attached to his shirt lapel and radioed dispatch. "We need an ambulance! Last Dollar Road. Six miles northwest of 145. Shots fired. Man down!"

Tony looked again in the direction of the shot, a rocky ridge in the distance, perched above the road. He saw Deputy O'Connor scrambling over rock, as nimble as a deer, taking cover behind trees and boulders as she made her way to the ridge.

He turned his attention back to Jack and looked for blood, relieved when he didn't see any.

"Martin," he said, putting gentle pressure on Jack's shoulder. "Martin, can you hear me?"

Jack coughed once and groaned. His eyes were screwed shut with pain. He tried rolling to one side, but Tony held him in place.

"Hold still, buddy," Tony told him. "Ambulance is on the way."

Jack groaned again. "What happened?"

"You were shot."

Tony ripped open Jack's shirt, sending the buttons flying, then laid his fingers on the black woven fibers that covered the Kevlar vest. He took in a deep breath and let it out slowly, trying to calm his nerves. He'd never seen a man shot before.

Jack coughed, then groaned again. "It hurts."

"Stay still."

Tony looked toward the ridge. Kim was getting closer. It had been a clean shot from around 150 yards out. The shooter was someone who knew what they were doing. Tony squinted, searching the woods again, but still didn't see anyone.

Kim had reached the ridge and was walking slowly, studying the ground. Finding useful footprints in all the rock would be nearly impossible. She would be hunting for a spent shell casing or some other clue.

Tony glanced down the road in the direction of town but knew it was too early for the ambulance. He looked again at Jack, who appeared to have passed out. The wait was excruciating.

He watched Kim search for several more minutes. He saw her pull something white from her pocket and shake it, then bend to pick something up.

There was a distant wail of a siren. The ambulance.

"I found something, Sheriff," Kim radioed from the bluff. "Looks like a Remington Ultra Magnum. One hundred eighty grain."

Tony whistled through his teeth. "Enough to take down the largest bull elk in the area," he radioed back. "Lucky he turned just as the guy squeezed off the shot and it deflected off the vest. He'd be dead if he hadn't."

Several minutes later Kim came stumbling out of the forest holding a rifle cartridge. "Is he all right?" she asked, staring down at Jack.

"I'm fine," Jack moaned. He started to roll to the side, but Tony held him down again.

"They're almost here, Martin. Hold on a minute."

The siren had grown closer.

Jack pushed Tony's hand off his shoulder and rolled to sit, clutching his side and groaning in agony as he did so. "I said I'm fine."

He didn't look it. His face was contorted with pain.

Kim handed Tony a handkerchief. "The cartridge is inside. You think somebody could have been hunting?"

"And hit Martin by mistake?" Tony finished for her. "I don't think so." He rolled the cartridge over in the handkerchief to look at it. "The shot was intentional."

Jack had struggled to stand and was squinting at the spent shell, still holding his side. "This wasn't a hunting accident." His voice was tight with pain. "Someone wants me dead."

CHAPTER 53

JACK'S BODY ACHED. The ambulance ride to the medical center had been excruciating. Each bump in the road sent a shock wave of agony pulsing through him. The pain on his left side made it difficult to breathe.

He was grateful he wasn't dead. If Tony hadn't insisted he wear a bulletproof vest, he would have been. Another mistake, Jack thought. He'd been running on adrenaline, not thinking straight, too wrapped up in his obsession with figuring out what had happened to the late congressman, a man he had never met. But now the shooter had made it personal. Jack was madder than hell.

At the medical center, the medics unloaded Jack from the ambulance and instructed him to remain on the gurney. But he felt ridiculous.

"I'm fine," Jack insisted, his jaws tense with pain that he struggled to conceal. "I can walk."

The medic in charge started to protest, but Jack interrupted. He thanked him and then walked himself into the hospital. The staff knew he was coming and met him at the door. A pretty young nurse pushed a wheelchair quickly toward him, but Jack waved her off.

"Just point me to where I'm supposed to go."

She looked flustered but rolled the wheelchair aside. "Follow me," she said, pushing open a swinging door.

Jack followed. He hated hospitals, hated anything to do with pain and suffering and death. The sooner he could get checked and cleared and get out of there, the better.

It still baffled him that he was there in the first place. He didn't know Cliff Roberts—wasn't sure if he'd even *heard* of the congressman before the plane crash. The former governor of Texas was paying him to find out what had happened. But Jack didn't know Buckley either—not really. Somehow, Jack had found himself in the familiar predicament of obsessing over someone else's bad guy.

Jack knew he should let the case go. People were murdered every day. What difference did it make to him that Roberts— and now Gerald Purvis—was dead? He had never known Cliff and had met Purvis only once. Their deaths shouldn't matter to him.

But they did.

Jack twisted on the exam table, trying to get comfortable, his left side aching like he'd been hit with a sledgehammer. If he could just get someone to prescribe him a few painkillers, he could get out of there and be on his way.

A half hour later, he'd been poked and prodded, x-rayed, and scolded for not following instructions. He was ordered back to the exam room and waited impatiently for the doctor who had first examined him, and reminded him of Annie Wilkes, the creepy character in the movie *Misery*, to return and release him.

There were voices in the hallway. Someone was arguing. Jack heard panting and clicking on the linoleum floor. As the voices grew closer, he recognized one of them.

The exam room door swung open.

"Otto?" Jack said, surprised.

Crockett bound from behind the old man and threw his front paws up on Jack's lap, his tail wagging furiously.

The young nurse followed behind, clearly agitated. "I'm sorry, sir. But we can't allow visitors... or dogs—"

Otto leaned on his cane and waved his free hand at her. "You're a pretty little thing, and I'm sure my friend appreciates your concern. But I bet he feels better just by the sight of us. Ain't that right, Jack?" Otto turned his crusty old face in Jack's direction and rolled his eyes.

Jack looked at the frazzled nurse. "It's all right. I'd like them to stay."

Otto nodded triumphantly.

The nurse stared at Jack a moment, then glanced at Otto, then Crockett, clearly unsure of what to do next.

"He said it's all right," Otto told her, shooing her out of the room with his free hand.

She scowled at him, then turned and left.

Jack waited for the door to close. "What are you doing here?"

"Heard on the scanner that someone was shot up on Last Dollar." Otto pulled a plastic chair from the wall and lowered himself into it. "I bet beers to doughnuts it was you. So here we are."

"What made you think it was me?"

"There ain't no one else in town worth shootin'." His crystal-blue eyes sparkled mischievously.

Jack smiled, still petting Crockett. "Thank you."

Otto nodded. He switched his cane from one hand to the other, trying to get comfortable in the chair.

"Did you walk?" Jack asked him.

"We did."

The medical center was on the opposite side of town—and uphill from the campground. Jack felt a twinge of guilt over the struggle the trip must have been for him—especially bringing Crockett.

"You didn't have to come."

"Well, of course I did," Otto said. "It ain't every day your best friend gets shot."

Jack felt a lump form in his throat.

The exam room door swung open, and a battleship of a doctor stepped inside. She pulled up when she saw Crockett. "I'm sorry, we don't allow dogs—"

Otto heaved a great sigh, interrupting her. "We've been told. Come here, Crockett. Sit."

The dog immediately went to Otto's side and sat with his back against the wall. The old man laid a hand on his head and looked up at the doctor. "Happy now?" he asked, a smug tilt curling the corners of his mouth. "We'll both be on our best behavior, Doc. Promise."

Jack suppressed a laugh. "What'd you find out?" he asked her, changing the subject and trying to head off further confrontation between the old man and Dr. Annie Wilkes.

The doctor raised an arched brow at Otto, clearly not happy, then looked at Jack. "You've got two cracked ribs," she said unapologetically.

She turned her back to them and began furiously stabbing at a keyboard set on a countertop. An x-ray image appeared on a monitor mounted on the wall above the counter.

"Here and here," she said, pointing to two spots on the screen with a pen. "You're lucky it's not worse. There's not much we can do except wrap the ribs and give you something for the pain. I'll have it called in to the pharmacy." She clicked her pen shut and left.

"A real peach, that one. Ain't she?" Otto remarked.

A half hour later, Jack had been released, and the trio was outside on the sidewalk. Jack walked slowly, letting Otto set the pace on their way back to the campground.

"What in the blazes were you doin' way out on Last Dollar Road?"

Jack told him about the anonymous text.

"Sounds like you made the wrong person angry, son," Otto said.

Jack agreed with him. The bevy of familiar faces ran through his mind again: Buckley Bailey, Susan Roberts, Lea Scotsman, Ted Hawthorne, and Eric Dale. Hank Wade, Elizabeth Mayweather, and Turner Biggs, the hiking guide.

Jack suspected that one of them didn't like him poking around asking questions about Cliff's murder and had wanted to put a stop to it... permanently.

But which one?

CHAPTER 54

AFTER FIFTEEN MINUTES, the trio had made it as far as the courthouse—almost halfway to the campground. Jack's side ached. He walked slowly, grateful for Otto's slow pace. Crockett lumbered between them.

As they walked, Otto spoke of summers past spent high above town. Jack was intrigued by the old man's secret mine. But no matter how hard he tried, Otto still refused to divulge the mine's location.

"Many a prospector has lost a fortune braggin' about their claim," Otto said, shaking his head. "Sorry, Jack, but I can't do it. John Fallon made that mistake once, but I won't."

"Is John Fallon a friend of yours?"

Otto chuckled. "I might be old, but I ain't that old. John Fallon was the first one to discover gold in these parts." He stopped walking and pointed his cane to a spot high above town. "Up there." He started walking again. "Found it in 1875. Enough gold to have made him one of the richest men in the world, but he couldn't keep it to himself, had to go running his mouth. Next thing he knows, prospectors were rushin' here from all over the world. Finland's where my folk came from."

Jack doubted what little gold or silver Otto found in his mine would set off a second global rush to Telluride, but he decided to keep the opinion to himself.

"When are you leaving?" Jack asked.

"Soon. A bit more snowmelt and I'll be on my way."

Jack couldn't imagine how the old man managed the steep slopes of the San Juans—especially alone. But the sparkle in Otto's eyes suggested he came alive when he was in the mountains digging for gold.

A white Tahoe pulled up beside them.

"Martin!" It was Tony Burns. "I've been looking for you."

Jack realized he hadn't turned his cell phone back on after leaving the medical center. "Well, you found me," he said.

"Y'all get in. I'll give you a ride. Where you headed?"

"To the campground." Jack opened the front passenger door for Otto and helped him in. When he opened the door behind, Crockett hopped in the back.

"I went by the med center looking for you. You got released quick. I figured you'd be there at least overnight."

"I think they were ready for us to leave."

Tony turned in his seat and looked over the two men and the dog. "I can see why," he said. "But seriously, you look good— too good for a man who was shot a few hours ago."

"I'll take that as a compliment."

Tony checked for traffic, then pulled away from the curb. "My guys picked up Eric Dale again. He's denying any involvement in shooting you."

"And you believe him?"

"I talked to him myself this time, but I don't know yet. There was more to his story than what we expected."

"Like what?"

"When I asked him where he was around the time Gerald Purvis was run off the road, he claimed to have been stuck on Last Dollar Road with a flat tire."

"Last Dollar?" Jack repeated, not buying it. It was too coincidental.

"That was my thought exactly," Tony replied. "We had him take us to where he claimed to have had it, and would you believe it wasn't ten yards from where you were shot. We ended up finding an oil spot on the road. Sure enough, when we checked, Dale's truck was leaking like a sieve."

"So he *had* been there?" Jack asked.

"At some point. It appears so. Anyway, when we checked his truck, we found a rifle and several boxes of ammunition."

"Remingtons?" Jack asked, remembering the cartridge Kim O'Connor had found at the scene.

"Nope," Tony said. "Winchesters—cheap ones. And they were the wrong caliber."

Tony pulled off Main Street into the campground and wound his way through the trees. He stopped in front of Otto's tent, and they all got out.

"Thank you for the ride, Sheriff," Otto said, shuffling toward the picnic table with Crockett close on his heels.

Jack turned in the direction of the lone tent still left at the activists' campsite. It was quiet. "It looks like most of the Wilderness Keeper folks have left. But Dale's still here," Jack said, wondering why Dale was still in town.

"I asked him about that. He said with Cliff dead, most of his *associates* had moved on. He told us that after Cliff died, a lot of the money they were getting dried up."

"Money from where?"

"That's the million-dollar question."

"Did he say why he was sticking around?"

Tony nodded. "He said that, as much as he knew I'd like for him to pack up and get out of here, until Hank Wade's land deal with the government was dead, he wasn't going anywhere."

Jack thought about it for a moment. During his time at the bureau, he'd had plenty of experience dealing with activists of all kinds. Left, right, it didn't matter. In almost every instance, the devout commingled with the opportunists. He suspected Dale was a member of the former.

"Well, you gotta give the guy credit for holding to his principles."

Tony harrumphed. "If you say so."

Although Jack admired Eric Dale's conviction, he still thought there was a good chance Dale was a killer.

CHAPTER 55

JACK WATCHED THE Tahoe disappear through the trees and realized he hadn't thanked Tony for insisting he wear the Kevlar vest. After Jack had gotten the text at Pandora Café, Tony had been relentless. First imploring Jack not to meet whoever it was that had sent it. "It could be anybody," Tony had said. "We've already had two murders in the county in less than a week. And if they want to commit a third, Last Dollar Road would be a good place to do it."

But Jack wouldn't relent; his curiosity had gotten the best of him. He was determined to find out who had sent the text and why. When it was obvious he wasn't going to back down, Tony had insisted on the Kevlar vest. Thank God he had.

And it wasn't just the vest. Jack had had no idea Tony and Deputy O'Connor were going to follow him. When Jack woke up lying in the road, he was surprised to find the sheriff at his side and was too embarrassed to admit he never knew they were there. He had been listening for an approaching car or truck, waiting to see who'd sent the text, and somehow never heard Tony or Kim. They were both stellar examples of law enforcement officers, and Jack was glad they'd had his back. But dammit, he should have thanked Tony.

He pulled his cell phone from his pocket just as it buzzed from an incoming call.

Archie Rochambeau.

Jack hoped he was calling to say who was behind the Caymans account. He wanted to know who Hank Wade had bribed.

"Jack!" Archie boomed when Jack answered the call.

"Hey, Arch. What do you have for me?"

"I've got an ATM machine that's addicted to money. It's suffering from withdrawals."

"Arch..."

"Yeah, yeah, I know. All business with you sometimes. I get it." There was no animosity in his voice, just disappointment.

Jack made a mental note to google bad financial jokes and find one for him the next time he called. The last thing he wanted was to alienate the best friend he had left in the bureau. Plus, Jack genuinely liked Archibald Rochambeau.

"Sorry I didn't call you yesterday," Archie began. "Got tied up on some legitimate work I'm actually being paid to do."

"Not a problem. What'd you find?"

"Frankly, I'm stumped, buddy. I've dug and dug and can't find out who's behind the Bridal Veil account, but I'm still working on it."

"Did you check the list of names I sent you?"

"I checked every blasted one—congressman and congress-*woman*. I can't find a single connection to the account. But that's not to say there isn't one. Like I said, I'll keep checking."

"All right, thanks."

"I *was* able to run a quick check on that bank there—Telluride Bank & Trust. I rechecked the dead congressman's accounts, but there still doesn't appear to have been any funny business going on. But there *was* a substantial withdrawal made on *another* account just this morning. It's probably nothing, but compared to the bank's normal daily activity, it definitely caught my attention."

Jack knew that loads of wealthy residents banked at Telluride Bank & Trust. He didn't hold out hope that a single withdrawal would mean much, but if it caught Archie's attention, he was curious what it was.

"How much was the withdrawal?" Jack asked.

"Half a mil."

Jack whistled. It *was* a significant amount. He thought of the wealthy people he knew in town. The amount would be too much for a luxury car and yet too little for even a small condominium in town. It had him curious, and he wondered which of his suspects banked with Ted Hawthorne. It could prove enlightening if the withdrawal had come from an account registered to Buckley Bailey, or maybe even Hawthorne himself.

"Do you have a name?" Jack asked.

"I do. Hold on." There was a rustling of paper on the other end. "Here it is. The withdrawal was made from the account of one Althea Scotsman."

"Althea?" Jack repeated. Then it dawned on him.

Lea.

She had been at the bank early that morning before it had opened. And she had avoided Jack when he'd called out to her.

What was she up to?

CHAPTER 56

Tuesday, May 17

JACK WAS ON the road early the next morning. The pink daylight spilling over the far end of the canyon promised it would be another beautiful day. But despite taking the pain medication, his side still ached, and he hoped the new day would be less eventful than the one before.

He drove slowly through Telluride, watching sleepy locals head to work and a couple of ambitious hikers already making for the mountains. It reminded him of Turner Biggs, Elizabeth Mayweather's guide. Biggs had called Jack the previous night and scheduled their upcoming hike. He told Jack he was busy but that he would block out the upcoming Thursday, and to plan on spending the entire day in the mountains.

Thursday was only two days away, but Jack was impatient. He wanted to know what Cliff had done the day before he died and had a feeling it would help solve the case.

In the meantime, there were plenty of other leads to follow. He wanted to talk to Lea. Earlier, he had started to call her but reconsidered. If he could catch her off guard, show up unannounced, he knew he'd have a better chance of getting the truth out of her. He wanted to know why she had withdrawn half a million dollars from her account. And why, when she saw Jack, she had avoided him.

As Jack passed Telluride Bank & Trust, he saw the door swing open and the activist Eric Dale step out. Ted Hawthorne locked the door behind him.

Jack slammed on his brakes and wound down the truck window. "Dale!"

But he was already running.

Jack watched in the rearview mirror as Dale ran in the opposite direction, then disappeared around a corner. He was holding something that looked like an envelope.

Jack glanced back at the bank and saw Hawthorne watching him through the window. When their eyes met, the nervous banker immediately turned and disappeared inside.

You're not exactly winning friends and influencing people, Martin, Jack told himself, referring to a self-help book he'd read years earlier in college.

He decided to let Dale go. He would find him later and catch him by surprise. And if he couldn't find Dale, there was always another option. He could sit on a bench across the street from the bank, watching who came and went.

Strange things were going on at Telluride Bank & Trust.

CHAPTER 57

AN HOUR LATER, Jack pulled to the front of Lea Scotsman's lodge and killed the engine. He spent a few moments looking up at the impressive log structure, wondering what secrets might be hidden within.

He laid a hand on the bandage still wrapping his chest and felt the dull ache of his cracked ribs. The last time he had visited Lea, her ranch foreman, Percy Ferguson, had been carrying a rifle. Jack reached over and took his 9mm from the glove box, tucked it in his waistband, and pulled his shirt down over it. Better safe than sorry.

He took the steps to the porch and, when he reached the door, was surprised to see Lea already standing at the threshold.

"What are you doing way out here?" she asked. She sounded surprised rather than annoyed. After she had avoided him the morning before, Jack was expecting the latter. She pushed open the screen door. "I heard you were shot."

"Word travels fast," he said, bringing a hand to where his ribs were wrapped.

She looked him up and down. "You look all right."

He nodded. "I am. Just a little sore."

"Come inside," she said, holding the door open wider. "Coffee?"

"That sounds great."

They made their way to the kitchen, where there was already a pot percolating on the stove. The aromas of coffee and bacon were strong.

Lea pulled a cup from a cabinet and filled it, keeping her back to him. There was an uneasy tension in the room. She was nervous, and Jack wanted to know why.

"Have a seat," she said, forcing a smile and gesturing to the long table. She carried his coffee and set it down in front of him.

When her back was turned, Jack quickly scanned the room as he settled into the chair. There was no sign of Percy. Or the rifle.

He studied her as he blew over the coffee and took a sip. She was fidgeting with a button on her flannel shirt, avoiding eye contact.

"Coffee's good," Jack said, wanting to ease into conversation.

"Thank you."

It didn't work. An awkward silence lasted several seconds. Jack knew getting information out of her wasn't going to be easy, but he had to try. He liked Lea—liked her a lot—but she was keeping secrets from him. She lifted her cup to her lips.

"I saw you leaving the bank in Telluride yesterday morning," Jack said, raising his cup for another drink and watching her closely.

Lea blinked several times as she swallowed, then set the cup down. "I didn't see you," she said, blinking again. She was lying.

"I called out to you. But I guess you didn't hear me."

The look of confusion on her face was forced, and Jack wasn't buying it.

"I'm sorry. I must have been in a daze."

"It *was* still early," Jack said, throwing her a bone.

"Yes, it was."

He wanted to keep her talking. "Do you bank with Ted Hawthorne?"

She looked surprised that Jack knew his name. "I do. My family has banked there for generations."

"You were there early yesterday—before it opened. That's some impressive customer service."

"Ted's an old friend of mine."

"So you get to do business *outside* traditional bankers' hours," Jack said. "It must be nice."

He saw her eyes harden. She was suspicious.

"Like I said, Ted is an old friend."

Jack had to tread lightly. He didn't want her to stop talking. But there was no easy way to ask what he wanted to know, so he got right to the point. "It's none of my business, but I'm curious why you were there so early. What business won't wait until the place opens?"

"You're right," she said. "It's none of your business."

There were several more seconds of awkward silence.

Jack cleared his throat. "I'm sorry for prying. But in my defense, butting into other people's business and asking inappropriate questions *is* what I do for a living." He watched for a reaction.

Lea stared at him. Jack was sure she was about to ask him to leave when the hint of a smile curled the corners of her mouth.

"Being a detective can't be easy." Her demeanor had relaxed.

"It's not that bad."

"You're being modest," she said. "I've read all about you. The consensus is you're a brilliant investigator." She raised her cup again, watching him. She was turning the tables, and it worked. Jack felt himself blush.

"I've been lucky."

"From what I've read, it doesn't sound like luck has had any-thing to do with it." She stopped talking long enough to drain the last of her coffee. "How is your investigation into Cliff's murder going?"

"Slow."

She nodded, then dropped her gaze to her hands and twisted the coffee cup in circles. "He was one of the good guys."

"So I hear."

She looked up. "Did you ever meet him?"

Jack shook his head.

"Then why are you doing this?"

"Doing what?"

"Trying to find out what happened. I mean, I know you're being paid by someone, but it seems like this means more than money for you. Why are you doing it? And after being shot."

Jack thought about it, trying to find an answer. He still wasn't sure himself. After a few seconds, he answered, "It's what I do."

The back door swung open, surprising them both.

Lea laughed. "Percy, you scared us half to death."

Percy Ferguson stood just inside the doorway, holding a rifle and frowning. "I hope I haven't interrupted anything."

Lea got up from the table. "Of course not. Come in. I'll get you a cup of coffee."

"Percy," Jack said, nodding.

Percy studied him a moment, then must have decided there was nothing to worry about. "Howdy, Jack." He propped the rifle against a kitchen cabinet and pulled out a chair. "I heard you were shot yesterday."

Jack kept himself from glancing at the rifle. "I was. But I was wearing a vest."

"And you're walking around already?" Percy asked. Lea set a cup of coffee down in front of him. "Thank you, Lea. I should have gotten that myself."

"Not while you're healing that ankle," she replied.

Jack glanced under the table. Now that she mentioned it, he had noticed an almost imperceptible limp. "What happened?"

Percy shook his head as if the question wasn't worth answering.

"Rolled his ankle yesterday," Lea answered for him.

"Stepped on a rock when I wasn't looking," Percy finished. Jack thought he detected a flush of embarrassment. "One of the pitfalls of gettin' old."

"You're not old," Lea said, sitting back down at the table.

Jack took the opportunity to change the subject. "That's a nice rifle you got there," he said, standing up and lifting the firearm from the floor. He opened the bolt and ejected a cartridge from the chamber and examined it, turning it over in his hand. It was a Winchester, not a Remington. And a smaller caliber than what he'd been shot with.

Percy eyed him suspiciously. "Thank you," he said slowly. "You a huntin' man?"

Jack replaced the cartridge and set the rifle carefully back on the floor. "When I have to be."

Lea turned to Percy. "Forget checking Angel's Pasture today with that ankle. I'll do it." Percy started to protest, but she continued. "Jack can go with me." She glanced at him. "Unless you're busy."

Jack *was* busy. He wanted to find Eric Dale, figure out why the guy kept running from him. Was it because he was surprised to see Jack still alive? Tony Burns had already questioned Dale about his whereabouts when Gerald Purvis was run off the road and when Jack was shot, but he wanted a chance to interrogate Dale himself.

He also wanted to talk to Ted Hawthorne again. Hawthorne had refused to reveal why Lea had been at the bank before it opened, but Jack wanted to try again. And this time, he would also ask the banker about Dale. Lea Scotsman had plenty of money and probably a sizable account with the bank, but what was Dale doing there? Jack doubted the activist was one of Hawthorne's regular customers.

There were other things Jack needed to do and people he wanted to talk to. And he'd left Crockett with Otto again. He needed to wrap up his visit with Lea and head back to Telluride.

"Well, Jack," she said, "want to come with me to Angel's Pasture?" She had locked on to him with her hazel eyes.

Jack couldn't help himself. "I'd love to."

CHAPTER 58

THE DAY HAD been one of the best Jack could remember. He went over it again as he drove back to Telluride.

After Percy left, Lea had packed them a picnic lunch of turkey sandwiches and fruit. She filled a large thermos with water, more than Jack felt would be necessary. But it had been a clue he later realized he'd missed that indicated how long they would be gone. He had expected a quick trip to Angel's Pasture, then lunch and a return trip to the lodge. He had been wrong.

Lea had insisted on taking her Jeep Wrangler, and it didn't take Jack long to figure out why. They spent the first hour climbing a washed-out, rutted road high into the mountains. On two occasions, Jack had to jump out and move boulders that had slid down the mountain and come to rest in the middle of the road.

It was raw, wild country. They saw coyotes, rabbits, a herd of elk, and a silver fox. Jack marveled at the beauty of the rocky crags and high-alpine meadows of the San Juan Mountains. He couldn't wait until more snow melted, and he could take Crockett and explore them further.

At some point, Lea parked the Jeep, and they got out.

"Why is it called Angel's Pasture?" Jack asked as they walked the fence line.

"My great-grandfather named it that years ago. He always said this part of the ranch was the closest he could get to heaven without leaving this earth."

Jack's gaze swept the snowy peaks on the horizon, then across the green slopes and down to the valley below. "I would have to agree with him."

They spent the rest of the morning—and well into the afternoon—driving to several locations, then walking the fence line on foot. Jack had lost track of time and forgot why they were there. But he didn't care. The mountains were beautiful. He followed Lea, taking her lead.

As they walked, she regaled him with stories about growing up on the ranch, the times she'd camped above the timber line, and stories about her family's history.

Her ancestors had immigrated to the mountains from Scotland a hundred years earlier and never left. Jack listened as she talked and realized Lea had become as much a part of the land as the animals they'd seen earlier.

After a couple of hours, they took a break and lunched along the bank of a tiny brook that trickled from somewhere high up in the mountains still covered in snow. They were above the tree line. The sun blazed in the turquoise sky, but it was cold. Jack pulled his Carhartt jacket from the Jeep and put it on.

"I told you you'd need it," Lea said, teasing him.

Jack swallowed a bite of turkey sandwich. "Tell me why we're up here again. Not that I mind."

"There's an old black bear that regularly tears up our fence up here. Every few weeks, one of us comes up here to check for damage."

"Does he wreck it often?"

"Once or twice a year," Lea replied. "We have to stay on top of it. You can't leave a fence down for long or you'll lose livestock."

"Why not trap the bear and relocate him?"

She looked at Jack as if the suggestion was unthinkable. "Because this is his home."

Jack had loved the time spent in the mountains that day and suspected he had enjoyed it even more because he got to spend it with Lea. Something about her had gotten under his skin.

He tightened his grip on the steering wheel as he made the roundabout a couple of miles outside of town, the dull ache in his side reminding him of his cracked ribs and bringing him back to reality.

He had a job to do. Someone had the gall to murder a sitting congressman and probably the congressman's chief of staff. Somebody who could do that had no right to be walking the streets. There was no time to get sentimental over a woman. There would be time for that later.

When Jack passed Telluride Bank & Trust, he noticed that it had already closed. He checked the time on his phone—seven o'clock.

He glanced in his rearview mirror and saw that the sun, which had been blazing over the mountains earlier, was setting low on the horizon. The day had flown.

He made his way slowly through town, stopping to let pedestrians cross at the corners, and glanced up a side street in time to see an attractive woman on the sidewalk headed uphill, away from Main Street. She was wearing a long camel-colored wool overcoat. Her blond hair was pulled back in a loose ponytail that fell to just above her shoulders.

He drove on but couldn't get the image of the woman out of his mind. Even at a distance, there was something familiar about her—her classy clothes, the elegant way she walked, not clomping around like so many tourists. It was then he realized it was Susan Roberts.

He turned off Main Street and headed up the hill, driving slowly. At the intersection, he looked but didn't see her and decided to circle the block and come in from the opposite direction.

As he made the last turn, he saw her climbing the stairs to a small white church. Jack was still some distance away but pulled to the curb and parked. He watched her open one of the large wooden doors and step inside, letting the door close behind her.

He got out of the truck and approached the church. It was pretty, with white-clapboard siding and green trim, and a tall, white bell tower with a steeple on top.

Jack climbed the steps, peered through a window in one of the doors, and saw her. She was kneeling in a pew near the front with her head down. It looked like she was praying.

Jack scanned the parts of the sanctuary he could see. It looked empty. But an assortment of lit candles on an altar just below a statue of the Virgin Mary was evidence that someone had come and gone.

He turned his back to the doors and stuck his hands on his hips. So, this was what he'd been reduced to—stalking a grieving widow as she came to church to pray.

He took the steps to the sidewalk and sat down on a bench nearby. He wasn't sure how long he'd been sitting there when the church door opened. He watched as Susan descended the steps. When she reached the sidewalk, she turned in his direction and stopped.

"Detective?" She looked surprised but not unhappy to see him. "What are you doing here?"

He stumbled over his words. "I—I'm sorry. I thought I recognized you going in. I..."

She smiled at him but looked sad. "Well, it's nice to see you again." Her voice was kind. "My husband's funeral is tomorrow. Will you be there? It's at the cemetery."

Jack didn't know what to say. "What time?" *Idiot,* he immediately thought. Like the time would matter. It wasn't as if he had a full schedule. He should have simply said yes or no.

"One o'clock. Do you know where the Lone Tree Cemetery is?"

"I do," Jack replied. "I'm staying at the campground right across the street."

She studied him for a moment, probably wondering what kind of famous detective stays at a campground. "I hope you can make it," she said. "It will be small—just close friends and family. Cliff wasn't one for pomp and circumstance. And it's supposed to be another gorgeous day like today." She looked up at the sky and looked sad again. "Just the way Cliff would have wanted it."

She turned to him and smiled, waiting for him to reply. When Jack didn't, she nodded. "It was nice to see you, Detective. I do hope I'll see you tomorrow."

Jack watched her make her way down the sidewalk. At the corner, she turned in the direction of her home, probably six or seven blocks away. It was a pleasant night for a walk, and Jack wondered if he should have offered to accompany her.

Susan had been surprised to see him but seemed genuinely happy that she had. And when he'd stumbled with an explanation for why he was outside the church, she could have quizzed him further, put him on the spot for an answer, but she hadn't.

She had been gracious and kind, even asking if he was planning to attend Cliff's funeral. It had been a pleasant exchange.

But something bothered him.

She hadn't asked how his investigation was going.

CHAPTER 59

Wednesday, May 18

IT WAS THE perfect day for a funeral. The sun blazed in a blue-bird sky dotted with clusters of cotton-white clouds. There was an easy breeze and no threat of rain.

The Lone Tree Cemetery was across Main Street from the campground. Spring grass blanketed the hillside that sloped upward to the base of the mountains that towered over town and marked the northern edge of the canyon. Old tombstones were scattered across the slope, some in rows, others placed in random spots here and there.

Jack pulled open the wrought-iron gate just off the sidewalk and stepped inside. People trickled in past him and headed up to where a small group had gathered in front of a coffin sitting above an open grave.

Jack was early. He stood for a moment, taking it all in. The cemetery was old. Many of the grave markers were worn and barely legible, many from the 1800s. He strolled past several, reading them as he went.

One gravesite was outlined in stone that was flush with the ground and had blackened with age. He read the chiseled name, *John C. Wolfe*, and saw that he had died in 1926. Jack didn't know why, but he felt the sudden urge to touch it. He reached down and ran his fingers over where it read *Murdered by an Indian* and wondered what had happened to John Wolfe so long ago. Had he been ambushed? Killed for a horse or a rifle? Maybe for money in his pocket or gold in his saddlebag? Had he squatted on the Indian's land?

Jack had learned from Judith and Otto that life in the early mining town had been treacherous. They had told him stories about early residents battling disease and avalanches, mining accidents and explosions, as well as Indians. The early settlers had been a different caliber of strong, Jack thought. He couldn't begin to imagine their struggles.

He straightened up and smoothed the front of his jeans, then glanced in the direction of the small crowd that had gathered around Susan. A tall, thin man stood nearby, the bottom of his black robe billowing in the breeze. From the white collar, Jack suspected it was the priest from the church where he'd seen Susan the night before.

The land around them was rugged and wild. And the town didn't look much different than it must have a century earlier. It resembled a scene from a Western. He imagined John Wayne emerging from the trees on horseback, hunting fugitive outlaws or hostile Indians.

Jack stepped closer to the crowd but was careful to keep his distance out of respect for Cliff's family and friends. In a way, he felt like an interloper; he didn't belong. But experience had taught him that killers often made appearances at their victim's funerals, especially if they had been related or were friends.

Jack remained apart from the rest, watching. Ted Hawthorne stood just behind Susan, fighting back tears. Was Hawthorne crying out of sorrow—or guilt? Susan turned and said something to him, and Hawthorne took several steps back, away from her.

Judith was there. Jack watched as she took a bouquet of flowers and laid them atop the coffin, then visited with an elderly couple he didn't recognize.

Jack turned again to the mountains, looking east, high up into the canyon. He breathed in a gust of wind that carried the musty smell of newly turned earth and didn't hear the soft footfalls in the grass behind him.

"I lift up mine eyes to the hills from whence cometh my strength." It was a soft, gentle voice.

Jack turned and saw Ivy Waggoner staring up at him, smiling. She wore a loose-fitting black dress and tall, black rain boots, and was carrying a bouquet of wildflowers.

"Hello, Ivy."

"Detective," she said with a slow nod.

Jack glanced behind her. "Where's your sister?"

"Opal doesn't believe in funerals. She thinks they're contagious."

Jack smiled.

"It's true," Ivy continued. "Opal swears they could be fatal for people our age—hasten our demise. I think she's afraid she'll get a foot caught in a grave and not be able to pry it loose."

Jack laughed. "But you're not afraid of funerals?"

"Oh, no," Ivy replied. "You might think I'm crazy, but I kind of like them. They put things in perspective, don't they?"

Jack thought about it for a moment. "They do."

Ivy patted him on the arm. "It was nice to see you again, Detective. I do hope you'll stop in the store again sometime."

Jack watched her amble up the hill toward the growing crowd that had gathered around the grave. He heard the wrought-iron gate below him click shut and turned to see Elizabeth Mayweather approaching.

"Hello, Jack."

"Elizabeth."

"Did you call Turner?" she asked, referring to Turner Biggs, the hiking guide.

"I did. He's taking me somewhere tomorrow."

She raised her brows. "Oh? Where to?"

"I'm not sure. He didn't tell me. I guess I'll find out in the morning."

"Well, I'd be curious to know. There are so many beautiful hikes in the San Juans. You'll have to call me and tell me which one you did. There aren't many that I haven't done."

Jack glanced again toward the end of the canyon. "As soon as the snow thaws, I plan on hiking Ingram Falls. I bet the view of town is beautiful from up there."

"It is. I've hiked it dozens of times. But it'll probably be another two weeks before it's safe to get up there." She thought of something. "In the meantime, have you hiked Bridal Veil Falls?"

"Bridal Veil?" Jack thought of the account in the Cayman Islands and felt the color drain from his face.

"You haven't heard of it?" Elizabeth looked surprised again. "It's a short hike, but beautiful. And the trail's open—the snow's already melted. Parts might be a bit muddy but nothing bad enough to keep you from hiking it."

"Where is it?"

Elizabeth pointed to the right of Ingram Falls. "It's around the corner there—just out of sight. If you drive a bit farther into the canyon, you'll see it. It's the largest free-falling waterfall in the Colorado Rockies. Three hundred and sixty-five feet..."

Jack was no longer listening.

Bridal Veil.

Bridal Veil Limited.

He turned and stole another glance at the grieving widow, then quickly searched the small crowd of mourners who had gathered on the quaint hillside cemetery to bury their friend.

He saw Buckley and Celeste Bailey mingling in the crowd with Ivy Waggoner and Judith Hadley. Ted Hawthorne was still trying to pull it together. And Tony Burns was there with Deputy O'Connor. Jack glanced next at Hank Wade and Lea Scotsman, each standing alone, off to the side.

Bridal Veil. Bridal Veil.

Jack rolled the words over and over in his mind.

It was then he knew.

CHAPTER 60

JACK CLOSED THE cemetery's iron gate behind him and started for the campground. He walked fast, his heart pounding in his chest. He pulled his phone from his pocket and searched for Archie Rochambeau's number.

"Jack!" Archie answered the call as if he hadn't talked to Jack in years instead of the day before.

Jack wanted to get straight to the point but slowed himself down. He needed to keep his FBI buddy happy.

"I've got one for you," Jack said, quickening his pace.

"One what?"

"Why is money called dough?"

Archie was silent a moment. "Huh?" He sounded confused.

Jack was surprised to find he enjoyed turning the tables on him. "Why is money called dough?" he repeated.

"I don't know. Why?"

"Because we all knead it. Get it? *Knead* it."

Archie roared on the other end. "Oh man. That's awesome." He laughed some more. "I'm going to borrow that one."

Jack smiled as he took the corner into the campground. Archie Rochambeau was a study in how to find joy in the simple—and sometimes ridiculous—things in life. Jack missed his old friend and would make a point to see him the next time he was anywhere in the vicinity of Texas.

"Seriously though, Arch. I've got some news."

"What is it?"

"Bridal Veil Limited. Someone connected with Telluride is behind it."

"What about the other congressmen on the house committee?"

"Forget about them. Set that list aside."

"Okay."

Jack could tell Archie wasn't sure which way to turn next. "Take these names down."

"Hold on a second." There was rustling on the other end. "All right, shoot."

Jack gave him the names of everyone in Telluride he could think of. He was sure one of them would be behind the Bridal Veil account. Archie said he'd get right on it, and they ended the call.

At the campground, Jack changed into comfortable clothes and hiking boots. He packed a water bottle and a collapsible bowl for Crockett in his backpack, locked the trailer door, and went to see Otto.

"Howdy, friend," the old man called out when he saw Jack coming. He was sitting beside the river, whittling.

Crockett was lying next to him but jumped up and ran to greet Jack.

"Hey, buddy," Jack said, scratching him behind an ear. "How about a hike?"

Otto set the stick down and stabbed the knife into the dirt on the riverbank. "Where you going?"

"Bridal Veil."

Otto thought about it, then nodded. "Snow should be melted and pretty near dried up by now. You two will be fine."

Jack glanced at the tattered hiking boots set against the tent. "Care to join us?" he asked, knowing Otto would probably refuse.

Otto pulled his cane from beside him and struggled to stand. "Back in the day, I would have jumped at the chance. Thank you for askin', but you two go on without me." He lumbered to the folding chair next to the picnic table and dropped into it. He looked sad, and Jack felt his heart clench.

Jack threw a leg over one side of the picnic table and sat, wanting to give the old guy a few minutes before he rushed off. "You have a date yet for when you're heading into the mountains?"

"Soon."

Jack sat with him a few minutes longer, then stood up to go. "You ready to go, Crockett?" He turned to Otto. "We'll be back in time for dinner at Judith's. How about it? My treat."

The old man smiled, his teeth flashing white in his gray beard. "That sounds like a fine plan."

Jack followed Elizabeth's directions, taking the road headed toward the end of the canyon.

Not long after he passed the cemetery, the falls came into view. He pulled up and stared at it in the distance. It was beautiful, a spray of white that did, in fact, resemble the shape of a bride's veil. The cascading water fell hundreds of feet from the base of a large white building perched precariously on the edge of a cliff face and disappeared into the forest below.

It took over a half hour to reach the trailhead. Jack found it on the edge of a small gravel parking lot half a mile from the canyon wall and well below the base of the falls. He glanced at an informational sign before they started up and found out the white building was a hydroelectric power plant built in 1907 to supply electricity to a nearby mine.

He scanned the sign for names of benefactors, politicians, anyone who might be associated with the Bridal Veil account in the Caymans but didn't see any. He set out, hoping there would be something at the top.

The terrain was rough and the ground uneven. It was a mostly vertical climb. The two hiked around giant boulders, past abandoned mining cables and fallen towers that once brought ore from the mountains above to the mill below.

It was almost a mile and a half to the bottom of the falls, mostly straight up. By the time they reached the top, Jack was out of breath. He took a moment to recover, marveling at the site of the water free-falling onto giant moss-covered boulders below. It was cold, the spray quickly soaking through his shirt.

He turned and studied his surroundings but couldn't see anything that could be related to a bank account in the Caymans. It was a dead end but had been a beautiful climb.

Jack stared down the valley, just making out the edge of Telluride. It was magnificent, nestled between the green canyon walls.

But somewhere in all that beauty lurked a killer.

CHAPTER 61

Thursday, May 19

BUCKLEY BAILEY WAS sound asleep when his cell phone buzzed on the nightstand. He turned over and felt an empty bed where Celeste should have been. *Where is she?*

Six twenty. The faint gray light of dawn filtered through the crack between the curtains. In a drowsy panic, he pulled the phone toward him.

The call was from Jack.

Buckley rolled out of bed and sat up. "Jack? What is it? Where's Celeste?"

There was silence on the other end of the line.

"What do you mean?" Jack asked. "You don't know where she is?"

The concern in Jack's voice matched what Buckley was feeling. He stood up and staggered toward the bathroom. "Why did you call?" he asked, glancing into Celeste's closet and then his own.

"I wanted to let you know that I was going to be out of pocket today."

"Why?" Buckley asked, stepping into the hallway. "Celeste!" he hollered, looking for her.

"Sorry, Buckley. If it isn't a good time, I can call back tonight."

"No, no, I just can't find her. I'm sure everything is all right. What did you say about tonight?" Buckley was distracted and growing frustrated.

"I'll call you tonight. I'm going to follow a lead, try to figure out what Cliff did the day before he died."

Buckley thought of Cliff and started down the stairs, his heart now pounding in his chest. *Where is Celeste?* "What did you say you're doing?"

"Following a lead."

"Okay." Buckley rounded the corner to the kitchen. The lights were on, which was a good sign. Or was it? He yanked open the door to the pantry with his free hand, half expecting to find Celeste murdered on the floor. But the pantry was empty. Thank God.

"Buckley, is everything all right?"

He shut the door and took in a deep breath, trying to calm his nerves. He was being ridiculous.

"Sorry, Jack. Everything's fine, but I'm kind of busy at the moment."

"No problem. I just wanted to let you know that I could be out of cell service most of the day."

Buckley leaned back heavy against the kitchen counter and dropped his head into his free hand, covering his eyes. He needed to get it together. "That's fine. Thank you for letting me know."

He ended the call and tossed the cell phone on the counter. He thought of Cliff, and the funeral the day before, then remembered Gerald Purvis, and panic threatened to surge through him again. *Where the hell is Celeste?*

Something darted past the kitchen window in the growing light. Buckley pushed off the counter and peered outside. Bo was running and loping at full speed, acting agitated. Buckley had forgotten about the dog. How did he get out there? Had someone broken into the house and let Bo out? But he would have barked.

Buckley ran to the back door and opened it. He was immediately hit by a gust of frigid air. His breath fogged in front of him.

Bo raced to Buckley and danced at his feet. He was happy.

Confused, Buckley stepped farther onto the porch, the flagstone cold to his feet. He scanned the yard but didn't see anyone. Bo barked once, then darted around the corner, and Buckley followed.

"Celeste!" Buckley let out a huge sigh of relief. "What in the blazes are you doing out here?"

She was bent at the waist, wearing gardening gloves, and had soil up to her elbows. "I couldn't sleep," she said, brushing hair from her face and leaving a smear of dirt across her cheek. "I figured I might as well get up and plant the lupine and marigold seeds that I should have planted weeks ago."

Buckley knew there was something wrong. She hadn't been herself since the funeral the day before. Too much death, he thought. First their friend Alice Fremont, four months earlier. Now Cliff. Buckley was sure it was what bothered her. He hadn't told her about Purvis and wondered if she had heard. Celeste wasn't one to pay attention to the news, and he hoped she hadn't. She hadn't known Purvis, but when she learned of his death—which was sounding like another murder—it would disturb her further.

Buckley kissed her on the top of her head, then went back into the house and shut the door. He realized the deaths had gotten to him, too. He was paranoid, jumpy. It wasn't like him.

He made a pot of coffee and carried a cup to the breakfast table. There was time now to think. He remembered Jack phoning, but he had been half-asleep and panic-stricken at the time of the call.

Jack had said something about following a lead—being out of cell phone range. For an entire day? Buckley frowned, trying to remember their brief conversation.

Jack hadn't said what he would be doing. Buckley's pulse sped up, wondering what he was up to and worrying about what Jack might uncover.

CHAPTER 62

AFTER THE CALL to Buckley, Jack walked Crockett through the trees to Otto's using the flashlight app on his phone. The sky was still dark. As they got closer, he heard music playing softly inside. It sounded like Tim McGraw.

Crockett stuck his nose through a gap in the zippered door flap, and Jack heard the old man laugh, then start to cough. He watched as Otto slowly unzipped it from the inside and emerge from the tent.

"I thought that was you," Otto said with a chuckle, laying a hand on Crockett's head. "Might near scared me to death. Took you for a bear."

"Morning, Otto," Jack said.

Otto stretched, putting a hand on his lower back as he did. "What's got you two up before the chickens?" he asked.

"I hate to ask you again, but I need a favor."

Otto looked down at Crockett. "So, it's you and me again, is it?" he said, bending slowly to pat the dog again. "Like I told you, Jack, anytime. Crockett and I are old pals, aren't we, old feller?"

Jack didn't know what he'd do without the old man. He had come to rely on him for help as well as his company. He appreciated both.

"Thank you, Otto. It might be for most of the day."

Otto waved a dismissive hand. "You take care of whatever it is you gotta do. We'll be fine till you get back—whenever that is."

Jack watched the old man step back into the tent and hold the flap open.

"Come on, Crockett. I was just about to fry up some bacon. How does that sound?"

The dog looked up at Jack, then stepped into the tent.

Jack hated leaving him again. But there wasn't time to worry about that now. Turner Biggs would show up at any minute.

Jack made his way back to the Airstream. As he was climbing the steps, his shadow flashed distorted across the silver skin of the trailer. Headlights. He turned and watched a dark Ford Raptor pull up to the campsite and stop. The driver's-side window slid down, and a man's head popped out, his face lit by the dashboard lights.

"Jack Martin?"

"Are you Turner?" Jack asked.

"Yep," the man replied. "Glad I found you. Let's go. We're burning daylight."

Jack would hardly call the faint gray dawn sky "daylight," but he agreed with the sentiment. He was ready to find out how Cliff Roberts had spent the last full day of his life.

He locked the trailer, pulled open the passenger's-side door, and got in, holding his side. His ribs ached, but Jack decided nothing good would come from telling the guide he'd been shot the day before. He would do everything he could to mask the pain and keep it a secret.

"Nice truck," Jack said, admiring the smooth leather interior. It still had a new car smell and was a nicer ride than he expected a hiking guide to drive.

"Thank you," Turner Biggs said, beaming with pride. "Ate beans for a year to save up for it, but it was worth it." He stroked the steering wheel affectionally, then put the pickup in gear.

It was almost an hour's drive to the trailhead. Turner spent the time talking about trucks. Jack spent the time listening. He heard the details about every truck Turner had owned since he started driving.

Jack tried changing the subject several times to no avail. He wanted to talk about Roberts and find out about that last day. But each time, within minutes, Turner changed the subject back again.

Jack stole occasional glances as the guide talked. He was average height and lean, with a grizzled beard and medium-brown hair that hung close to his eyes. Probably in his early forties, but mountain-aged to look older.

Turner was saying something about putting a grill guard on his truck when he interrupted himself. "Almost there," he said, pulling from the highway onto a dirt road. "About five miles from here to the trailhead."

They bounced along, Jack's ribs throbbing with each jolt of the truck. He thought he'd try to change the subject again. "How do you know Elizabeth Mayweather?"

Turner grinned. "Elizabeth is one of my best clients. Known her for years. I don't remember exactly how we met. Probably on our first hike. Seeing as how I'm the best guide around—I grew up in these mountains—she probably heard about me and looked me up. But I can't remember."

"What do you know about her?"

"A lot. She's from Arizona. Her husband croaked and left her a wad of cash. But she's not like most of the other rich women around here. Got a third lung, I think. Has no problem keeping up with me. I take her fishing, too. She's caught more trout in these rivers than just about anyone I know. I'll give her that."

"And how long had you known Congressman Roberts?" Jack hoped he could finally learn more about Cliff.

Turner pursed his lips. "Never met him till the day I brought him up here. Elizabeth gave him my number. Just like she gave it to you. He told me where he wanted to come and what he wanted to see, and I said sure. I know these mountains like the back of my hand. So I brought him up here."

"Did he tell you why he wanted to come? Or what it was he wanted to see?"

Turner shook his head. "Nope. Never hardly said a word. He didn't say, and I didn't ask."

Jack didn't doubt it; it was easy to imagine Turner Biggs doing all of the talking. Jack had hit a dead end with the guide. He hoped what he saw on their hike would help him understand what Cliff was thinking the day before he died.

They had been hiking for hours. Turner's Raptor was thousands of feet below them. Jack was out of breath, his ribs were throbbing, and his thighs were on fire.

"How much farther?" he asked, stepping over a rock, careful to avoid a rolled ankle.

Turner spun around, not even breathing hard. How was that possible? Jack suspected he was part mountain goat.

"We're getting closer. Keep comin'."

It was easier said than done.

"I need to stop for a minute," Jack said. He took off his baseball cap and wiped sweat from his forehead.

Turner raised his eyebrows in understanding. "Gotcha. You need a pit stop?"

"I do."

"I'll wait for you here."

Jack stepped off the trail and toward a large fir tree. It was on the crest of a small ridge that sloped downward a ways before it angled back up just a few yards away. He relieved himself, zipped up his pants, and never heard Turner sneak up behind him.

"Don't make a move." Turner's voice was a low, menacing whisper. He was close enough that Jack thought he felt his breath on his neck. "Stay right where you are."

Jack froze. A succession of quick thoughts flashed through his mind. It was an ambush. He had been tricked again. Turner had lied about where he'd guided Cliff. Had he been the shooter on Last Dollar Road? The mountainside was remote. It would be the perfect place for a murder. No one would ever find his body.

Jack's heart thumped in his chest. He should have known better than to trust a stranger. He was just so damned eager to find out what had happened to Cliff Roberts. He had made a grave mistake.

Turner laid a firm hand on his shoulder.

But Jack wasn't going down without a fight. He was on the verge of wheeling around when the guide pointed to the other side of the draw.

"Do you see it?" Turner asked.

Jack was confused.

"Look there," Turner whispered. His voice had lost its menacing tone.

Jack glanced at where he pointed and saw it. A bear. It was huge, black as night. And only a few yards away.

Jack watched it, fascinated. He went to take a step forward, but Turner held him in place.

"Wait a minute," the guide whispered. "There. Look there."

Jack saw two cubs emerge from the brush and fall in step with the larger bear. He could hear the snorting breaths of the mother. She stopped, sniffed the air for a moment, and then, to Jack's relief, moved on.

Jack let out the breath he'd been holding. "How did you know?"

The guide was grinning. "Heard her in the trees. You didn't hear the commotion? The cracking branches?"

Jack was embarrassed that he hadn't.

"When I saw her," Turner went on, "she was too close for me to holler at you. You don't want to spook a mama when she's with her cubs. Man, we got lucky."

It was then that Jack noticed Turner was breathing shallow and fast. The climb hadn't done it to him, but running into a black bear and her cubs had.

The two men continued their climb, and the air got colder.

"How much farther?" Jack asked after another half hour.

"What's wrong?" the guide said, looking down. "Can't be that your feet hurt. Those are some fine-looking boots." He continued to talk as they hiked. "Good boots are your best friend up here. That and a satellite radio, since we're pretty much off the grid most of the time. If there was an accident. . . "

Jack wasn't listening. He studied the top of his boots with each step, remembering when he'd bought them months earlier. The salesman at the mountain gear store had said they were among the best. Jack thought of Otto's worn, mismatched pair and felt a stab of guilt. He wondered how the old man managed summers high in the mountains with boots that were falling apart.

"We're here," Turner announced without fanfare.

Thank God. Jack didn't think he could have gone much farther. He stopped, took in several deep breaths, and looked over the ridge at the large basin below. The mountains sloped down and away on several sides. He hadn't noticed, but they had hiked past large patches of snow. Somehow, Turner had been able to thread the needle and had found the only route up the mountain that avoided climbing in it. Jack was impressed.

A turquoise lake still rimmed with ice was nestled in the basin below them. The first buds of vegetation were visible in the bare patches of earth, speckling it with hints of green. The wind blew gently over them, carrying the scent of snow and clean air. It was cold, but Jack barely noticed.

He stood there a moment, drinking in the majesty of the mountains in the distance and below him. He had spent most of the hike looking down, trying not to roll an ankle on loose rock, and hadn't realized they had climbed to the summit.

It was perfect. The deep blue sky, the mountains. The patches of snow and the signs of spring. It was all perfect.

"Where are we?" he asked Turner.

"This is what Cliff wanted to see. Down there is Hank Wade's ranch. See the house and barns?"

Jack looked to where he was pointing and saw the cluster of buildings in the distance. They looked like miniatures from so high up the mountain.

"Do you know Lea Scotsman?" Turner pointed in a different direction. "That's her place over there."

Jack squinted, but the lodge blended in with the trees. It took him a moment to find it. "You know Lea?"

"No," Turner replied. "I know *of* her. Her family is legendary in these parts."

Jack swept his gaze over the mountain range and down the basin once more, and he finally understood why the congressman had changed his plans, delaying his trip to see it all.

The hike to the summit changed everything.

CHAPTER 63

BY THE TIME Jack and Turner returned to Telluride, the sun was quickly dropping below the horizon. The streetlamps had kicked on, casting the town in a hazy glow much like when they'd driven through that morning.

They had spent the entire day in the mountains. Jack's legs were heavy and weak, his feet swollen and sore, and his ribs were on fire. Nothing sounded better than a cold beer and bed, but he had Turner drop him off just shy of the campground. He had an errand to run before he went back to the trailer.

He paid Turner, hoping Buckley wouldn't balk at reimbursing him. A private guide for a day of hiking just about drained all the cash Jack had left. He would have to dip into emergency savings if Buckley wouldn't pay him back.

Jack thanked Turner and waved as he made an illegal U-turn on Main Street and headed home. On their way back to town, Turner had done most of the talking again. Jack had learned a lot about him, and despite Turner's proclivity for carrying on one-sided conversations, he had grown to like him.

The lights inside Pandora Café were burning bright. Jack smelled Judith's famous meat loaf when someone pulled open the door as he walked by. His stomach growled and he was tempted to stop in, but there wasn't time. He needed to get to the mountain gear store before it closed.

Twenty minutes later, he staggered past the trailer and stepped through the trees to Otto's campsite. The old man was sitting at the picnic table, the ash of his cigarette glowing orange in the dying light.

Crockett leapt to his feet and ran to him, wagging his tail.

Jack shifted the box he was carrying and bent to pet the dog. "Hey there, boy. Have you been good?"

"He was perfect," Otto said, blowing out smoke. As Jack got closer, Otto squinted, studying him. "You look like something a mountain lion drug in. What in tarnation have you been up to?"

Jack was too tired to explain. He handed Otto the box.

"What's this?" the old man asked, his cigarette bouncing at the corner of his mouth as he spoke.

"Just a little something for taking care of Crockett."

Otto reached out with both hands, took the box from him, and set it on his lap. He lifted the lid and laid it on the table, rifled through the tissue paper, and pulled out a hiking boot.

"Is this for me?" he asked. There was a catch in his voice.

"For you," Jack said. "I couldn't have my best friend spending the summer in the mountains wearing those old things." He nodded at the mismatched pair set near the tent.

Otto pulled the second boot out of the box and held it next to the other. "They match."

Jack laughed and nodded. "They do. I checked your old ones the other day for your size. They should fit. If they don't, I can exchange them."

"They'll fit." Otto studied the boots for a while longer, then looked up. "They're mighty fine, Jack. I thank you. I can't say that I've ever had any better."

Back at the trailer, Jack had lost all interest in food or beer. He was exhausted. He peeled off his clothes and got into bed. Crockett settled in at his feet.

He switched off the light, but as tired as he was, his mind was racing. The hike into the high country had been one of the hardest things he had ever done. But it would pale in comparison with what he had to do in the morning.

CHAPTER 64

Friday, May 20

JACK HAD TOSSED and turned most of the night, cobbling together only a couple of hours of sleep. Then, just before dawn, he'd finally sunk into the deep slumber of the dead.

He wasn't sure how long he'd been out when he woke with a start, surprised by the beams of daylight pouring through the gap between the curtain and the wall of the trailer.

He reached for his phone on the floor, wondering what time it was. Muscles he hadn't felt in years were either stiff or ached, and his cracked ribs felt like someone was trying to jam a knife between them. He pulled the phone up, squinted at the screen, then rubbed his eyes and squinted at it again. Nearly eight o'clock. He hadn't slept that late in years.

He started to lay the phone back down but noticed there were two missed calls. He opened his voice mail and listened to one from Archie Rochambeau.

Call me, buddy. I think I've found something for you.

The second message was from Lea. Jack began listening to it and was out of bed before it finished playing.

Jack, it's Lea. I'm sorry, I know it's early, but I need to speak with you. It's urgent. Please call me as soon as you can.

She had called nearly an hour earlier and sounded upset.

Jack called Lea first.

She answered on the first ring and talked fast, her voice shaking. "Jack, I got a letter from Cliff. It—"

"Wait a minute," Jack interrupted. He didn't think he had understood her correctly. "From Cliff?"

"Yes." Jack heard her draw in a deep breath before she continued. "I picked up the mail this morning in Ridgway. I didn't notice it in the stack until I was back home. But Cliff had changed his mind. He wasn't going to vote for the land trade."

"He was going to vote *against* it?"

"Yes."

Jack wasn't surprised. Standing on the summit the day before with Turner Biggs, he realized that Cliff had taken Lea's advice and gone to see the land before he handed it over to Hank Wade.

Between Aspen, campgrounds outside Frasier and Durango, and now Telluride, Jack had lived in the mountains for almost two years. He knew their beauty. But something about the hike the day before had been different.

The San Juans had affected Jack in a way he found impossible to describe. Standing on the summit the day before had been spiritual in a way that Jack still didn't fully understand. He was sure Cliff would have felt the same way when he stood in the same spot only a few days earlier, especially after having grown up in the mountains.

Jack was curious who else knew that Cliff had changed his mind about the vote. And wondered if it could have been the reason he was killed. He thought of Eric Dale. If word had gotten out that Cliff was going to vote against the trade, could it have actually *saved* his life?

There were still too many questions to be answered.

"When did Cliff send the letter?" Jack asked.

"It's postmarked the day he died. He must have mailed it that morning."

"Before he got on the plane," Jack said, thinking out loud. It could explain why the flight had been delayed. That and his argument with Buckley. "Can you take a picture of it and text it to me? I'd like to read it myself."

"Sure. I'll do it right now."

Jack waited a few seconds and heard the ding of an incoming text. He pulled the phone from his ear and checked. "I got it," he said, then scanned the letter.

"Does it mean anything?" Lea asked. "That Cliff had changed his mind?"

"It might," Jack said, then thought of something. "Lea, do you know if Cliff had a bank account in the Cayman Islands?"

"I don't have any idea, but I wouldn't think so. For as long as I've known him, he's banked with Ted. Why?"

"Just curious."

"He must have other investment accounts somewhere, but I can't imagine why he'd have an offshore one. Isn't that usually for hiding money?"

Jack needed to ask Lea a more difficult question and hoped she wouldn't hang up. "There's something else," he said.

"What?"

"I saw Eric Dale leaving Telluride Bank & Trust Tuesday morning, exactly twenty-four hours after I saw you there." Jack thought of the $500,000 Archie said had been withdrawn from Lea's account. "I know you gave Dale money."

There was silence, then Jack heard Lea sigh. "I gave it to Wilderness Keepers, not Eric Dale."

It had been a bluff, but Jack's hunch had been right. "Why'd you do it?"

"To keep Hank from getting his hands on the land."

"But half a million dollars?"

"I would have paid twice that. I thought when Cliff died the deal would be over, but it wasn't. Hank isn't giving up, and I didn't want to take any chances." She paused a moment, then shrugged. "I was desperate."

"But Wilderness Keepers? They've been accused of violence, including bombings in Montana and burning down Hank's barn."

"*Accused*," Lea pointed out. "They haven't been found guilty of anything. And in the case of the land trade, they're fighting on my side."

She was right, and Jack dropped the point. After the day spent with Lea in Angel's Pasture, he understood her love for the land. It was generational—something that had been bred into her. He didn't doubt for a minute that her intentions in giving Wilderness Keepers the money had been sincere. For her, choosing Eric Dale over Hank Wade had been the lesser of two evils.

"If that's all, Jack," she said, "I need to go. There's someone I need to see."

They ended the call, and Jack dropped the phone onto the bed. He pulled on a pair of jeans and grabbed a shirt.

It was going to be a tough morning, but he knew what he had to do. He would call Archie on the way, to confirm what he had discovered.

But his gut told him the call wasn't necessary. He already knew.

CHAPTER 65

AFTER JACK FINISHED dressing, he dropped Crockett with Otto and started for town. He typically walked, but this morning he drove.

He pulled his phone from the seat next to him, found Archie Rochambeau's number, and touched it.

"I've been waiting," Archie said. His tone was serious. "And wondering."

"I slept in."

"Well, that's a first."

Jack passed Telluride Bank & Trust and glanced through the window. It was closed, but he thought he caught a glimpse of Ted Hawthorne inside. Hawthorne was no saint, and Jack didn't like him, but he knew now that he wasn't a killer.

"What'd you find?" Jack asked.

"A humdinger, that's what."

Jack took a right off Main Street and headed uphill. "Tell me," he said, and turned the next corner.

"Bridal Veil Limited. I checked the names you gave me, and by gum, I finally got a hit."

"Who?" Jack parked along the curb and shut off the ignition.

"Roberts," Archie said. "Not Cliff, but a Susan. Susan Roberts."

It confirmed what Jack already knew.

"And get this," Archie continued. "I ran a search on Susan. It wasn't easy—do you know how many Susan Robertses there are? Anyway, *this* Susan Roberts has an account with a small bank in Cape Girardeau, Missouri. And a rather significant sum of money landed in the account on the same day of the withdrawal from the Bridal Veil account in the Caymans."

Susan Roberts, the mystery person behind Bridal Veil Limited, the grieving widow. Hank Wade had transferred a small fortune to her offshore account. But why?

"Thanks, Archie," he said, looking up at the large blue Victorian. "I owe you one."

He got out of the truck and crossed the street, then started up the sidewalk.

Cliff Roberts hadn't taken a bribe, but *Susan* Roberts had.

Had Wade paid her to influence Cliff's vote? Or worse, had he paid her for her husband's murder?

CHAPTER 66

JACK RANG THE doorbell and waited, looking down at his boots and knowing the next several minutes would be ugly.

A few seconds later, the door opened and Susan Roberts stood before him. "Hello, Detective."

"Susan."

She stood holding the door. There was a long, awkward silence that Jack let happen. He wanted her rattled, or at least back on her heels, when he questioned her, knowing that when someone was nervous, they were more likely to reveal something they hadn't intended.

"Is there something wrong?" she asked.

Jack saw her swallow. "There is. Can I come in?"

She hesitated a moment, then pulled the door open wider. "Of course."

In the living room, she gestured for Jack to have a seat in one of the chairs. She took the sofa.

"Is it about Cliff's accident?" she asked.

"It might be." Jack leaned toward her. "Tell me about Bridal Veil Limited." He saw the color drain from her face.

She blinked several times. "I—I don't know what you mean."

"It's time to cut the crap, Susan, and tell the truth. I know about your account in the Caymans."

She glanced nervously to one side of the room and then the other, as if searching for an explanation. Jack watched her clasp and unclasp her hands in her lap and almost felt sorry for her. Almost.

"Look at me."

She did, and blinked several times, her chest rising and falling with short rapid breaths. "I'm sorry. I just—"

"I know about the money transferred from Hank Wade."

She tensed, and there was panic in her eyes. Then her body relaxed, and she slumped back onto the sofa. She looked defeated and dropped her gaze to her hands, where she twisted her wedding ring.

"It's true," she finally said. "Hank promised me the money if I could get Cliff to vote in his favor."

"For the land he wanted?"

She nodded, still staring at her wedding ring.

"But he paid you after Cliff was already dead."

"I was going to influence Gerald to vote in his favor. Hank was still going to pay me."

"Why did you do it?"

Susan took a moment. She stood up and walked to a window, then laid her fingertips on the glass. She stared into the distance, looking toward Savage Basin, where Cliff had died.

"I never wanted to live in the mountains." Her voice was distant, like she was talking to herself. "It was Cliff's idea. Everything was always Cliff's idea."

She was silent a moment, then turned to look at him. "This town. This house—everything in it." She swept her arm around the room. "It was all Cliff's idea. I didn't want to move here, but I didn't want to live in DC, either. I'd had enough."

She floated across the room, running her hand along the furniture as she spoke. "The money was going to give me the chance to get away. Go somewhere *I* wanted to. Live where *I* wanted."

Jack studied her, not sure if he felt pity or revulsion. "Why not just divorce him? Why take the bribe?"

She turned to him with an eerie stare and cocked her head to one side. "You don't divorce a Roberts in this state, Detective."

"You could have," he replied. "If it weren't for the photographs."

Susan stared at him, confused, then realized what he was saying. She opened her mouth to speak, but Jack got to it first.

"Buckley told me about the photos. He tried telling Cliff, but he wouldn't listen. They're proof that you were having an affair. Not exactly what you'd want to come to light during a divorce trial."

He was pushing her, hoping she would break. He wanted her to admit the affair with Gerald Purvis. Then he would ask about Purvis's murder.

Her face burned scarlet. Jack was sure she was about to erupt in a volcanic rage, but instead, she burst into tears.

She fell onto the sofa and buried her head in her hands. "It wasn't supposed to happen this way."

Jack wanted to keep her talking. He wanted her to admit the affair. It was the opening he needed to get her to confess to the murders.

"It wasn't supposed to happen *what* way?" he asked.

"Cliff and Gerald," she said, still crying. "None of this was supposed to happen."

"You were having an affair."

She looked up, her eyes red and swollen.

There it was. The pause that meant she was searching for a reply. She was going to deny everything. Jack expected that whatever she said next would be a lie.

Susan had stopped crying, but she couldn't look at him and, instead, dropped her gaze to the floor. Her reply was a whisper. "It's all true."

She began to cry again, softer this time.

It was difficult, but Jack gave her a moment. He was reeling with questions. Had she hired the guy who paid Ronnie Bugler to stash the bomb on the plane? Why murder Purvis? If she was having an affair with him, why did he also need to die?

She rubbed her eyes with the back of her hands. Jack pulled a tissue from a box on the side table and handed it to her.

"Thank you." Her voice was shaky and weak. She dabbed at her eyes. "Do you remember when I ran into you? Outside the church the night before Cliff's funeral?"

"I do."

"Do you know what I was doing, Detective?"

Jack shook his head.

"I was praying. Praying that somehow I wasn't responsible for everything that's happened. I cried out to God that night, begging him for forgiveness, even though I knew I didn't deserve it. Deep down, I'm afraid that the things I've done have somehow gotten Cliff and Gerald killed."

In some convoluted way, she was attempting to deflect the blame, acting as if she hadn't been directly responsible. But Jack wasn't going to let her get away with it.

"Why did you murder them?" he asked.

"What?" She frowned, confused.

"Did you kill Cliff for the money when you found out he'd changed his mind about the vote? You thought you could influence Gerald instead?"

She shook her head. "What are you talking about?"

"Cliff's decision not to recommend the swap with Wade would have killed the deal, wouldn't it have? And you wouldn't have gotten your payoff unless you could have convinced his successor."

She was still frowning.

"But why murder Gerald?" Jack asked. "Did he find out about the bribe? Was he going to expose it?"

She put her hands to her ears and shook her head. "None of that is true."

"Why did you kill them, Susan?"

"I didn't!"

"I've had sociopaths look me in the eye and swear the same thing."

"But I'm telling you the truth."

"I understand why you felt the need to murder Cliff," Jack said. "For the money. He was going back to DC to vote against the deal. But why kill Gerald? Was he threatening to expose you? Or did you kill him in a jealous rage? Was he going to break up with you because of the bribe?"

"Break up with me? What are you talking about? I wasn't having an affair with Gerald. He wasn't the one."

She'd said it emphatically, without blinking. And Jack believed her. He sat for a while in stunned silence. He'd thought he had it all figured out but realized now that he had been wrong.

"The photographs?" It was all he had. If not Purvis, then who?

"I should have known better than to trust him." Susan had started to cry again and buried her face in her hands.

"Trust who?" Jack asked.

"He ruined everything. How could he do it?"

"Do what?"

"Kill them."

"Who killed them?"

She wasn't listening. "I shouldn't have trusted him."

Jack grew frustrated. "Who are you talking about, Susan?" he asked, his voice raised. "Who shouldn't you have trusted?"

She shook her head, still crying. "I can't."

"Yes, you can. Other people could be in danger."

He let her cry awhile longer, then pressed again. "It's over, Susan. What's done is done. It's time to do the right thing. Who are you talking about? Who were you photographed with?"

She looked up at him, her eyes swimming with tears. "Hank."

Jack froze, letting the name sink in. He leaned back on the chair, no longer paying attention to her crying on the sofa.

Her affair had been with Hank Wade. Had she been foolish enough to tell him that Cliff had changed his mind about the vote?

"Susan, listen to me."

She looked up but didn't speak.

"Did you tell Hank that Cliff had changed his mind?"

She stared at him a moment, then buried her face in her hands again.

It was all the answer Jack needed.

Susan Roberts was lost in the rubble of her own making. It was as if a bomb had been detonated inside her.

Jack saw her shoulders shake with each sob and knew her life would never be the same again. She was shattered. And like Cliff's plane, she would never be made whole again.

There was no reason to hang around and watch.

CHAPTER 67

JACK CROSSED THE street and jerked open the door to his truck. He needed to talk to Tony Burns. Hank Wade didn't live in Tony's jurisdiction; he lived in Ouray County. But Tony would know what to do next.

He shoved the key into the ignition and turned it, starting the truck, then pulled away from the curb. Then it dawned on him.

Ouray County.

Lea.

When she had ended their call earlier, she said there was someone else she needed to see. She had been angry; Jack had heard it in her voice.

At Main Street, he turned in the direction of Ridgway.

Jack hoped to God that Lea hadn't taken the letter from Cliff and gone to confront Wade. But his gut screamed she had. He dug his phone from his pocket and dialed her number.

"Come on, Lea. Pick up."

The phone didn't ring but went straight to voice mail. If she was on Wade's land, she wouldn't have service.

He tried again.

"Pick up, pick up." But the call wasn't answered.

Adrenaline pulsed through him. Something was wrong. He pressed his foot down hard on the accelerator.

CHAPTER 68

LEA SAT IN Hank Wade's kitchen. But not by choice. Hank had tied her hands and held a rifle on her.

She stared at Cliff's letter just out of reach on the table. Hank had taken it from her after he'd made her sit.

He was leaning against the counter, watching her. "I would take care of you myself," he said, "but I don't get my hands dirty. That's Brody's job."

She had listened earlier as he radioed Brody, telling him to get to the ranch, that he had a *project* for him. Lea knew she was the project. The rope that bound her hands was rough and cutting into her skin.

"It's a shame that you couldn't just mind your own business," Hank started in. He propped the rifle against the counter, and Lea glanced at it. "We could have been great neighbors."

"You never wanted to be my neighbor," Lea replied. "You wanted my land."

Hank raised his eyebrows and nodded. "That's true. But we could have handled this amicably," he said. "Now I'll get your land anyway. When you're gone, it'll be sold to the highest bidder. And guess who that'll be?"

He smiled at her in a way that made her skin crawl. She had never liked Hank, but now she hated the man. He was a monster.

"How did you do it?" Lea asked.

"Do what?"

"Kill Cliff."

A smug look crossed his face. "That wasn't planned. But it did turn out brilliantly if I do say so myself."

"How did you do it?"

Hank stared at her. Lea knew he was debating how much to tell her, but she hoped his arrogance would outweigh his common sense. No rational person would admit to killing a sitting congressman, but there was nothing rational about Hank Wade. If Lea was going to die, she wanted to find out what had happened to Cliff first.

"First of all," Hank began, "*I* didn't do it. I told you, I don't get my hands dirty."

"Brody did it."

"Of course he did."

"But Brody isn't smart enough to have pulled it off on his own."

The smug expression was back. "You're a smart woman, Lea. It's too bad you have to die." He hopped onto the kitchen counter, his legs dangling next to the rifle he'd left on the floor.

Lea glanced at it. It was too far away. She wouldn't be able to get to it in time. She needed to lure him away from it.

Her hands were tied, and she rested them in her lap. But even bound, Lea was confident that if given the chance, she could sight the rifle and pull the trigger.

"It was my plan," Hank continued. "Some thug made the pipe bomb for me in Grand Junction. I was going to use it to blow up the barn, but darned if Cliff didn't go and change his mind about how he was going to vote."

Lea felt bile rise in her throat. "And you knew he was leaving the next morning, so you killed him."

Hank nodded. "I already had the bomb. It was an easy decision. I was going to use it on the barn, but I figured I could just as easily set the thing on fire and say I'd seen that envionmentalist in the area when it happened, and bingo—same result. The fact that people might assume he had put the bomb on Cliff's plane was the icing on the cake."

"How did you find out that Cliff had changed his vote?"

"From Susan."

"Susan?" Lea was stunned. "Why would she tell you?"

There was a sly look on his face. "When you give a woman what she wants, she'll tell you anything." He paused for effect, watching Lea for a reaction.

She refused to give him the satisfaction. But her heart lurched thinking about Cliff. She wondered if he had known about Susan and Hank before he died. She hoped he hadn't. It was all such a tragedy—such a waste. And for what?

"Why did you do it?" Lea asked, her stomach turning in disgust. "Just for the land?"

"There's nothing *just* about it. The land means everything. You of all people should know that."

"But I don't. Tell me."

He heaved a sigh. "I'm disappointed in you, Lea. I expected more. Then again, you've been handed everything you've ever had. You've never had to fight for anything. You've never had to claw and scrape your way to the top while others tried to pull you back down."

He kept talking. "The land is a way to keep score. And, by all accounts, I'm winning. When the government takes the worthless property close to town and gives me the high country, this ranch will be the most spectacular one in the country. It won't be the largest, but it will be the most significant. Who else has a ranch with thirteen- and fourteen-thousand-foot peaks? Nobody. Who else can boast elk and deer, bears, mountain lions, and now moose?" He waited for her to answer. When she didn't, he added, "Nobody."

"So it's an ego thing for you."

She saw a momentary flash of rage, but it passed quickly.

"It has nothing to do with ego," he said. "I told you. It's keeping score. And I like winning."

He was a psychopath. Lea strained to listen for an approaching vehicle, hoping Brody was still miles away. She needed time. If only she had told Percy or Jack where she was going. No one knew where she was.

"You shot Jack." It was a guess, but she wanted to keep him talking.

"Jack?" He frowned.

"Jack Martin."

"Ah, yes. The nosy detective." He smoothed his jeans over his thighs. "That was a rare miss. Of course, I wasn't the one who shot him."

"Let me guess," Lea said. "Brody."

Hank made his fingers into the shape of a gun, then winked and pretended to shoot her. "Now you're catching on. That Martin fellow was starting to get in the way. He was asking too many people too many questions. Everyone thought Eric Dale was responsible for Cliff's murder and torching my barn. Nobody would have ever suspected *me*. But the detective was going to ruin it." He raised both palms in the air. "So why not kill two birds with one stone? Shoot the detective and frame the environmental wacko."

"You burned down your own barn?"

He shrugged. "It was old and falling down and on the land I'm trading. It was no use to me and a great way to frame Dale and get him off my back."

Lea couldn't believe what she was hearing. Hank had destroyed his own barn to frame an innocent man. He had killed two people with no remorse, like he had been checking items off a to-do list. And Lea knew she would be next unless she could come up with a plan.

"Why kill Gerald Purvis?"

"Because he was a fool," Hank spat. "I had people already lobbying the governor to appoint him to Cliff's seat. It was a done deal. But then he goes and finds a conscience, thought Susan was hiding something. Somehow he suspected Cliff had changed his mind and came out to ask me about it. *Me!*" Hank laughed. "What a moron. It's ironic, though. Gerald came out here because he didn't trust Susan. But his greatest mistake was trusting me."

He was amused with himself. There was no hint of regret or remorse. Lea's skin crawled as he continued talking.

"It was going to be a no-brainer," he said. "Purvis gets in, votes for the land swap, and we all get what we want. If he had just stayed the course, hadn't gone and gotten curious about things—hadn't come out and asked me about it—we would have all gotten what we wanted. I would have gotten the land, Purvis would have gotten a seat in Congress, and Susan would have gotten her money."

"What money?"

Hank's eyes narrowed. "The money I sent her for Cliff's vote."

"But you killed him." Lea was confused.

"There was still Gerald Purvis," Hank said. "Or so I thought. But now all bets are off. Cliff's dead, Purvis is dead, and I'm already working on the other members of the committee. I'll get that land. And Susan doesn't know it yet, but she's going to give the money back, or else."

"Or else what?"

He made a gun with his fingers again and pretended to pull the trigger.

Lea thought she heard a car approaching in the distance and glanced at Wade's rifle. It was still too far away.

CHAPTER 69

JACK CALLED JUDITH on his way out of town, hoping she would have Percy Ferguson's cell number, and she did. Jack called him, but Percy said he didn't know where Lea was. He was at home in Montrose, over thirty minutes from the lodge, but while he was still talking to Jack, he jumped in his truck and started that way.

Jack had just enough time to fill him in on what he'd learned about Hank Wade.

"Is Lea in danger?" Percy asked.

Jack heard the fear in his voice. "She could be."

The connection dropped when Jack started down the valley. He wouldn't regain service until he was almost to Lea's. For the next half hour, there was nothing he could do but drive.

As he neared the entrance to Lea's ranch, he tried her again but got no answer. He slowed the truck but, at the last second, decided to stay on the highway. Percy would go to the lodge and look for Lea.

Jack had a different idea.

He drove farther, then swung the truck off the highway onto Wade's ranch. As much as he hated to admit it, there was a good chance Lea was there.

Rain had dampened the gravel road, cutting down on the dust. Jack drove fast but was careful not to be seen. He slowed the truck as he rounded one of the last corners before reaching the house. He still didn't have a plan, but if Lea was in danger, announcing his entrance wouldn't be part of one.

He entered a grove of trees and immediately braked, surprised to see Percy's truck parked just off the road. Percy was crouched behind a large spruce, clutching his rifle and staring at Wade's house about twenty yards away.

Jack killed the engine, pulled his pistol from the glove box, and jumped from the truck.

He squatted down beside Percy. "What are you doing here?" he whispered.

"I could ask you the same thing."

Jack studied the house. Lea's tan Tahoe was parked at an odd angle just off the porch. Red, Wade's hound dog, was tied to a fence post and lay lounging in the yard.

"I thought about what you said," Percy told him, "and I figured there was a good chance Lea had come here to confront him, not knowing he had killed Cliff."

"Have you seen anyone?"

"Not a soul. But I heard some yelling inside. Sounded like Wade. He must have been yelling at Lea. As far as I can tell, there's nobody else here." Percy turned and looked up the road toward the highway. "Let's hope one of his guys doesn't show up before we get her out of there."

"We should call the sheriff."

"Already did that," Percy replied. "They're tied up on the other side of Ridgway but said they'd get someone out here as soon as they could."

"That might be too late."

"My thoughts exactly."

"What's your plan?" Jack asked him.

"I was hoping you had one."

Jack took in and released a deep breath, wondering what to do next. He was holding his pistol in his right hand and used his thumb to unlock the safety.

"All right," Jack said. "I'll try to make it around back and see if I can get inside. You stay here and cover the front. Fire a warning shot if any of Wade's men show up."

"That's all you got?"

Jack could tell Percy was hoping for a more sophisticated plan.

"That's all I got."

Jack set out and kept his distance as he made a wide arc around the house, careful to stay within the cover of trees. He chose the opposite side from where Red was tied, hoping the dog wouldn't see him and start barking.

Branches hidden in the pine needles snapped under the weight of Jack's boots as he sprinted from tree to tree. He stopped at each one to glance at the house, making sure he hadn't been spotted.

It took several minutes, but when he reached the back, he studied the yard and realized there was no way of getting to the house without being exposed. The house sat in a clearing, with no adjacent trees on any of the four sides. There was a large propane tank not far off the porch, but to reach it, Jack would have to leave the cover of the trees and be exposed in the open for several seconds.

He furiously searched for another way, turning back and glancing again at the side of the house, where the yard was deep. There would be nowhere to hide if he came under fire.

He sat gripping the pistol hard and straining to hear, but the house was eerily quiet. A magpie chattered at him from above, and Jack knew it was time to make a move.

He took another quick glance at the house, then leapt from behind the tree and sprinted to the propane tank, keeping his head down as he ran. He crouched behind the tank, holding his breath, and peered over the top. He scanned the porch, then the windows on the second floor. The house was still quiet.

Lea had to be somewhere inside, but where?

Jack squinted, shielding his eyes from the slanting rays of the morning sun. He searched the shadows again. Where were they?

Red barked once, then fell quiet. Jack hadn't heard an approaching car, and Percy hadn't fired a shot. Had Lea and Hank walked outside? Were they out front? Was Hank taking her somewhere?

Jack quickly calculated his odds and pushed off the tank. He had made it only a few feet when he heard someone rack a shell into a rifle chamber.

"Stop right there, Martin." It was Hank. He was hidden somewhere in the shadows.

Jack froze and squinted, searching the porch. He put up his hands, still holding the pistol. "Don't do anything stupid, Wade."

"Looks like you're already doing it."

Jack ignored him. "Lea?" he hollered. "You all right?"

"She's fine," Wade said, stepping farther onto the porch, the lower half of his jeans now exposed in the morning sun. "I tried throwing you off the scent the nice way."

Jack thought a moment. "The flyer on my trailer from Wilderness Keepers. You were trying to frame Dale."

Wade sighed. "And when that didn't work—"

"You shot me."

"Not me. But I have to admit, I *was* disappointed that Brody missed."

Jack didn't mention the Kevlar vest. He held the pistol aloft but had his finger still on the trigger. His heart was in his throat, knowing their predicament was his fault. He should have waited for law enforcement. Now it was too late.

"I'm here, Jack," Lea hollered from somewhere in the shadows of the porch.

Jack still couldn't see her. He stared at Wade's legs and calculated the distance. Probably thirty feet. Too far for a shot from a pistol. And he could hit Lea by mistake.

He took a step closer. "It's over, Hank."

"Says the man with his hands over his head." Wade laughed.

"It's over," Jack repeated, stepping slowly forward.

"For the two of you it is. Drop the gun behind your back. You get to come inside while we all wait for Brody."

Jack took another step toward the porch, his finger still on the trigger. He glanced at Wade's jeans and calculated twenty-five feet. He searched the shadows and saw the faint figure of a woman standing to Wade's left. Her hands were pulled in front of her and looked like they were tied. Wade had her arm near the shoulder with his left hand and held the rifle with his right.

There was a porch chair next to her.

"Lea, you shouldn't be standing on that bad knee," Jack called out.

There was a moment of silence.

Jack held his breath, hoping she would understand. He needed her out of the way to get a clean shot at Wade.

"You have a bad knee, Lea?" Jack heard Wade ask in a tone devoid of sympathy. "How thoughtful of Martin to care."

Jack squinted, still watching her. *Sit down, Lea. Sit down.*

He heard Wade sigh. "I'll give you one more chance, Martin." His voice had grown hard. "Keep your hands up and drop the pistol behind your back."

Sit down, Lea.

Jack held his breath, then, to his relief, saw Lea slowly lower herself into the chair. Wade let go of her arm and placed his left hand under the stock of the rifle, supporting its weight.

"Let her go," Jack said, trying to give Wade one more chance.

But he laughed. "Or what?" Jack saw him sight the rifle on his chest. "Too late, Martin."

"Hank!"

The voice came from inside the house.

Wade wheeled around, still holding the rifle.

There was an explosion, and Lea screamed.

Wade flew backward off the porch, landing in the yard.

Jack had ducked and rolled to the side, setting his cracked ribs on fire. He glanced up and saw boots step onto the porch and out of the shadow. He threw up his pistol, sighting it on the shooter, but stopped when the figure stepped out farther into the sun.

Percy.

He was holding his rifle, the end of the barrel still smoking.

CHAPTER 70

IT WAS ALMOST two o'clock, and Jack still hadn't been released from the scene. He sat on the steps of Hank Wade's front porch. Red was still tethered to the rail and lay at his feet.

Jack could hear Lea talking to a medic inside, insisting that she didn't need attention despite the abrasions on her wrists from being tied.

Wade's ranch hand, Brody, had finally shown up and immediately turned around when he saw the commotion, but he had been quickly apprehended and taken in for questioning. Jack knew that after the Ouray County Sheriff's Office was finished with Brody, he'd be turned over to the feds. And if Ronnie Bugler identified him as the man who'd paid him to plant the bomb on the plane, Brody's days as a free man would be over.

For what seemed like an eternity, an army of deputies and men in white coats from forensics scoured the house and yard. A photographer had come and gone. Wade's body had been loaded into an ambulance and whisked away to the morgue, or God knows where—Jack didn't care.

Not long after the ambulance left, Percy had been taken in for questioning. Jack was sure it was just a formality and that he would be out before nightfall.

The sheriff of Ouray County had sat with rapt attention as Jack recounted what had happened and everything he suspected Wade was guilty of. When Jack finished, the sheriff had sat for a moment, letting it all sink in. He shook his head and mumbled, "This is going to be one hell of a report to write."

Jack had been told to hang around in case they had more questions. He had obliged, taking a seat on the steps next to Red. That had been over an hour ago.

A female deputy had moved Jack's truck and parked it in front; another had driven Percy's away. Lea's Tahoe was still parked askew, the way they'd found it earlier. It had been searched and dusted but left in place.

Jack's side ached, and he was starving. He needed a meal and his pain meds. But most of all, he wanted to get back to the trailer. He thought of Crockett. He'd been without cell service all day and had no way of letting Otto know where he was or what had happened.

Jack smiled to himself, thinking the old guy was probably sitting at the picnic table glued to his scanner. But unless he had it tuned into the frequency for Ouray County, instead of the one for San Miguel, he wouldn't know what had happened. Jack would fill him in later.

A deputy stepped out onto the porch. "You're free to go, Martin."

Jack stood up and slapped the dust off the seat of his jeans. The dog at his feet got up and looked at him expectantly.

Jack turned to the deputy. "What's going to happen to Red?"

"Red?"

"The dog."

The deputy looked down and frowned, thinking about it a moment. "I guess we'll keep him secured here at the scene until animal control can come get him."

Red stood stoically at Jack's feet, then stole a glance toward the truck as if looking for Crockett.

Jack bent to pet Red, and he wagged his tail. It didn't seem fair. A life spent on the ranch, and now he faced one in a shelter. Jack wondered what would happen to him.

After several seconds, he heaved a sigh. "Ah, hell," Jack said, straightening back up. "Can I take him?"

The deputy looked at the dog a moment, then shrugged. "Suit yourself."

Jack untied the rope from the porch rail and led the dog to his truck. He pulled open the driver's door, hoping he wouldn't regret what he was about to do.

"Let's go, Red. There's an old man I think you need to meet."

CHAPTER 71

Saturday, May 21

THAT NIGHT, FOR the first time in months, Jack slept like a baby. He woke the next morning slowly, coming in and out of consciousness, bouncing between dreams of a mountain lodge and a beautiful woman and his solitary aluminum reality. The dream came and went several times before Jack was finally fully awake.

He dragged a hand down his face and noticed Crockett curled and sleeping at his feet. His gaze left the dog and swept the tiny trailer, taking it all in. It wasn't a mountain lodge, and Crockett wasn't a beautiful woman, but Jack was happy.

Outside, a dog barked, and Crockett bolted upright. The dog barked again, and Crockett leapt to the floor.

Jack tossed the covers aside and got out of bed. "Hold on a minute," he said, pulling on his jeans from the day before. It was time to do laundry, but he was tired and sore. The laundry could wait another day.

When Jack opened the door, Crockett dashed from the trailer. Jack followed through the trees in his bare feet. When he reached the edge of the adjacent campsite, he stopped to watch.

Otto was seated in his folding chair and threw a stick toward the river. It fell just short of the bank. Red barked once, then darted for it. He snatched it up, but then leapt into the water and frolicked for several seconds, jumping this way and that, before he returned it to Otto. The old man doubled over, laughing in delight at the antics of his new friend.

Crockett had watched it all and stood wagging his tail.

Jack smiled.

Otto threw the stick again, and Crockett joined in this time, both dogs romping in the flowing river. Otto laughed, coughed, and then laughed some more.

"He can stay?" Jack asked, holding his breath.

Otto sat watching the dogs play, a wistful grin creasing his old face. "For as long as he wants."

A half hour later, Jack was back on the road, this time with Crockett sitting on the seat next to him. Jack had decided the night before that he would take the day off, hang around the campground with Otto and the dogs. But his plans changed—they always changed.

He needed to call Buckley, but he would do that later. Jack had called him briefly the night before and filled him in on what had happened. "Well, I'll be damned," Buckley had replied to the news of Hank Wade's death. "I can't say that hell is better for it, but the devil's got himself some formidable company."

Buckley had insisted Jack stop by the next day, saying he wanted to settle his bill and that he was going to give him a bonus. After everything that had happened, Jack wasn't going to refuse.

He passed Pandora Café and resisted the urge to stop. He would pop in on his way back to the campground later. Judith would have questions about what had gone on the day before, wanting him to fill in the gaps of the gossip she had no doubt already heard. His stomach growled. Judith's breakfast was tempting, but there was something pressing on him harder than hunger.

When he reached Telluride Bank & Trust, Jack slowed the truck and peered inside. He saw Ted Hawthorne scurrying around, getting the bank ready to open. Jack kept driving; there was no reason to stop. The nervous banker would have to live with what he'd done. Hawthorne had been a bad friend to Cliff, but he wasn't a killer.

Next, Jack reached the street that led up to the Robertses' home. He caught a glimpse of it as he drove past and wondered what would become of Susan. Along with Cliff and Gerald Purvis, she had been caught in Hank Wade's murderous web, and her life would never be the same. Jack turned his attention back to the road when he realized he didn't care. He'd probably never see her again, and that was fine.

For the next hour, Jack was lost in thought as he drove the tilting curves of the highway, nearly missing the entrance to Lea's ranch. He turned in and took the gravel road to the lodge, passing a herd of elk grazing in the distance along the way.

He shut off the engine and spent several seconds staring up at the impressive log structure and the mountains it was nestled in.

Jack opened the door and got out. "This won't take long," he said, leaving the dog in the truck.

As he approached the porch, Percy stepped around the side of the house with a bundle of kindling in his arms. When he saw Jack, he dropped the wood and came striding toward him with an outstretched hand and a smile.

"Howdy, Jack." He pumped Jack's arm. "Lea expecting you?"

"No. Last-minute decision to come out."

The screen door opened, and Lea stepped outside. She smiled when she saw him.

"Jack." She took the porch steps to the ground. "I was hoping you'd stop by."

Percy picked up the kindling and made an excuse about getting back to work. He touched the brim of his hat and nodded, then told Jack goodbye.

"Coffee?" Lea asked.

Jack shook his head.

"Let's sit, then." She led him up the porch steps, where they settled into a couple of rocking chairs and sat for a while in silence.

"Why'd you come?" she asked.

Jack stared at the snow-capped mountains in the distance. "I'm not sure."

They sat for a while longer, rocking.

"Althea?" Jack asked.

Lea looked confused, then smiled. "It's Greek."

"I thought you were Scottish."

She grinned. "Althea was a Greek woman who saved my father's life in Italy during World War II. He was still just a boy—seventeen, I think. He spent the rest of his life referring to Althea as his very own guardian angel."

Jack watched her as she talked. "I can see the resemblance," he said, and saw her blush.

An easy silence fell between them.

"Where does this insatiable need to right the world's wrongs come from, Jack Martin?"

He thought about it a moment, then shrugged. "Just doing what I can."

Lea spent the next several minutes filling him in on some of the details that Hank Wade had admitted to before he died. They were the pieces to the puzzle that Jack still needed.

She told him about Wade setting fire to his own barn and attempting to cast suspicion on Eric Dale. At the same time, his foreman, Brody, had lured Dale to Last Dollar Road, making sure he was busy with a flat tire in the middle of nowhere, ensuring he wouldn't have an alibi.

Jack remembered the matching radios that Wade and Brody carried and realized they'd pulled the same stunt on him—an ambush at the same spot. Jack would suggest Tony Burns get with the sheriff in Ouray and compare the ballistics of the cartridge Deputy O'Connor found to any rifles owned by Brody and Wade. Jack was sure there would be a match.

"I better get going," he said, getting up from the chair.

They took the porch steps to the yard.

Jack turned to look at her. Lea was everything he'd ever wanted in a woman. She was older than him, but it didn't matter. She was strong and kind, and Jack thought she was beautiful.

He turned, letting his gaze sweep over the ranch and remembering his dream. He could be happy here. Although he knew nothing about ranching, he could learn.

"What is it?" Lea asked.

Jack realized she'd been watching him. He turned to her and opened his mouth to speak but hesitated. Then he shook his head, dismissing the dream.

"It's nothing," he said. "I should go."

She stared at him a moment longer, then smiled gently and nodded. "Well, don't be a stranger."

Jack glanced in the rearview mirror as he drove away and saw Lea take the steps to the porch and disappear inside. He took in and released a long slow breath, squeezing the steering wheel.

Crockett sat on the passenger seat beside him. The dog was quiet, almost sullen, a mirror image of Jack's mood. A lot had happened in a week and a half. Jack was tired and sore and wanted to rest.

He navigated a grove of pine trees, then laid a hand on the dog's back. "I believe we've earned a few days off, Crockett. What do you think?"

The dog barked, and Jack smiled.

They would rest. Then, when Otto and Red left for the mine, Jack would pack up, and he and Crockett would head up into the mountains. He would find a blue alpine lake like the one he'd seen in the high basin, where they could camp. They would eat and sleep under the moon and stars.

As he thought about it, Jack's heart rate slowed. He let his grip on the steering wheel relax. He noticed tiny buds on several aspen trees. A few wildflowers along the road were beginning to show their heads. Jack rolled down the window and drew in a breath. It was going to be a great summer.

But a few minutes later, as Jack was pulling onto the highway headed back to Telluride, his cell phone rang...

ACKNOWLEDGMENT

Murder in the San Juans depicts several real locations in and around Telluride, Mountain Village, and Ridgway, Colorado, but all events and characters are entirely fictional. Anything negatively portrayed is done so purely for literary effect.

I purposely didn't research security at the Telluride airport to avoid disclosing something I shouldn't. And it's a safe bet that I vastly understated their actual security—trespass at your own risk. You've been warned!

I also took liberties with the historic Mahr Building, which is the site of Butch Cassidy's first bank robbery. The San Miguel Valley Bank that Cassidy and his gang robbed in 1892 is long gone. The Mahr now houses an art gallery. But the building is one of my favorites, and its history was too good not to use in the story. So Telluride Bank & Trust it became!

Following the publication of The Killing Storm, I had several readers message me that they wanted to visit Telluride and eat at Pandora Café. I hated to tell them the café was fictional. I wish it weren't. I'd love to eat there, too!

Writing and publishing mystery novels has been a fantastic adventure, although a mostly solitary one. For each story, I have spent hours, day after day for months, alone in a world of my own conjuring. But I have been blessed with invaluable help and support along the way.

As always, thank you to Kristen Weber, my editor par excellence. I am eternally grateful for her invaluable guidance and encouragement. My books are so much better because of your help!

Thank you to my father, Roger Hopkins, a veteran flight instructor with the United States Air Force and former commercial pilot (our family's very own Top Gun), for answering aviation questions. And I asked some weird ones! Like radio procedures, flying in inclement weather, different types of private aircraft, and where to effectively plant a bomb. Thanks for your help, Dad!

I also want to thank my brother-in-law and long-time banker, Sid Cauthorn, who generously gave his time and knowledge, answering countless financial questions while I was writing Murder in the San Juans. Obviously, any banking mistakes that might have made it into the story are mine, not his!

Thank you to my friend and fellow Telluridian Janet Jacobs for letting me use her middle name and likeness for the character of Lea Scotsman. Janet said she hoped Lea wouldn't be killed or turn out to be the killer. To which I replied, "No promises. It's a murder mystery!" I had a lot of fun writing Lea. I hope you liked reading about her!

To my husband, Chris. Thank you for both your praise and constructive criticism, and for knowing to give much more of the former than the latter. You are a very wise man, and I love you.

And last but never least, to you, the reader. As long as you enjoy reading about Jack and Crockett's adventures, I'll keep writing them. Thank you again for your messages, letters, comments, and reviews. I love hearing from you!

29050150R00217